Readers 1

Touchstoı

CW00520590

"So good has got into my drear
Finney, the master in time travel,
vein I cannot wait..."

"An engaging time travel story, gradually demanding more concentration and weaving itself into more than simple there and back again stories."

"I ordered the whole set and was glad I did. The stories were fantastic..."

"From the first book to the last in the first season I was hooked. Some nights went to bed intending to read just a chapter or two but found myself not being able to stop reading..."

"Engrossing and never quite does what you expect..."

"Superb. Really enjoyed this series. Can't wait for more!"

Touchstone (1: The Sins of the Fathers) [1912]

"I couldn't put it down…"

"Makes for an interesting, enjoyable and easy read, and opens the reader's eyes to a time in Moseley long forgotten. It draws your attention to details of how the area was 100 years ago: the beautiful old buildings, the steam tram, how the Village green was actually green…"

"An extremely riveting short book that I didn't want to end and would have loved the book to be longer..."

"I have read a few time travel books but this one really got to me. I thought it was going to be a typical teenage romance but it certainly wasn't. Absolutely gripping…"

"I was rapt up in the story, couldn't put it down."

"I didn't expect to be so blown away as I was with this... I felt I could go and visit and really see these places. I love the characters and simply adored this book."

"Tried this out on a whim, very pleased I did, crisply written, engaging and thrilling, enjoyed it so much, I bought the series!"

"I must admit I love any books that have time travel in them, and this one didn't disappoint either. To make things even better, was to get to the end of this book knowing there were more to come. I ended up purchasing all five of the books and reading them one after the other over the space of a couple of days."

"A story to make you feel you have gone back to Birmingham in 1912. I could not put it down and can't wait to get into the next adventure."

Touchstone (2: Family at War) [1940]

"A very good short book that kept me riveted through the whole story — I never wanted it to end."

"Brings home to one what life must have been like on the Home Front, in cities suffering nightly air raids. Doesn't flinch from the true horrors of the Blitz, nor the petty squabbles amid the rubble..."

"The historical detail in these books is fantastic, found myself wanting to know more about the area and the times."

"Initially thought it purely for children, but pleasantly surprised by the author's convincing style and obvious research into the time period concerned... all in all much better than expected, will be looking out for more by this author."

"Although the Touchstone books may have been written for a younger audience, I assure you; if you are a true fan of timeslip reads these will not disappoint! Each went by far too fast and I find myself waiting in anticipation for the next instalment. Rachel and Danny, along with the characters they meet on their 'journeys' are real, likable and completely caught up in the craziness that's so drastically changed their lives. Delightfully, Andy Conway has a unique way of throwing in twists and turns when least expected. For the price, you won't be better entertained, and soon, you too will be as hooked as I am."

"Basically, it's a wonderful read — I just love these time travel books, whatever shape or form they have. This one was special… I believe it's one of the best series of its kind."

Touchstone (3: All the Time in the World) [1966]

"I've read all three of the *Touchstone* stories now and each brings the period, in this case the sixties, to life. By concentrating on one area of the world, Moseley, Andy Conway has given it a depth and realism. He turned my preconceptions of the swinging sixties upside down a couple of times."

"As per the previous two in this series, it is an interesting concept and is developing the story nicely with obviously more time eras to come with all the central characters and now this new introduction of some sort of monitoring team. Who are they? What is their function? I'll need to keep reading the series now I'm hooked."

"Enjoyable storyline giving a bit of an insight into people and life during these times. Some historical events creatively written."

"I really enjoyed Touchstone 1 and 2 so much that today while in Birmingham I went to Moseley village to see if the place were real. Thank you for writing the books…"

"Loved this one… I got so engrossed in it that I lost track of time completely (excuse the pun) and finished this in three to four days! Highly recommended to anyone who loves a good time travel tale."

Touchstone (4: Station at the End of Time) [1959]

"A cracking, spooky read with some great twists… oozes atmosphere, reminiscent of old TV shows like Sapphire and Steel or the Twilight Zone… As ever, it's a cracking read which never really stops for breath, exactly like the freight train bearing down on the protagonist's grandmother… also comes with a bonus short story which is a real head-wrecker."

"Best one yet. I really love this series of books and this is the most gripping yet. Although not familiar with Birmingham it is still fascinating to hear of the old Kings Heath station and the images it creates in my mind. Also take the time to read the short article at the end."

"This was a good read, enjoyed the whole series."

"Just read Touchstone 1-4 in one sitting. Unfortunately, I have now time-travelled up to your writing speed. Looking forward to Touchstone 5."

Touchstone (5: Let's Fall in Love for the Last Time) [1934]

"I've thoroughly enjoyed every bit of this series… this is an incredible story. If, like me, you love time travel novels, you'll love this."

"The plot is definitely thickening. Over the course of the five books, with the brilliant slight diversion of book 4, I have fallen deeper and deeper into the story of Rachel and Danny and the stories of the people around them."

"I am by far a *huge* fan of anything time travel related, and this series of time travel books had me hooked from book number one."

"What a find! I have never read anything by Andy Conway before — but I'm now hooked! Not only was the story thoroughly enjoyable, it was also very thought provoking. Andy Conway certainly makes you think about how ordinary people lived and how their values and belief systems have changed so dramatically over the past 100 years."

"Waited, waited, waited and waited for this. Now read it. Loved it. Can't wait for the next one. Also looking forward to the spin off sequels. Amazing story."

Touchstone (6: Fade to Grey) [1980]

"This series has had me hooked from start to finish. I'm sad it's ended but glad it's not the end. I'm now looking forward to the next season. It's a magnificent story."

"A great series and a fine final episode, probably the best yet and by far the longest. Can't wait for series two, I am going to miss going to bed with this book at night!"

"Absolutely Superb! I have thoroughly enjoyed the whole *Touchstone* series and I have to say I've been eagerly awaiting this one, the last in the series. I wasn't disappointed in any way! If you haven't read this series yet — you simply must! Go and download *Touchstone 1. The Sins of the Fathers* — but beware — you will be hooked!!"

Buried in Time [1888]

"Inventively brilliant alternative history. Enjoyed the first Touchstone series and this is deeper, darker and more inventive."

"Everyone loves a good Jack the Ripper tale. This is one."

"A brilliant book again from Andy Conway."

"Very good."

"Cracking read."

"Great read, and thought provoking on whom Jack the Ripper really was. Look forward to reading series 2."

"Another riveting read. Another excellent book from Andy Conway."

Bright Star Falling [1874-87]

"I have been waiting for the release of the eighth novel in the Touchstone series and this fabulous book definitely did not disappoint. It immerses the reader in the fascinating and tragic world of the Native Americans whilst still keeping the Touchstone theme. A brilliant and enjoyable read, I couldn't put it down!"

"Fantastic story . A world away from the Birmingham of season one but the Wild West and time travel what a brilliant combination."

"We had to wait a while for the next instalment in the Touchstone series. But it was well worth waiting for."

"As a huge fan of time-travel fiction and film I devoured the first Touchstone series, and Season Two has certainly got off on the right footing. From Jack the Ripper to the Wild West via a hipster Birmingham suburb… I love the way the series is so close to home, whilst effortlessly dancing over centuries — and the globe… with truly educational and sensitive depictions of the Lakota, and the events and skirmishes leading up to what is known as "Custer's Last Stand"… it's a great book."

"A good read. One gets the impression that the author has done his historical homework, so one really seems to get a 'feel' of the time and so learns something in addition to being well entertained."

"Well written and immersive with a real sense of place and time. You feel that the author has really done his research. Great storytelling as always, can't wait for the next one."

Bright Star Rising [1887]

"Touchstone saga at its best. Absolutely brilliant and highly recommended."

"Another brilliant book in the Touchstone series. The story twists and turns, with so much detail and strong links to Birmingham in another time."

THE GHOSTS OF CHRISTMAS PAST

Andy Conway is the novelist, screenwriter and time traveller behind the Touchstone series. He wrote the feature films *Arjun & Alison*, *An American Exorcism* and *The Courier* and runs a publishing empire from a loft in Birmingham.

Read more at andyconway.net

Photography: Ian Davies iandaviesphoto.com

THE GHOSTS OF CHRISTMAS PAST

WALLBANK

This paperback edition 2019
1

First published in Great Britain by
Wallbank Books 2019
Copyright © Andy Conway 2019
The right of Andy Conway to be identified as the author of this
work has been asserted by him in accordance with the Copyright,
Designs and Patent Act, 1988 © Andy Conway 2019

ISBN- 9781679300691

Cover design by Sean Strong
www.seanstrong.com

To Stacy

The woman who sleeps under the bridge

Mrs Hudson was lost again. That familiar feeling of coming to her senses and not knowing where she was or what she was doing.

She looked around the busy concourse of New Street Station. They had changed it in recent years and now called it something else. What was it again? She clenched her fists, trying to recover the name. So many names just out of reach lately.

Grand Central. That was it.

She smiled at her success. The relief, when you were struggling for a word, fighting the frustrating fog in your mind, and then it cleared and the word came to you — a precious lost jewel suddenly there before your eyes, gleaming in the light.

It was the new name for the station. Yes, that was right. Except it wasn't. They still called the station New Street Station. Grand Central was the name of the shopping mall they'd built on top of the old station.

There had been a grand unveiling, she remembered, a couple of years ago. A new iconic train station for Birmingham. Except it wasn't. It was just a new shopping mall.

The smell of coffee grounds from the cafes greeted her, warm and homely. A brass band played *Hark the Herald*

Angels Sing, the men in top hats and frock coats, the women in bonnets and bell-shaped dresses. A nostalgic Dickensian Christmas pantomime for the hordes of shoppers. The carol echoed round the giant atrium. A giant fir tree decorated with gold ribbons and twinkling fairy lights.

Mrs Hudson looked around, wondering if she was due to meet someone.

She couldn't remember.

Was she heading home? Home was in Moseley, she was absolutely sure of that. She hadn't moved, even though she'd sold the shop, Pastimes. That time was over. And the mission too. Yes, that came flooding back to her: that awful taste of failure.

Things had all gone so terribly wrong.

Why was she here?

She dug into the handbag on her arm and pulled out a pocket diary. This would tell her, but what was the date? She looked up at the Departures board: a row of TV screens with amber text, a dizzying array of place names and times, all different, and the screens kept changing.

There, at the bottom right of each screen was the current time. 7:08. She glanced up at the atrium roof to see it dark. It was night. Seven in the evening.

The screens did not show a date.

People walking past, almost all of them reading their phones as they walked. She didn't have a phone. She had had one, once, she remembered, but there wasn't one in her bag. She checked the pockets of her camel hair coat. No. If she had a phone, she had left it at home. But perhaps she didn't have one anymore.

How to find out the date? She could ask someone.

No one looked at her. A young man caught her eye and, at the gleam of recognition in her face, he looked at the floor and passed on. She saw herself as they might see her — a strange old lady asking for help. Had he thought she was a beggar?

A WH Smiths store over there. A newspaper would tell her.

She walked over and entered the store, crowded with shelves of books and confectionary and almost no space between the aisles. She went to a stack of newspapers in a plastic stand and peered closely to check the date.

Tuesday, 24th of December, 2019.

She walked out, back to the concourse and dug her pocket diary from her handbag, thumbing through the gilt-edged pages.

It was Christmas Eve. Each page of the diary contained her scribbled instructions. Quite detailed. When a woman was forgetting everything, she made an effort to instruct herself.

1000. Make smoking bishop.

1200. Buy Christmas wreath at florists.

1300. Visit parents' grave at Brandwood End Cemetery. Leave Christmas wreath.

That would have been earlier today. Had she done that? She cringed and felt her shoulders tighten. Yes, there it was, a memory: standing in the cold cemetery in bright sun and placing a wreath at the granite stone that bore her parents' names. She'd had a flask of something warm. Yes, Smoking Bishop. This was her Christmas Eve tradition. She made the drink every morning on the 24th December, with a Seville orange stuck with cloves. The pungent smell of cinnamon, mace and Allspice with the port and red wine. The scent of every Christmas of her childhood.

She looked down the list of things to do for today. But there was a blank space and then a single line.

Theatre Royal, New Street, 1842.

But it was gone seven and this said a quarter to seven. She was late.

She turned and headed across the concourse towards the New Street exit. Strictly speaking it came out on Stephenson Street, behind New Street. There was a tram line there now,

5

another new feature.

As she walked up the ramp to the row of glass doors that ran the length of Stephenson Street, she remembered that the Theatre Royal had been demolished years ago. 1956, wasn't it? When she was a young woman in her 20s studying History. And the time in her diary was strangely specific. 1842. Forty-two minutes past six, not forty-five. Why was that? And she'd written the time at the end of the line, not at the beginning, like every other entry.

She walked along the concourse, glancing out through the row of glass doors to Stephenson Street in the gloom.

The building opposite was the one she expected to see: it had been the rear of the Midland Hotel most of her life and still bore the name carved in stone, then it had been a Waterstones bookshop and more recently an Apple store. The shops behind the old Midland Hotel, still a hotel but with a different name now, she couldn't remember what. Hudson's bookshop had been there in that block. Birmingham's major bookshop that had borne her name. She had always laughed off jokes about being heir to the Hudsons bookshop fortune, or that she'd opened a vintage clothes emporium in Moseley instead of a bookshop. And Hudsons had died in the 1980s. Waterstones had come along and taken its throne.

As she glided along, the shop fronts in the stately stone building seemed to shimmer and fade, the signs turning to ornate lettering in gold and red.

And as she headed for the glass door at the foot of Lower Temple Street, her palm out, she swooned, as if the floor were giving way. She thought for a moment that it might be an earthquake.

She plunged through and found she wasn't in 2019 anymore.

She sensed it immediately, even before she saw the physical evidence and her conscious mind could assert the fact. Her heart skipped a beat and she caught her breath, as it always happened, as if slipping through time meant her body died in one time for a second and was revived in another. A little death.

Then the odour hit her. It was like walking into a farmyard.

The street was a muddy track, not a tram line.

She looked behind to check where she'd come from, as any startled traveller finding herself in the wrong place would do, but there was just a row of dingy hovels, rickety wooden tenements that looked like they were about to collapse.

New Street Station had disappeared.

— 2 —

Fred Smith surged forward into a flurry of windmilling fists. He didn't feel the first punch. He landed a few punches himself. He socked a man in a black polo-neck on the nose and watched him crumple and fall back, a red rose blooming from his face.

Fred fell too. Without even seeing himself fall, he was on the floor, trying to get up and he couldn't get up, as if something was blocking him.

A placard on the ground, trampled by boots. Someone's trilby hat.

A black boot lunged for his face and he jerked his head back.

A kick. Yes. A kick in the head.

The mob scattered like a starling murmuration, shrieking and screaming. He was on his feet, running, pushing through the throng. He ran past the Register Office, his place of work. His keys jingling in his pocket. He could slip inside and wait for the demonstration to disperse.

He glanced over his shoulder. A bunch of Blackshirts chasing. He ran past the Register Office and on down Paradise Street to the Town Hall.

Their boots drumming the pavement behind him faded and he slowed to a trot.

He passed the Greek columns of the Town Hall and edged

along Victoria Square where motor cars and buses belched out fumes as they made the turn at the island before the Council House and snaked down New Street.

The uproar was well behind him, but he thought he could hear the clamour of violence crackling under the drone of traffic. Perhaps the riot was tumbling down from Broad Street all the way to New Street, following him.

He stopped running and broke into a nonchalant stroll. To run was to give yourself away. He was safe now on New Street among the crowds. He was a normal man walking the street, just like all these nice, innocent shoppers. The trick was to slow down and pretend to be a young man out on a Saturday morning, not a demonstrator fleeing a riot. If you didn't run, no one could chase you.

Up ahead, the pavement was crowded with people. Was it an outlying crop of the demonstration? No, it was the Theatre Royal's matinee performance emptying out a herd of people. He could duck in and lose himself in the crowd, but ushers in purple livery were waving people out.

Walking in front of him, two beautiful young women in silk stockings and cloche hats turned at the shouts echoing down from Victoria Square.

"Some sort of demonstration."

"That bloody Oswald Mosley's lot at Bingley Hall."

He smiled and shrugged, as if none of that had anything to do with him, and one of the girls smiled back and then frowned in disgust. She pulled her friend closer and they scurried across the street, weaving through motor cars to the other side.

Something was pouring into his eyes. He wiped a slick of sweat from his forehead and examined his hand. His fingers were stained scarlet.

Blood. He was bleeding.

Walking down New Street pretending to be a shopper and blood pouring down his face.

He glanced back over his shoulder. A gaggle of Blackshirts

running down the street alongside the motor cars. Had they seen him all this way? The blood on his face was a beacon calling every shark.

He plunged into the Theatre Royal crowd, lost in it for a moment, pushed through and ducked into Lower Temple Street. A short slope down to the New Street Station entrance. Twenty yards away. He could run right in and hop on the train to Moseley. He winced at the cruelty of the joke: that the nice suburb where he lived had the same name as the fascist bully he despised. The bully he was fleeing.

He blinked and wiped more blood from his eyes. One eye closed now.

He glanced in a shop window and saw his reflection. A dark stain down one side of his face. He yanked out his handkerchief from his breast pocket and wiped it, and focused on the display beyond his reflection.

Golden timepieces and carriage clocks glittering. He froze, beguiled by the beauty of it.

Shouts and commotion on the corner. The Blackshirts pushing through the theatre crowd.

He turned and ran and as he reached Stephenson Street he walked smack into someone coming around the corner.

He jerked back, reeling. A pair of hands grabbed hold of him. An old lady.

"Oh, excuse me," she said.

He didn't register her face, because he was staring at what was behind her.

New Street Station wasn't there. The grand Victorian facade of the Queen's Hotel wasn't there.

None of it was there. Just a hovel in brown dusk.

— 3 —

"You're bleeding," the old lady said. "What happened?"

A rich voice with the brittle edge of age. Kind eyes. A wave of warmth came off her and Fred felt safe for a moment, as if New Street Station hadn't just disappeared.

"Mosley's lot," he said, jerking a thumb behind him. He looked back, but they weren't there. The New Street of motor cars and beautiful women with cloche hats and dresses that fell over the knees just wasn't there. No men in trilbies and overcoats. No Blackshirts chasing him.

A horse and carriage sailed past in the gloom up there. A real carriage, pulled by a horse. A couple passed in its wake, the woman in a bonnet and a gown that ballooned down to her feet, the man in a top hat and frock coat. It was as if the Theatre Royal had been staging *A Christmas Carol* and the cast had spilled out onto the streets. Or it was…

Not now, he thought. Not when he needed to run from the Blackshirts.

"Moseley?" The woman said. "You're from Moseley?"

"Yes, I am. But not that. I was talking about Oswald Mosley. The British Union of Fascists. The demonstration at Bingley Hall."

He hooked his thumb again in the general direction of Broad Street, though he knew Bingley Hall wasn't there.

"Oh," the old lady said. "That Mosley."

11

She looked up and down the street, still holding on to him. "You're not a Blackshirt, are you?"

"What? Lord, no. I was fighting them."

"Oh, that's a relief."

"Except I don't think I'm much of a fighting man."

"Evidently."

"In fact, I've never been in a fight."

"Who are you?" she asked.

"I'm Fred Smith," he said, his eyes roaming from her kind face to the entrance to New Street Station behind her. But it wasn't behind her. What was there instead was a row of Jerry-built wooden hovels that looked like they had been thrown up by a family of architects engaged in a bitter feud. No building resembled its neighbour.

The woman followed his gaze and looked over her shoulder, and at that moment it seemed a dark figure came out of the gloom to greet her — a man in a crumpled stovepipe hat — as if one of the buildings across the dirt road had belched him forth. Across the street, where New Street Station had been, more figures emerged: skulking men in the shadows of that hovel.

"We'd better go," the old lady said. "I don't like the look of this."

Fred didn't move, despite her pulling on his arm. He was frozen, his eyes locked onto the man in the crumpled stovepipe hat approaching, a club in one hand. He looked like Bill Sykes walking out of the pages of *Oliver Twist*. But this man had nothing of the comic caricature about him. He was mean and grim and the threat of violence came off him like the stink of sewage.

"Fred!"

He came to, and let her tug him away, guiding him as they scooted along the row.

Up ahead, more men crossed the street to block their way. A feral gang of Dickensian ruffians.

He was hallucinating. This was all a waking dream. He'd

been cornered by the Blackshirts and they were going to beat him up, but his addled brain was seeing them dressed as characters from a Christmas card. It wouldn't matter in a minute, because he would be unconscious. If he was lucky, he'd wake up in hospital.

Five steps ahead, a door opened and a young woman popped her head out. She threw a bucket of something into the gutter with a sickening splosh. She looked both ways and stiffened as she caught the scenario: a gang cornering a pair of helpless victims: an old lady and a young man covered in blood.

Fred had just a moment to register she was quite beautiful: a girl in a ball gown, her dark hair pinned up in ringlets around her pretty face.

She looked both ways again. The gang closing in.

"In here!" she called.

The old lady yanked him forward and they ran to her.

The men darted for them.

The old lady bundled into the doorway and Fred stumbled in after her.

A hand grabbed at his collar, snatched and missed. The girl slammed the door. Someone yelped. She slammed it again. A scream from the other side.

"My bloody hand!"

A rain of blows on the door.

The girl slammed a bolt across it.

They banged and kicked some more.

The girl leaned back against the door, as if to keep them out all by herself.

Fred looked into her eyes. "Oh. It's you."

A ghost from the past. The ghost he'd seen last Christmas Eve at New Street Station, walking up the dark end of Platform 3. Through steam and shadow, a dark-eyed young woman emerged, a hood over her head, her porcelain white face staring at him, just as she did now. A Victorian ghost in 1933. She had gazed on him and opened her mouth to speak and he'd turned and ran.

This was that same face.

Fred slumped to his knees, his head swirling. He looked to the ceiling, saw stars and fainted.

— 4 —

"Why is the station here and not there?" Dickens said, alighting from the train and stretching his legs.

Birmingham Station was a small affair. A few lines of track terminating in a cube of a building — a Roman temple with columns and a flat roof. Passengers streamed along the platform and through the building, strange spectral figures in the clouds of steam. He tucked the image away. He would think later of the exact wording with which to paint it.

"I'm not sure I follow you, Charles," John Forster said.

Forster was fumbling with his pockets, perhaps searching for the tickets, looking up and down the platform with the air of a man who has forgotten something and can't quite remember why he is where he is, how he got there and what he should do now he was there. He checked the three pockets of his waistcoat, the five pockets of his jacket both inner and outer, and the five pockets of his greatcoat, also inner and outer, before delving into his trouser pockets. The only thing he hadn't checked was his top hat.

"I was merely wondering why they built the station so far from the centre of the town?"

"I'm not sure I know the answer to that, Charles," John said.

"I suppose one could ask why they didn't build the town around the station."

15

"The station is only three years old. The town significantly older."

"Yes, quite. But the mystery persists."

Forster pulled the tickets from his inside jacket pocket, holding them aloft in triumph. "Here! At last."

A thick wad of paper fell out of his pocket and slapped to the stone pavement. An envelope, unsealed, and inside the unmistakable edge of banknotes. Like a book made of money, Charles thought.

Forster let out a pained moan and crouched to retrieve it but a boy darted in and scooped it up. For a moment, Charles thought the boy was going to dash off with the money, and he was going to watch it happen without doing anything, merely observing in stasis, noting the scene and finding the words to describe it. But the boy held the wad of money up.

Dickens saw a ghost.

The memory of another wretched boy reaching out with dirty hands, reaching out to Charles, his sunken eyes appealing, as if to say *take me with you from this hell. Don't leave me here.* And also to wave him on to a better life. It was the moment young Charles Dickens had turned from Master Green and walked out of Warren's Blacking Factory forever, never quite wiping the mud from his feet, the cold from his bones and the hunger from his stomach.

Forster snatched the wad of money from the boy with a yelp of relief and shoved it inside his greatcoat, looking all around to see if anyone had seen. "Thank you, boy. How kind of you."

The boy smiled up at them. Dickens stepped back, recoiling. It wasn't Young Master Green at all, a ghost come to haunt him, it was just a boy like any other. His suit was smart but his shoes had seen better days — the telltale sign of poverty — with an alarming tide mark of black mud. He wore an enormous baker boy cap nestling on his brown curls that he might grow into in a few more years. Charles couldn't help but think of little Oliver, the child he'd created in his imagination and set loose on the world.

"Good morning, sir," the boy said, tugging at Forster's coat. "Are you the gentleman from London, Mr Charles Dickens, sir?"

Forster put a gloved finger the width of the boy's arm to his lips. "Shhhhh, boy! You are not to mention that name! I gave instructions."

"They said I was to come and look for a fat man and a short, young man with long hair, and that would be Charles Dickens."

Dickens fought to hide a chuckle.

"Boy, you are not to say that name again, to anyone. Do you understand?" Forster checked all around to see if anyone had overheard, but it seemed no one had caught the boy's utterance over the hiss of steam, the shouts of porters and the chaotic rabble of passengers fighting their way to the exits.

"I'm from Showell's Printing House, sir."

Forster put his finger to the boy's lips now. "And don't mention printers, either."

The boy stared up at Forster as if he were mad, which was not far from the truth.

Forster beamed a grin, and said, "What's your name, young man?"

"Tim, sir. I'm Tim Cratchit."

"What a delightful name. And what a delightful, intelligent boy you are. Now, I'm Mr Forster — the man you seek — but you are not to say the name of Charles Dickens aloud. It's a deadly secret, isn't it?"

Forster looked to Charles for support, not more than a minute into his deception and already floundering with a child.

"It's a magic spell," said Charles, "that will cause untold calamity should you say it three times. Do you understand?"

The boy nodded and looked from Charles to Forster and back again as if they were the mad ones. Which, of course, was indubitably right.

"I understand, sirs," he said.

"Such an intelligent boy," said Forster. "Now, lead on, young master Cratchit and show us the way."

Charles was about to follow the boy through the crowd when a woman cried out.

"Oh, it's you, isn't it?"

A pretty young woman in a pretty blue bonnet, her pretty blue eyes bright with recognition and adoration. She held out her hand and gripped his sleeve.

"It's Mr Dickens, isn't it? Charles Dickens!"

Charles coughed and looked up and down the platform, as if someone might come to rescue him.

"I'm afraid there's been some mistake, madam," Forster said, stepping between the lady and Charles, the bulk of his massive frame shielding the author, so he quite disappeared behind him.

"It is," the lady cried. "I know him! It's Boz! Dear Mr Dickens!"

"No, madam, I assure you it isn't," John wheedled in his Northumbrian tone.

"Wait a while. I have a copy of *Oliver Twist* right here in my case. I must have him sign it!"

Forster took Charles's arm and dragged him away after the boy. "You are mistaken, madam. This isn't Charles Hmm-hmm at all, no, not at all."

They were leaving their cases behind. "John, our cases."

"We'll send for them," Forster muttered through the side of his mouth.

"It is. I'm sure of it!" The woman was delving into her case, pulling out her clothes.

"You are mistaken!" Forster called. "Come now, Ch— er, come now, John."

Forster presented their tickets at the barrier and they rushed into the Roman temple, a grand atrium with a ticket office to one side and two marble staircases curving in an embrace. They dashed straight through and out the other side to a gloomy street, the boy leading the way.

"So much for our incognito trip to Birmingham," Dickens said.

"I shouldn't have brought you. Your fame is too wide."

"My star is fading fast, John," Dickens grumbled. "I'm sure you've noticed."

"Well, we're here to arrest that fall."

Forster waved his cane in the air to hail a cab, and saw there were none. The only cabs in sight were the convoy of carriages thundering off in the direction of the town.

"I think we've missed all the cabs, sir," the boy said.

"That wretched woman," said John.

"She was rather comely," said Charles. "Perhaps the only reader I have left, and you spoiled it for me."

"We don't want a repeat of our Cornwall debacle, do we?"

"John. What happened in Cornwall stays in Cornwall."

The boy looked up at Dickens, grinning inanely, understanding nothing. Charles rubbed the knot of tension between his eyes. This whole affair was ghastly.

"Charles," Forster hissed. "May I impress upon you the absolutely top secret nature of our mission here?"

Dickens laughed and rolled his eyes. They were no more than two dozen steps into Birmingham and already the secret mission had descended into a Christmas pantomime. "Young Master Cratchit, how far is it to our hotel?"

"It's a short walk, sir. Less than a mile. We might saunter it in a quarter hour."

"Then we shall saunter it."

"I'll get a porter to send the baggage on," said Forster. He rushed back into the Roman temple, pushing against the tide of human traffic all emerging and complaining at the lack of cabs.

Dickens knelt down to the boy. "And which direction do we go, Master Cratchit? Point it out to me."

The boy pointed up the hill beyond the immediate cluster of soot-black dwellings and workshops, from which came the glow of furnaces. "That spire there is St Martin in the Bull Ring, and that spire in the distance; that's Christ Church."

"I suppose I'll want the one that is farthest?"

"Christ Church is at the top of New Street next to the Town Hall. The New Royal Hotel is up that way."

"But a mere quarter hour, you say?"

"For young gentlemen like us," said Tim. "It might take longer with your friend."

Dickens smiled despite himself. He had been nursing a surly countenance since they had set out on the six o'clock train from London, and it had soured the closer he'd got to Birmingham. He'd been rather enjoying being surly and mean and fully intended to luxuriate in it. But the boy, despite his ragged appearance, was intelligent and a wit to boot. Charles reached behind the boy's ear and pulled out a shiny new half farthing. The boy's eyes lit up and he shoved the coin in his trouser pocket, as if someone might take it from him, or the magic might take it back.

The lady in the pretty blue bonnet came running out, a porter lugging her case, from which a scrap of bright green material peeped out and flapped like a flag. She had a book in her hand. "Where is he? Where is the great author?"

Dickens sighed, rose to his feet and stepped toward her.

She halted and her face brightened with joy. "Oh, there you are!"

She thrust the book at him with a metal pen.

Charles turned the pen over in his hand. "Exquisite craftsmanship."

"Yes, Mr Dickens, and made right here in this town."

She had the Birmingham twang to her voice. These Brummagem folk talked differently to your Sam Weller cockney types. It was quite rounded and melodious, as if they were all eating some sort of gooey, chewy item of confectionary. It was quite fetching.

"Ah yes," Charles said. "We're in the home of the pen." He signed the frontispiece and gave the book back to her.

20

She read his signature and held it to her breast, squealing with delight.

He tipped his top hat and said, "Delighted to make your acquaintance."

"Charles Dickens, here in Birmingham! I can't believe it."

She ran off and joined the crowd of stranded passengers waiting for cabs.

Forster came running out. "I've arranged for the cases to be sent on. Is there no sign of a cab?"

"Why did you choose *John?*"

"I'm sorry?"

"When you were looking to call me a false name, you called me John."

"It was the first thing that came to mind."

"But you're John, John."

"I'm not as quick with my imagination as you, Charles."

"It *is* my second name, I suppose. Perhaps you should utilize both of my middle names and call me John Huffam."

"Two Johns might be confusing."

Dickens tapped his lips with his finger. "I wonder if I might have made a better way in the world with the name John Huffam?"

Forster patted him on the shoulder, to wake him from his reverie. "Anyway, thank goodness we avoided you being recognized. It would not do if anyone knew you were here. If word got out, our venture would be compromised."

"No one will know," Charles said. "Come on, let's walk."

"We might still get a cab. I'll demand the first one that comes."

"By using my good name, John?"

The boy skipped down the stone steps and Dickens followed.

A beggar woman sat on the steps. He had mistaken it for a pile of rags and only now realized it was an old woman, holding out a withered hand. Her eyes flared with entreaty — or was it recognition? — did she too recognize the author of

Oliver Twist? Or the stain of blacking on this gentleman? The stain that betrayed him as one of her kind: a stain he could never wash off.

With a bitter taste in his mouth, Dickens patted his pockets and passed on, following the boy up Curzon Street.

— 5 —

Fred opened his eyes to find the ghost looking down on him.

"He's awakening," she said, turning back to someone else.

"A faint, nothing more," came a voice. An old lady's voice.

Fred tried to see her, craning his neck to glance over the way. A sharp pain flared through his temples.

"Shhhh. Stay still," the ghost said.

An old lady had bumped into him on the street corner, yes, and this ghost was the dark-eyed young woman in Victorian costume who'd opened the door to them. She appeared quite real. His eyes rolled up to the ceiling. Gold stars with a crescent moon painted on a sheet of indigo cloth.

The Theatre Royal had been playing *A Christmas Carol* and the actors had spilled out as if they'd taken the entire production onto New Street. That was the last thing he remembered. He closed his eyes.

"He took a knock to the head," the old lady said. "He'll be all right soon."

"You're lucky I came out when I did. The street behind us is the edge of the Froggery. It can be a dangerous place even in the morning. What is this gentleman's name?"

"I don't know."

"Oh, I thought you were…"

"We just bumped into each other. I've never seen him before in my life. At least, I don't think I have. My memory's been a little… impaired of late."

"Oh, I see." The angel left him. Fred sensed her shift away from him and felt bereft. Her footsteps crossed the room. "My name is Miss Isabelle Ruth. People call me Belle. I'm pleased to meet you."

"Mrs Hudson," said the old lady. "Susannah Hudson."

They whispered together and Fred couldn't catch their words. He strained to hear and moved to get up but a wave of nausea swept through him and he slumped back into the plush cushion of the sofa.

A familiar sense of dread gripped him. It was happening again. The thing that had happened so many times before. The thing he was scared to let anyone know, it was so weird.

Mrs Hudson's warm voice whispered on. Was she the same? Was she from another time as well? Perhaps she was also…

He choked on the words. Even in his mind he hesitated to say them. The phrase he'd conjured for his impairment, his disability, this malady that he knew he had but had never told anyone about, including, for most of his life, himself.

This old lady suffered it too, he could tell. She was, just like him…

Chronologically-impaired.

A blush of shame fluttered through him. His dark, dirty secret. The cancer inside he was afraid to mention. Because saying it aloud, even acknowledging it to himself in his thoughts, would make it real. He had always put on a cheerful disposition and pretended there was nothing different about him, that he didn't see ghosts from the past, that these insane visions were just the memories of dreams.

Delusions. This was all a delusion. He would snap out of it soon. He always had done. It had just never happened for so long before.

No. He'd been knocked out in the fighting. This was an hallucination. Vivid, yes, but all hallucinations were vivid. Hallucinations were absolutely real to the people experiencing them. That's why they were hallucinations. They felt no different to reality. He was Fred Smith from 1934 and had gone along to the anti-fascist demonstration at Bingley Hall to protest against Oswald Mosley.

That's right. He'd been hit in the fighting. He'd surged forward with a crowd of anti-fascists and it had been a flurry of windmilling fists. He'd been punched and had felt nothing, only knowing he'd landed a few himself.

And then Fred had fallen too. Without even seeing himself fall, he was suddenly on the floor, trying to get up and he couldn't get up, as if something was blocking him. A kick. Yes, He remembered that. There had definitely been a kick in the head.

No wonder he was seeing things.

Belle came back, sitting on the sofa beside him and resumed wiping his brow.

He was seeing a beautiful young Victorian woman dabbing his brow with a cloth. The dark-eyed young woman whose ghost he'd seen on the station platform last Christmas. She dipped the cloth into a pan of warm water from the stove. The soothing heat on his head. Her face close to his and the pleasing scent of her, of lavender or something: a feminine fragrance, something floral and pleasant.

Her face close to his, intent on the wound. Their eyes met and she focused on him, holding his gaze. There was nothing but the intense electricity that passed between them, nothing else in the universe. And then she blushed and lowered her eyes, fidgeting with the cloth and pan.

She bustled out and Fred listened to her steps down a passage and off to a room somewhere on the right. The creak of floorboards and the clatter of noise from a scullery.

Mrs Hudson had a strange little sad sort of smile on her face. She was sitting on a chaise longue across from him. A jumble of props all around.

"Where are we?"

"We appear to be in the Theatre Royal," she said.

"Christmas Eve, 1842."

"None of this makes sense." He stroked his forehead and felt it slick and wet. His skull throbbed and his neck was made of steel, weighing heavy on his shoulders.

"It's not *that* Theatre Royal," she said. "Well, it is. But not the one you know. Nor the one I remember."

He closed his eyes and groaned. Perhaps this was just a peculiarly vivid dream and he would wake soon.

"You understand we're in the wrong time?"

He opened his eyes. She had said it right out loud, as if she were a radio presenter giving a running commentary on his nightmare. *And back to square one.* There was no escaping this or pretending it was a dream. He wasn't going to wake up from this.

"Has this happened to you before?" she asked.

He shrugged and looked at the splodges of blood on his brogues. "I don't know what you mean."

"It has, hasn't it?"

He met her gaze. She could see it in his eyes: the thing he'd been dreading to admit, even to himself. It was happening again and with greater detail than it had ever happened. He was right in it.

"But not to this extent," she said. "Am I right?"

He nodded. A violent spasm of pain. He stiffened and held his forehead, shuddering as the agony faded.

She came across and sat next to him. He was on a chaise longue too. She patted his knee. "Don't worry. We'll muddle through somehow. This kind of thing happens a lot when you first find your… ability. You learn to control it."

"You mean we can go back to normal?"

"Yes. If I can remember how. I've been forgetting things a lot lately. Sometimes I think, well, if I'm here, perhaps there's a reason. You see this?" She dug in her handbag and pulled out a little pocket diary, sweeping it open with the bookmark ribbon.

He focused on the page, frowning, the print blurred.

26

"I wrote down this place and this year, you see? So I must have intended to come. I just can't remember why I wrote it."

"This is 1842?" he said.

"Yes, obviously."

He turned the diary over to examine the front cover. "And you're from... two thousand and nineteen?"

She nodded. "You're from some time in the 1930s, I'm guessing."

"It's 1934," he said. "This is a dream. I'm going to wake up."

"Not yet. Perhaps we have to do something here. Perhaps we can't leave until we've done it."

Belle stood in the doorway, staring at them.

Mrs Hudson shoved her pocket diary into her handbag and snapped the brass clasp shut.

Had Belle heard any of that? It seemed she'd just appeared in the room and not approached. No footsteps creaking up the corridor. The sure sign of someone who had been listening at the door.

There was a blush of alarm on her face, the shamefaced bloom of one who has heard a terrible secret and now must pretend she knows nothing.

— 6 —

Tim Cratchit walked the gentlemen to New Street, running alongside the young man who was never to be called Charles Dickens, though they had not yet told him what he *was* to be called. The young man who wasn't Mr Dickens had a long stride to him and was a good walker. The fat man who was Mr John Forster huffed and puffed a good twenty paces behind and several times called out for them to slow down.

When he did, the man who wasn't Charles Dickens would stand and wait and gaze up at the surrounding buildings or at passing people. He didn't look at Tim, not once. He sneered, an unfriendly chap who didn't care to be in this place at all. The fat man called John would catch up, wheezing and ask if they were nearly there yet, and then the man who wasn't Mr Dickens would walk on and the whole thing would happen again.

Tim trotted alongside him and told him at which corners to turn. Within a few minutes, they were on New Street, walking under the stone portico of the Hen and Chickens Hotel, at which the man gave a guffaw, and then they passed the grim facade of King Edward's School, which, at night, always seemed to Tim like a haunted castle. He rushed on ahead, crossing Peck Lane and King Street, both of which led down to the Froggery — the dark place they couldn't guess at from this stately street — and eventually he came to the main

28

road that dissected New Street — Temple Street. The Theatre Royal sat there opposite the foot of Bennett's Hill.

"This is the theatre, sir," Tim said.

The man who wasn't Charles Dickens paused and looked up at the white columns and arches of the front of house. "Look at this, John," he called to the fat man. "A little hut like this is what counts as a Theatre Royal in this town."

"It looks grand enough," said Mr Forster, gasping for breath.

"The hotel is right next door, sir," said the boy.

He thought the man who wasn't Mr Dickens might say something bad about this building too, but he paused and took in the grand edifice, with its elegant pergola. He nodded and hummed and walked in.

Mr Forster patted Tim on the head, said, "Thank you very much, lad," and followed him in.

That was it. His job was over. He clutched the coin in his trouser pocket, brought it out and examined it, so shiny and new.

The words *Half Farthing* under a crown and numbers *1842*. Some flowers at the bottom. A rose, a thistle and a shamrock. On the other side a plump girl's face with a knot of hair tied up with ribbons. He edged the coin around to read the words *Victoria D:G: Britanniar: Regina F:D:*

Gripping it tight in his fist, he turned down Lower Temple Street and walked over to the Froggery, along the mean cluster of shabby streets and lanes.

His step quickened. His mother would be home before the hearth, preparing father his lunch before rushing back to Mrs Jowett's to attend to the old lady. They would hide their disappointment at the half farthing.

"Perhaps a penny," his father had said. "Two esteemed gentlemen from London. Perhaps even a shilling!"

"Don't fill the boy's head with such high hopes," his mother had said, though she'd laughed and he could read the hope in her eyes as well as his father's.

29

That hope would be swallowed like a lump of bread that stuck in your throat and wouldn't go down.

A shadow leapt from the blackness and grabbed him by the collar.

"Here, boy! Where you going?"

Slogger Pike leered down at him and Tim recoiled at the stink of saveloy from his mouth, the debris of it on his teeth.

"Home, Mr Pike, sir," Tim said.

"What have you got for me, boy? I've been waiting."

"They walked from the station. No cabs."

Tim writhed in his rough hands as he yanked him this way and that, checking his pockets.

"What did they give you? Hand it over."

Tim opened his fist. "This."

"Half a farthing? Is that it?"

"Yes, sir, Mr Pike."

He took the boy's collar in his fist and pulled him close. Another blast of foul breath. "You lying to me, boy? He gave you more than that, rich knob like him."

"No, sir. A half farthing. That was all."

Tim gulped hard, knowing that Slogger Pike would do to him what he'd done to old Jacob Marley. What everyone said he'd done to old Marley.

Pike shoved him away. "Why, the dirty old miser."

Tim rearranged his collar, his fingers feeling the hem. There was a tear. His mother would be upset and have to patch it up as best she could. The thought of her squinting over his torn shirt in candlelight, sighing and simpering and straining her eyes, was too much to bear. Tears sprung to his eyes and he rubbed his face to wipe them away.

"Who is he and what's his business?"

"Dickens, they called him. Someone important from London. A lady got him to sign a book. A book he wrote."

"A writer? What's he doing here?"

"Something about the theatre, he said, but there's another man with him here to talk business with the print shop.

That's why they sent me to meet them."

"What kind of business?"

"Something important, because my father is all a flutter about it. A big investment, he said."

"So they've money on them?"

Tim gulped. He should say nothing of what he'd seen, but in Slogger Pike's grip he had the urge to let everything tumble out of him, his tongue desperate to betray everyone in the world and befriend this man.

"Come on, little Tim," Slogger Pike said, suddenly friendly and soothing. "You can tell me."

"He dropped an envelope full of money. I picked it up for him."

"Money, eh? How much money? How many coins and what type? Did you see? Not half farthings, I hope."

"Not coins. Notes. About this thick." Tim held up his thumb and forefinger in a C shape to indicate the width of the envelope, picturing it in his hand as he did so. "Heavy. Like a book."

Slogger Pike licked his lips. "You find out what you can about that money, you hear? You tell me everything." He dug into his pocket and pulled out the shiny half farthing. "And here. This is yours. A little something for helping out old Slogger Pike. For being a good boy. You keep this."

Tim took the warm coin and shoved it in his pocket, while Slogger Pike brushed him down.

"Now you go home, boy, but remember what I said. I want to know more about those gentlemen and that money. And when you know it, you come to the old Dungeon and let me know all about it."

"Yes, sir," he said.

Tim turned and ran down the mean street, muttering a silent prayer under his breath that he might reach home without seeing any more dark spirits.

— 7 —

"You poor people," Belle said. "I do so wonder how I can help you."

"You've already helped us," the young man answered. "I think you might have saved us from certain death."

"I'll get you some bandages. And you, dear lady, have lost your skirts. I must find you something to cover your legs."

The old lady looked down at her legs and seemed surprised to find that her coat only came down to just below her knees, exposing her stockinged calves and her strange fur-lined bootees. Belle reached for a blanket and threw it over the old lady's lap. It covered her modesty enough. "The wardrobe," she said. "I'll find a dress from the wardrobe."

She pointed to the adjoining room, as if they knew where it was. She was flustered, embarrassed. This was all too much. Her eyes fell on the clock and her heart jumped. She would be late for Mrs Jowett and one could never be late for Mrs Jowett. Unpunctuality was the sin she would not countenance.

The strangers sitting in her lounge looked up at her, so lost and forlorn: a half-dressed old lady who'd forgotten her clothes, and a handsome young man who'd been bashed on the head by Slogger Pike. Belle had saved them. She checked the swell of pride in her bosom. Was it pride? A warm, fuzzy feeling inside her at helping the young man. She didn't know what it was, but she was certain it wasn't pride, so it couldn't be sinful.

"I'm deeply sorry," she said. "Please do not think me rude, but I have to leave."

The young man went to stand up, then groaned and slumped back on the chaise longue.

"No, please, stay," she said, perhaps a little too forcefully. "I have a most urgent appointment, but I shall return in an hour. Perhaps a little more than an hour."

"Are we all right to stay here?" the old lady asked.

"Most certainly. I insist on it." Belle reached for her cloak and clasped it around her neck, pulling the hood up over her head. "But please do excuse me for the moment."

The young man stood again as she went to the door, which was handsome of him. Belle found she was smiling. She paused at the door and said, "Please don't leave."

She blushed as she stepped onto the street behind the theatre. She wasn't sure why she had said that again and so forcefully expressed her desire that they should stay, but she knew now that she certainly did feel it, with all her heart, and not merely because the young man had evinced in her an overwhelming desire to protect him and tend to his poor head.

Queen Street was safe now that it was nearly midday and the criminal elements had faded like insects crawling under stones. Belle crossed the muddy street, holding her skirts up as much as she could, and walked down the length of the street till the crossroads where Peck Lane divided Queen Street and changed it into Colmore Street, like a sword cutting a snake in half and creating two snakes. She turned down Peck Lane and entered the maze of streets that were known variously as the Froggery, or the Hinkleys, after two particular streets, the part standing in for the whole. Some called it the Rookeries also. The Froggery's narrow streets were busy with life. A jumble of streets here at the foot of a hill, as if the new Town Hall had shoved out the poor and they had all tumbled down

Pinfold Street to land in a heap at the bottom of the hill, like Jack and Jill.

Like her strangers, Belle thought, turning. A man and a woman who had fallen down the hill, the boy with a broken crown. She hadn't learned his name and now wondered if he might be called Jack. Should she mend his head with vinegar and brown paper?

A strange sense of destiny fluttered in her heart.

It wasn't simply that the young man was handsome, nor that it was Christmas Eve and she felt some of the seasonal spirit that no one seemed to care about. There was something else. The old lady too. These strangers had awoken something in her: a sense that these unearthly visitors might solve the puzzle of her life on this very day.

A cold wind bit at her cheeks as she came to Dudley Street. The air whispered the threat of snow. So many of the town's wretched poor might be caught in the bitter cold.

The Connexion chapel stood right on the corner of Peck Lane and Dudley Street, a gleaming beacon of hope at odds with the jumble of run-down tenements all around and the Dungeon that faced it on the opposite corner: the spikes on its wall and the grim grille on its gate that always made her shiver with dread.

The gruff old bell of St. Martin's church struck twelve as Belle rapped the old brass knocker of Mrs Jowett's rectory house.

Mrs Cratchit, the housemaid, let her in and took her cloak and Belle rushed to the drawing room, hoping the excitement of her morning visitors did not show on her face. She entered the drawing room only seconds after the twelfth toll of the bell.

Mrs Jowett looked up from her chair and glanced at the clock above the mantel. Her grimace betrayed she was unhappy with Belle arriving three seconds late. But she said, "Ah, Miss Ruth. So punctual."

A man rose from the sofa and Belle paused, startled at the

unexpected presence. An old man. So old he must have been forty or forty-five, in a grey suit that matched his grey face and greying hair. Ebenezer Swingeford, Mrs Jowett's brother. A man she had seen only a few times. He was immaculately turned out and well-dressed, but as genial as an icicle. His reputation around town was that of a ruthless businessman with no heart. A man she was glad she had managed to avoid.

"Miss Ruth," said Mrs Jowett, "you know my dear brother, Mr Swingeford."

The man bowed. "My pleasure, Miss Ruth."

Belle shook the man's cold hand and took her seat. She saw it now. Mrs Jowett's expression when she had arrived was not displeasure at her being three seconds late, it was the discomfort at the presence of this man, her brother. She had a ghastly pallor and her mouth had curled into a bitter gash.

"Very pleased to make your acquaintance, Mr Swingeford," Belle said. "And if I may, the greetings of the season to you."

"What's that?" the man said.

Belle wondered if he might be a little deaf. "I say a Merry Christmas to you, and to you too, of course, Mrs Jowett."

"Christmas?" said Mr Swingeford. "Bah."

Mrs Jowett allowed herself a wry smile. "You must forgive my brother, Miss Ruth. He does not partake of the joys of the season and I believe has never cared much for it. You shan't expect him to attend your show this afternoon."

"Humbug," he snarled.

Belle thought he must be joking with his sister. No man could be so rude, surely?

"You might think he has called to wish his only remaining family the greetings of the season, but no. I do believe he doesn't even know what day it is."

"Indeed I do," said Mr Swingeford. "It is the day before every man, woman and child in my employ takes it upon themselves to pick my pocket and expect a day's pay for a day of idleness."

35

Mrs Jowett seemed pleased at this outburst, a glimmer of malice in her eye, as if she delighted in pushing her brother to condemn himself with his own tongue.

Mrs Cratchit brought in a silver platter of cakes and poured tea, breathing heavily, as if she'd been running, the poor woman.

"Mr Swingeford was on the verge of telling me the reason for his visit, when you arrived," said Mrs Jowett.

Mr Swingeford grunted, shoving a cream scone into his mouth, struggling to speak.

"But you might be interested to know, or rather appalled," Mrs Jowett continued, "that my brother has secured a controlling interest in the Theatre Royal. I fear today's Christmas Harlequinade for the poor children of this neighbourhood might well be your last."

Mr Swingeford swallowed hard and thumped his chest. "My sister attempts to blacken my name in your good graces, Miss Ruth."

"I do nothing of the sort! Your own words blacken what name you have left."

Belle felt the colour rush to her cheeks and wondered if she should get up and leave these squabbling siblings to their row.

"No one is more surprised than I to hear of your patronage of the theatre, dear brother. You have never seemed like a man who cares for the arts."

"It is a business interest, no more. A trifle in my affairs."

Mrs Jowett purred with glee. "And yet you also own a printing house. Are you not secretly a man of letters?"

Belle looked at her lap to hide her smirk, fought desperately to clear it and raised her head to put on as stony a countenance as she could muster.

Mr Swingeford's eyes blazed defiance. "The railway is my main business. The railway that will wipe away all of this." He waved a hand around as if to indicate the drawing room, the chapel, or the town of Birmingham beyond the windows.

"What on earth do you mean?" Mrs Jowett asked, the grin falling from her lips.

It was Mr Swingeford's turn to smile. He sipped his tea and held the silence in the room, cosseting it like a bag of gold coins. "I mean there is a problem with this town, and it is that our station is on its outskirts."

"That is where stations should be," said Mrs Jowett. "Ghastly, dirty things."

"No, I say. The town needs a train station that is central. A grand, central station."

"Here?" said Mrs Jowett. "This is what you have come to tell me?"

"You are the first to know," said Mr Swingeford, with the smile of a cobra.

Belle shifted uncomfortably in her seat.

"Curzon Street is too far out. *Here* is where our station should be." Mr Swingeford pointed to the rug between them. "Right here, just off New Street. This is the heart of the town, and a train line is the main artery that pumps the life blood to it."

"Here?" Mrs Jowett cried. "You would build a train station next to my chapel?"

"No, I would not, dear sister."

"I am glad to hear it."

"I would build it right over this chapel."

At his sister's aghast face, Mr Swingeford merely sipped his tea and shrugged. "It is nothing personal. Do not assume that. It is simply progress."

"But this chapel. You would build it here and nowhere else."

"I fear you misunderstand the nature of this station," Mr Swingeford said. "It will be ten times the size of that pathetic Roman folly at the end of Curzon Street. A vast cathedral. The largest building in this entire town. The largest roof in the world."

"Bigger than the new Town Hall?" Belle asked.

"Five times bigger. A vast construction that will sit over this entire neighbourhood. Everything that the locals call the Froggery. I shall wipe it away and replace it with something grand."

"You plan to wipe out the entire neighbourhood?" Mrs Jowett asked.

"It is a fetid swamp. I say wipe it off the face of the earth."

"But what will happen to these poor people?" Mrs Jowett now waved her arm to indicate the maze of streets outside.

"They will make way for progress."

"But where will they go?"

"They'll move out to places more suitable. To Cheapside and to Small Heath. Push them out there, I say, where we shall no longer have to smell them."

"The poor are not vermin."

"They are a threat to our health. They spread disease like rats. They live among rats. The very air we breathe is heavy with pestilence from the labouring classes."

Despite this shocking news, Mrs Jowett looked to Belle and back to her brother and allowed herself a satisfied smile again. What was going on here between them? It somehow seemed to involve Belle, but she could not think why, other than she was witness to the childish one-upmanship of a sibling rivalry.

"My dear brother," Mrs Jowett said, pointing to the portrait on the wall of an old woman in a plain dress and a white bonnet. "This is a Countess of Huntingdon chapel. She may be resting with the angels now, but she has left a legacy, a formidable organization that has built a hundred or more chapels around this country and far and wide across the empire. Why, there are thirty-two almshouses on this very site — rooms for poor destitute women — bought by the Lench's Trust. We shall not be as easy to move on as the wretched poor you despise so much."

"It will go, like every other building in these three acres."

"There's a new synagogue too," Belle said.

38

"That will also go." Mr Swingeford pointed to the portrait of the Countess of Huntingdon. "Even she will make way for progress. The railway is the greatest achievement of the modern world."

"And have you forgotten," Mrs Jowett said, "what lies behind this chapel?"

Swingeford looked at the rug and shrugged. "I have not."

"Though this chapel be new, the graveyard behind it is old, and it bears the grave of your wife. Would you disturb her bones?"

"I was married a mere year and that was twenty years ago. She is gone. Her bones mean nothing to me."

"And your child."

"Who never took a breath on this earth."

"Dear God, you monster. I hope your dear departed wife haunts you."

"Ghosts," Swingeford sneered. "Humbug."

Belle fought desperately to stay her tongue. She had heard the rumours of Swingeford's tragic past, and it had seemed to lend him an air of doomed romance. This, perhaps, was what had made him so mad at the world. But could even such a tragedy as this be a reason for such cruelty, when it was something he dismissed so easily? She held her breath and stayed quite still, in case these squabbling siblings were alerted to her presence and asked her to leave.

"Dear, Ebenezer," Mrs Jowett said. "All of this money you will make, and you will never spend it, only hoard it, like a sad, old miser."

"I did not come here to be insulted," Mr Swingeford said.

"I know why you came here," Mrs Jowett snapped.

Mr Swingeford rose from his seat and bowed to Belle. "Miss Ruth. It was a pleasure to make your acquaintance. I only wish the encounter might have been in more pleasant circumstances."

"Go," Mrs Jowett said. "Go back to building your mountain of gold." She rose and followed him out, shouting after him, her voice echoing back to Belle. "But that mountain will slide and bury you, Ebenezer! Mark my words! It will bury you!"

A door slammed. Mrs Jowett returned and slumped against the doorjamb. Belle put her teacup aside and rushed to help her.

"My life, I feel all faint."

"Come and sit down, Mrs Jowett."

Belle walked the old lady to the sofa and sat her down. She reached for a fan and wafted her face.

"Forgive me, Isabelle," the old lady said. "I'm sorry you had to see that."

"It's quite all right, Mrs Jowett."

The old lady grabbed her wrist. "No. Let it be a lesson. That man is evil, and you must avoid his company. Shun him like the devil himself. Nothing good will come of any intercourse with him, as you have just witnessed."

Belle wasn't sure what possible company she might ever endure with Ebenezer Swingeford and was certain she would never see him again, nor wish to.

"It's quite all right, Mrs Jowett. I shall heed your warning."

And, to Belle's astonishment, Mrs Jowett wept. Real tears. Belle had never seen her show any form of weakness in all the days she had known her — and that had been her entire life — from her time at the orphanage when she had first seen the old lady introduced as a benefactor to whom they should all be eternally grateful. In all these years, this benefactor had never shown an ounce of weakness. Not until her brother had called on Christmas Eve.

Belle sat by her side and held her hand. Mrs Jowett squeezed her fingers gratefully and sobbed into a silk handkerchief. Belle comforted her in silence and wondered how long she must stay before she could return to the mysterious strangers at the theatre.

The clock ticked away and Mrs Jowett calmed herself and

fell into a slumber.

As Belle got up to go, Mrs Jowett let out an anguished sigh in her sleeping state and cried, "What have I done?"

She fell back into slumber and Belle crept out to the hall, where Mrs Cratchit let her out to the street.

Belle stood on the corner, pulling her cloak around her at the stark cold of the morning, and tried to imagine all of this gone and a railway station in its place.

A man stood on the other side of the street, watching her, standing before the spike-topped great gate of the foreboding Dungeon, the old prison building that stood opposite, glowering over the Froggery like a gate of Hell, in stark contrast to the chapel which sought to offer the alternative. It was rumoured that the Dungeon was now occupied by criminal lowlifes and vagabonds, Slogger Pike among them, but Belle didn't know if that was a child's rumour.

But the man standing before the Dungeon gate was not Slogger Pike. It was the young man she'd rescued. He must have followed her from the theatre.

He stood and stared at her with a look of wide-eyed amazement.

Belle stepped into the dirt road but before she had gone three paces the young man retreated, a look of terror on his face.

A horse-drawn dray came thundering down the hill, the driver cursed and Belle jumped back to the pavement, mud spraying her dress.

The young man was gone.

She froze, startled. How was that possible? He couldn't have gone through that enormous gate in those few seconds the dray had blinded her.

She looked up and down the street but he was nowhere to be seen.

Shivering at the thought she'd seen a ghost, she turned up Peck Lane and rushed back to the theatre.

— 8 —

Fred woke with a slap to the face. He jerked back. The old lady standing over him.

"You can't sleep," she said. "Not after a bang on the head. At least I don't think that's wise for a while, anyway."

His head pounded. Awful now. Throat dry. She hadn't slapped him, just a gentle pat on the cheek, a nudge, exaggerated by his sleeping state.

A blanket of stars on the ceiling. A Victorian lumber room. The nightmare of his timeslip came back to him. Not a dream. He was here, living and breathing. The girl called Belle had rescued him, tended to him and said she had to go. He groaned and wondered why he felt such a deep sense of loss.

"Come and see," Mrs Hudson said.

She walked out to the next room, taking an oil lamp with her, an elegant, slim column with a glass bowl that gave off a warm pool of golden light. Fred pushed himself up off the chaise longue and followed, shadows leaping along a corridor ahead of Mrs Hudson's silhouette. She turned to face him at the open door to an adjoining room and he was struck by her face lit up so brightly like a ghost.

"In here," she said.

He followed her into a great, dark room and the lamp cast a pool of light over racks of clothes, hanging solemn and silent.

"It's the wardrobe," she said. "I suggest we dress in something more era-appropriate."

He groaned again. "Is this really happening?"

"Oh, yes," she said. "I'm afraid so."

There was something about the finality of it that made his heart sink. This was no dream from which he might awaken. He was truly here, trapped, out of time.

She put the lamp to one side and set it on a table that seemed designed and placed for the purpose. It gurgled quietly to itself.

"What is that?" he asked.

"It's a Carcel lamp. I'm afraid we don't get paraffin lamps for a few more decades." She was rifling the racks of ladies gowns, assessing them swiftly.

Fred went to a row of gentlemen's clothes and flipped through them. "You seem to know a lot about it."

"Yes," she said. "I suppose I do. I can't remember yesterday but I seem to be rather good at history."

"You've done this before. You're... at home with this."

She pulled out a black gown and held it against herself. "I've done this many times. Far too many times. I wonder if I've spent more of my life in the past than in the present."

Fred chuckled. "Don't we all spend more of our life in the past than the present, when you think about it?"

"Yes, I suppose you could say that."

He heard her shuffling off her clothes, hidden behind a rack two rows beyond, and thought he should do the same. He pulled out a pair of dark check trousers that looked like they might fit him, a white shirt, a plaid waistcoat and frock coat with tails, all hanging together — a ready-made costume for a character he would play: a young, Victorian gentleman out to make his fortune, like Pip Pirrin or Nicholas Nickleby. He threw off his baggy suit and blood-stained shirt and tie and squeezed into his costume and felt ridiculous. The trousers were absurdly high-waisted and flat-fronted with no pleats at all, and so tight. The clash of patterns was garish, even though it was the most sombre outfit on the rack. He was definitely one of Dickens' more comic characters, not the young hero.

"That looks fetching."

The black gown looked like Mrs Hudson had been wearing it her whole life. She topped it with a black cloak and pulled the hood up over her head.

"I look like a Scottish Widow," she said. "Or the French Lieutenant's Woman." She saw his nonplussed shrug and added, "Neither are particularly comfortable places to be."

"I feel ridiculous," Fred said.

"You'll need some shoes. I'm keeping my boots on under this. They're nice and warm. But you need something that looks right."

She went to a shelf where rows of shoes sat and pulled out a pair of black boots, sizing one against the sole of his feet. He squeezed into them.

"A little tight, but not so bad. The whole outfit is tight."

She fiddled with the cravat tie he'd hung loose around his neck. "Come here. You need to tie this up. Do you know how to tie a cravat?"

"Do I look like I know how to tie a cravat?"

She pulled and tugged at it, patting it in place. "There. Splendid. Now get a hat."

She pointed to a high shelf with what looked like leather buckets. Top hat boxes. He scanned the numbers until he came to 56, his size, and pulled one down. A hat suspended upside down. He pulled it out, put it on his head, and felt it swamp him.

"Too big," she said.

He tried three more till he found the right size and looked at himself in a full-length mirror. A character from a Victorian novel looked back at him, one that had somehow stolen his face.

"Is this real?" he asked.

"You'll get used to it."

"You've been here before?"

She thought about it and seemed lost for a long time. So long he wondered if she'd forgotten his question. "Not *here* exactly. Not this time. I know that. But I knew I'd come here one day. I was told, you see, by someone who saw me here."

"Who was that?"

"A girl. A girl with red hair." She frowned and screwed up her eyes. "I can't remember her name."

Fred turned from his reflection and flapped his arms open as if to say, well, here we are, then.

"She knows," said Mrs Hudson.

"This girl you can't remember?"

"No. The girl who rescued us. The girl here. Belle."

"She knows what?" Fred asked.

"She knows about us; where we're from; what we are."

"Oh, great," he said. "Perhaps she can tell me, then."

They both jumped at the sound of a door wrenched open and banging shut again. The door to the rear of the theatre.

— 9 —

Fred panicked, as if caught stealing. Belle came through from the rear entrance of the theatre and stopped short at the sight of them standing facing her.

"Oh," she said. "You're still here."

Fred snatched the top hat off his head; a child caught playing dress-up, guilty and afraid he was about to be told off. It was sort of stealing. In her absence, they had helped themselves to the contents of the theatre's wardrobe.

Belle smiled. "My, you look transformed. What a picture you make!"

"We thought we should…" He faltered, not sure what to say. *Thought we should dress more era-appropriately, seeing as we're not from your time.* He couldn't say it.

"We thought we should dress more era-appropriately," Mrs Hudson said.

Belle considered this, frowning, and then nodded. "Yes. I agree. You look splendid. And I am so glad you've remained."

She went through to the lounge where she'd taken them earlier — a lumber room of props in which she seemed to have made a home — and she placed an enamel urn on the table. "Please sit down. I should love to play host to you, even in this shambles of a room. You must forgive the state of my abode."

"You live here?" Mrs Hudson asked, taking a place on the

chaise longue, flouncing her skirt out as she sat, as if she had worn that type of gown all her life.

"It is my home, temporarily. The committee have been happy to turn a blind eye to my living here as it has solved the matter of security and maintenance. I am a caretaker requiring little to no remuneration."

As she talked, she took glasses from a cupboard and filled them with dark brown liquid from the urn. Fred thought it must be tea but no steam came off it.

"Though I fear that my circumstances are due to change. A new person who has invested in the theatre would take a dim view of this. And the theatre might not be here much longer."

"What do you mean?" Fred asked. "The theatre will be here for another hundred years."

Belle turned to him and stared. How could he possibly know that? Unless he'd come from a hundred years in the future and seen it for himself. She gave them a glass each.

"Please, do take a drink. You must be thirsty."

Fred sniffed at it. Not tea. "It's beer."

"Yes," Belle said. "I'm sorry I had nothing in earlier."

"It's a bit early for beer, isn't it?"

"Is it?" Belle asked. "Why?"

"They don't drink water here," Mrs Hudson said. "It's not safe."

Belle took her own glass and sat beside Mrs Hudson. Fred took the other chaise longue.

"Where have you come from, where people drink water not beer?"

Mrs Hudson coughed and looked away. Belle searched their faces for an answer.

"You know where we're from," Fred said.

"I don't think you should—" Mrs Hudson began.

"She heard us earlier. She knows. You do know where we're from, don't you, Belle? Or is it Isabelle?"

She looked to Mrs Hudson.

"Miss Ruth," Mrs Hudson said, "may I introduce Mr Fred Smith to you?'

"Certainly. I'm pleased to make your acquaintance."

Fred stood and bowed. 'I'm sorry. I don't really understand all this formality."

"It is not regarded as respectable for you to address a young lady by her first name," Mrs Hudson said.

"Really? Never?"

"Not until you are engaged."

"I've always thought it a great deal of humbug," Belle said. "I don't think anyone would count me a lady, being so low in life — an orphan foundling and the subject of charitable education — and I sense the customs of this time are not yours. My name is Belle. This is what I've always been called."

"Belle," said Fred. "I'm honoured. But let's be honest with each other. You heard us, didn't you? You know where we're from."

Belle nodded. "You are from Christmas Yet to Come."

Fred and Mrs Hudson looked at each other.

"Yes. I see it from your faces."

"And what do you know of this future?" Mrs Hudson asked.

Belle leapt up and went to the door. She was going to run out. Fred noted a sudden pang of loss in his heart. He didn't want her to leave. But Belle peeped out and looked both ways down the corridor outside, slammed the door and leaned back against it, a hand to her mouth as if she might say too much and wished to stop herself. She stared at the floor for a moment and when she looked up her eyes were bright with defiance.

"I have seen it sometimes. I believe. I was never quite sure that what I saw was real or an hallucination and that I might be insane. I've kept it secret for many long years, ever since I was beaten at the orphanage for being fanciful."

She winced, as if the memory of that beating was too much to bear. She turned away again and Fred thought she was going to leave but she slumped onto the moth-bitten chaise-longue. Mrs Hudson took her hand.

Fred leaned forward in his seat, dearly wishing he'd been the one to sit with her and hold that delicate hand.

"It's all right," Mrs Hudson said. "You're with people who believe you. We've both had similar experiences and I rather think we might all have suffered the same confusion about what we've seen through our lives."

Belle looked across at Fred and there was such a bright light of entreaty in her eyes. He nodded and tried to smile to give her encouragement, and was pleased to note that she smiled and nodded and looked at her lap.

"It will sound like the ramblings of an insane person," Belle said. "It is the sort of thing for which they put people in the asylum."

"But it's real," Fred said.

She looked up to him again with a blazing light of trust. He wanted to be the man she would trust to the end of time.

"You have seen the same things?" Belle asked.

He nodded. He'd never seen the future, but many times he'd thought he'd seen the past. As a child, the night he'd woken and seen the girl on the landing. She had seen him and been just as scared of him as he was of her. He'd asked her name and she'd walked away, right through the wall. Sometimes the uneasy feeling that time had slowed and he would look around and see something out of place: an antique shop in Dale End that hadn't been there before and wasn't there again when he sought it out. And that strange afternoon he'd rushed along a platform at New Street Station and seen...

"You," he said. "I saw you."

Belle frowned and shook her head, confused, fighting the raging torrent of thought, then she nodded, accepting it. She had seen the same thing. She'd recognized him.

"Tell us some of the things you've seen," Mrs Hudson said.

Belle rose, and again Fred thought she was going to leave, but she paced the rug that lay between them.

"Once, I was walking along Queen Street about to enter the Froggery — this neighbourhood behind the theatre — and in a moment, it was gone. A giant silver dome took its place. It lasted no more than a few seconds before everything was normal again. Another time I was at the top of New Street. Christ Church disappeared and was replaced by a fountain in which sat a great stone effigy of some pagan goddess, guarded by other stone figures of mythical beasts with human faces — people, so many people, dressed in strange attire; the kind of clothes that you were wearing. I thought you might disappear, like all those people had, but you are here and as real as this hand of mine. You are the people from my deluded waking dreams and it seems now that they are real after all."

"We are real," Mrs Hudson said. "Have no fear of that. Quite real."

Belle looked up with such a vulnerable gaze that Fred fought the urge to jump up and embrace her, but he nodded and sipped at his beer.

"I thought these things fancies, visions, hallucinations — the product of a troubled and defective imagination. I have long thought there is something wrong with me to see such things when I know that no one around me sees them. Or perhaps I was strangely attuned to see phantoms, ghosts that no one else could see."

Mrs Hudson patted her hand. "Those things you see are no fantasies. You have travelled through time, that's all. It is a great gift, and nothing to fear."

Belle looked to Fred. He didn't know what to say. He needed Mrs Hudson's words as much as Belle did.

"They're not ghosts, you see," he said, feigning certainty. "Only the ghosts of the past and the future."

A knock came at the door. A feeble rap so weak that Fred thought at first that it couldn't possibly come from the rear

50

door to the theatre — it must be the door to this room.

Belle shuffled out down the corridor and answered it. A bolt slid and the door creaked open. Muttered words and the ring of activity out there — the hum and grind of a city awake. Belle came back with a pale boy whose cap came to her waist, and only then because it was a rather large cap.

"Little Tim, I'd like you to meet two friends of mine who have come to take part in the play today. They have come from a very long way away."

She looked to them, eyes earnest, appealing.

Mrs Hudson put out her hand and the surprised boy shook it with a shy smile. "Mrs Hudson. Delighted to make your acquaintance, young Tim."

Fred strode across the rug and did the same. The boy's grip was as weak as a sparrow's. "Fred Smith. Very pleased to meet you, Tim."

The warm smile on Belle's face pierced Fred's heart. She was so grateful that they had played along with her lie. So pleased that this tiny boy had believed her.

"Now, my friends," said Belle, "we are to meet a very important person who's here to write about our play, aren't we, Tim?"

"Yes, Miss Belle," the boy said. "He's right next door in the New Hotel Royal. I took him there myself."

"Come along," said Belle. "All of us."

She led the way and Fred followed them out to that back street where the girl had rescued them. He was stepping out to his city almost a hundred years ago. His head swam as he crossed the threshold to Christmas Eve, 1842 and wondered who on earth they were about to meet.

— 10 —

John Forster unpacked in his room and as soon as he was ready, knocked the door to the adjoining suite and entered.

Charles was sitting at the desk, scribbling on sheets of vellum, holding up a hand for silence.

"I'm sorry. I didn't know you were writing."

"Not writing," Charles muttered. "Just a letter to the donkey."

He finished with a flourish and looked up, not with a smile. Still a little lost, as if he belonged in that world of his imagination and didn't much care for this real world outside his pages.

"The donkey?" Forster asked, taking a seat.

Charles folded the letter and tucked it in an envelope. "My dear, sweet Catherine."

"Charles, that is rather unkind."

"Nonsense! A term of endearment, John. If you were married, you would understand."

He laughed, a little cruelly, Forster thought. His heart grew dark at the memory of his broken engagement. Ten years gone and it still hurt. His friend could be a monster when this mood was on him.

Forster had seen the waves of discontent in him, and this one had crashed with greater force than usual. 'Donkey' was a new low in the casual contempt he gave for his wife. But then it might be the new work, *Chuzzlewit*. He was always a little monstrous when he embarked on a new book and wasn't sure what it was all about; the characters not yet allowing him into their world, shutting him out.

Charles scribbled his home address on the envelope and rolled the ornate blotter over it.

"There is a wonderful new Post Office behind us. A huge affair."

"Oh, is there?" Charles looked out of the window at New Street.

"Not that little cottage across the street as it used to be. Too small. The post is a booming business, and they transport it by rail now, not coach. Your letter will be with your dear wife this afternoon, quite possibly. The wonders of the age."

Charles leapt up and paced the room.

"Nice rooms," Forster said. "I'm afraid we can't afford *the* Royal Hotel up the top of the hill but this is not so bad at all. In fact it might even be better."

"You know it isn't, John."

"Come now, Charles. It may serve our mission to be less noticed."

"And you keep calling me Charles."

Forster lowered his voice. "I doubt anyone can overhear us here."

Charles was pacing the drawing room like a caged tiger in Regents Park, like he always did when a new novel was germinating. All the tell-tale signs were there: the restlessness, the impatience, the surliness. But this ferocious impatience with his family was a little more pronounced this time. It was concerning.

"Don't be so hard on the place," said Forster. "You don't want to treat it as harshly as you treated America."

"I'm 'dear Boz'," Charles said. "I made my name writing biting satire. They love me for it."

"People don't like it so much when that biting wit is turned on them. They buy your books here too, Charles. A great many, in fact. Hopefully, some of them will also print them, eh?"

"So I'm to blunt my pen for these dull provincials?"

"Be kinder, that's all."

"A little gentle mockery is all I have in mind," said Charles. "I think these people know full well they live in a second-rate town. It will take more than a railway from London to elevate it to the level of a metropolis."

"There are grand things happening here, Charles, you will see. Great investments. It's a town that has great expectations."

"Humbug," said Charles. Then he had that faraway look. "Hmmm," he said. He went to the desk, snatched up his notebook and scribbled something. No doubt some grammatical error John had made that would go into a story. "If even this backwater is booming, why is there such a depression in the book trade?"

Forster looked at his boots. "It is most likely as you say, Charles. With this dreadful government, people have little money for literature."

"You might think they would want an escape all the more."

Forster checked his fob watch. "Come along. It's time."

Charles reached for his jacket and tucked the notebook in his pocket. He threw on his muffler and his top hat, pacing, eager to be out of this place.

Forster rose, feeling the call of the street. Anywhere but here in this room with his friend's worry that his career was a flop. The failure of *Barnaby Rudge,* so dreadful that even the periodical it had been serialized in had folded. And the looming bankruptcy.

There was a timid knock at the door. Forster answered to find the boy, young Tim Cratchit.

"Look at this. Right on time."

"I'm to take you to the place I'm not supposed to say aloud," the boy said.

"Intelligent boy," said Forster. "Come along, Cha— er, John. We're off to Showell's printing house."

Dickens was out the door in a flash. Forster patted his pockets and felt the wad of money. Best to leave it here.

"A moment," he said, retreating to the bureau and opening a drawer.

"What is it?" Dickens said.

"I don't like to carry it around on the streets. It's quite safe here."

He placed the wad of cash in the drawer, disturbed that there was no key. But it would be quite safe in a respectable hotel like this.

"Quite right," said Dickens. "In a negotiation, it would be vulgar to flash the money."

Forster shuffled to the door and stepped out to the corridor, turning his key in the lock. There. The room was locked and that meant the money was safe.

They walked along the plush corridor, the boy ahead.

"Perhaps it might not be a depression in the book market at all," said Forster. "Perhaps public tastes are changing."

Dickens turned, suspicious, his eye twitching involuntarily. He put his hand to his face to stop it.

"What if the public are moving on from the, er... kind of story you have previously tended towards, hmm?

"Is this another conversation where you try to talk me out of writing a picaresque adventure?"

Charles tramped on down the corridor to the stairhead and Forster followed, already behind pace.

"I'm just saying, Perhaps the public desire a more immediate experience..."

"Nonsense."

"They want things now, Charles, today. They want to go out and buy a book and consume the whole thing in a week or weekend, not have it doled out to them in little bites every month over two years."

They skipped down the ornate sweep of stairs to the

lobby.

"It is bingeing, nothing more, John, and you know it. Literary gluttony, and, and, and impatience, yes. The speed of life moves so fast in these industrialized times that they want everything now!"

"Exactly."

They walked out of the hotel doors to a blast of frigid air and strode up the length of the elegant pergola that reached for the street.

"*The Pickwick Papers* was a roaring success. It built my name. And *Nicholas Nickleby. The Old Curiosity Shop* enthralled the world. *Martin Chuzzlewit* will be the same, mark you. I rather think this will be the book I shall be known for. It will outshine all the rest. Even *Oliver Twist.*"

Forster held up his arms in surrender. "*Pickwick*, yes, I grant you. But *Oliver Twist* is your biggest success and that is a straight novel. And *Nickleby* is the same."

"They are picaresque adventures and you know it."

"More so novels, I say. It is the novels the public wants. The picaresque style has rather died out, I feel. Except in Spain. Its time will come again, no doubt, but for now, think of a concentrated tale with a single line of action. Sub-plots, yes, but unity of action. That's the thing."

"Like a play."

"Exactly that. Perhaps even a shorter work — a novella — to win your audience again?"

"Novellas. Humbug. No one takes them seriously."

"Thackeray serialises lovely novellas. His *Samuel Titmarsh and the Great Hoggarty Diamond* was a roaring success in Fraser's Magazine."

They came to the pavement and stopped. Forster looked around for the boy. Where on earth was he?

"There's no money in novellas, John," Charles scoffed. "Why do I have to tell you that? Long form serialised fiction is what keeps the people coming back for more, month after month — a story over a year or two, not done and dusted in four months. Monthly, even weekly, instalments. Why, if I could, I would put before the public an episode every single day, so that every person in the land could go home from their work, take their supper, and gather round the hearth to experience a nightly entertainment of myriad characters and storylines. Imagine it. A periodical that was never ending. One endless rolling panorama of everyday life, say of a single street or a square and all the characters in it. A street opera."

Charles pointed his cane to the west and all the way down to the east end of New Street as if it were his rolling street opera.

Forster was about to respond that there would never be a fashion for such a story and that Charles should focus his mind on something more palatable, when the boy tugged at his coat. He had reappeared from nowhere as if he were a mischievous Christmas spirit.

Forster was highly conscious that the longer they tarried, the more likely it was Charles might be recognized. They had been on New Street a mere moment when all his hopes were dashed, because he had not even opened his mouth to urge the boy to take them on to their destination, when Charles was mobbed by a group of readers.

"Mr Dickens!" a young lady cried. "Mr Charles Dickens, if I'm not mistaken!"

— 11 —

Tiny Tim led Miss Belle and her strange new friends round the corner onto New Street, passing the front of house and along to the hotel.

The young man who'd called himself Mister Fred looked all pale and was sweating, though curiously, he was also shivering in the cold. Tim wondered how someone could both shiver with cold and also sweat at the same time. Perhaps he had the ague and had come from the marshes or the tropics. Mrs Hudson tended to him, and Miss Belle gave her a pretty blue handkerchief so that Mister Fred could wipe the sweat from his brow.

"I'm not sure I ought to have told you this," Tim said. "I might get into trouble."

"Don't worry, Tim," Miss Belle said. "I won't reveal that you have said anything. You may pretend you've never seen me in your life before."

"Wait here, then, and I'll get them."

He walked down the red carpet under the pergola, as bold as brass, and right through the lobby, so ornate it was like a palace. He informed the gentleman on reception he was here to collect Mr Forster and Mr Huffam, and the gentleman waved him through to Room 102.

When he came back with them, he walked ahead so he could warn Miss Belle.

"This is them," he said.

They came walking up the red carpet under the grand pergola: the big fat man with grey hair and whiskers and the young man with wild, dark hair and vivid blue eyes, stalking ahead, almost marching, still arguing about books.

"This is them," Tim said to Miss Belle. He tugged at Mr Forster's coat, as a signal, sort of like a Judas kiss, though it was obvious who the two gentlemen were.

Miss Belle cried out, "Mr Dickens! Mr Charles Dickens, if I'm not mistaken!"

Mr Forster's eyes bugged out of his head and he let out a little cry of fright, as if Miss Belle had leapt at him with a cudgel. "Boy! Lead on, and quickly!"

He shoved Tim ahead so that he found himself marching down New Street in the direction of the printing house.

"Mr Dickens! Please!" Belle cried.

"I'm afraid you're mistaken, madam," Mr Dickens said, tipping his hat and rushing on. "My name is John Huffam."

Why did grown-ups behave in such odd ways? Belle wanted to ask the nice man from London who played magic tricks to help her, but when Tim brought her to him as she'd asked him to, she pretended it was all an accident and a coincidence that they'd met.

The nice man from London said he wasn't Charles Dickens, but Tim knew that wasn't true because he'd heard them say how important it was that Charles Dickens pretend to be John Huffam. But Charles Dickens had been happy to be Charles Dickens when the woman at the train station had asked him to write his name in her book. They'd joked in that strange way grown-ups did — when what was being said was simple but what was happening was more than what was said. But then when his fat friend Mr Forster had returned, Charles Dickens had turned back into John Huffam and pretended nothing had happened.

Tim feared he'd never understand it.

And now that Miss Belle did the same to Charles Dickens,

he pretended to be John Huffam again. Was it because Miss Belle didn't have a book in which he could write his real name? Or was it that Mr Forster was present, and Charles couldn't be Charles when Forster was there? Perhaps that was the point of the game, like a Christmas game of Blind Man's Buff or Charades, when someone had to guess what you were. Perhaps all the grown-ups in the world were playing such a game and only when Tim became a man would the rules of the game be explained to him.

Tim crossed the street at Cornish's bookshop and the two gentlemen followed swiftly, though Charles Dickens was not really following, more walking right alongside Tim with his hand on his shoulder and pushing him onward.

Miss Belle gave chase, just behind, but Mr Fred stopped in the street and stared up at the shops. Mrs Hudson dragged him out of the path of a horse and cart.

"But, please, Mr Dickens, I beg you. You are to write of my theatre performance later today and I urge you to come and talk to our players, to fully acquaint yourself with the work we do here."

"I'm not him, madam," Charles Dickens said.

Miss Belle tried to run, but she was aware of Mrs Hudson falling behind, because Mr Fred walked like an old man, as if with each step he was afraid the ground would fall away under him, or like he was swaying on a ship. Perhaps he was a sailor used to voyaging the tropics and dry land made him queasy.

The printing house was up ahead and Tim wondered if Miss Belle and her friends would follow the two gentlemen of London inside. For the first time he feared he might get himself into trouble for revealing the identity of the mysterious guests. The trouble might also extend to his dear father working under Stingy Swingey.

They came to the printing house and Tim waved the two gentlemen to the door, calling, "In here, sirs."

Miss Belle reached out, almost to grab at Mr Dickens' coat tails but stopped short. "I want my play to have a fair hearing, that is all."

As they bustled through the door and the printing house bell chimed their entrance, Charles Dickens turned, astonished, and said, *"You* wrote the play?"

But Miss Belle could not answer, because the door slammed in her face. The two gentlemen from London were safely inside and Tim thought it best to stay out here and make sure Miss Belle and her friends didn't follow them. He stood before the door.

"It is him. I don't know why he's pretending it isn't," Miss Belle said, stamping her foot.

"He looks so young," said Mrs Hudson. "I was expecting the older man."

Miss Belle gave her a curious look. It was indeed a strange thing to say. How could one expect to see an older version of a man if he wasn't yet old? Perhaps he had a father by the same name.

Mr Fred caught them up and stood wheezing, looking back down the street. "Corporation Street wasn't there," he said. "It should be there round about where Cornish's bookshop is, but it's just a straight row of shops. It isn't there."

"Not yet," said Mrs Hudson.

"Why would he pretend to be someone else?" Miss Belle said, ignoring their strange comments about streets that didn't exist.

"It's the same with my father," Tim said, trying to be helpful. "Papa comes home from a hard day's work and tells Mama what a nasty, spiteful miser Mr Swingeford is. He's the meanest man in all of Birmingham. But when he's at work, he speaks very nicely of Mr Swingeford and is very polite to him. It's a pretend game that all grown-ups play. I don't know the rules yet. They're very complicated."

The grown-ups stared at each other and Tim sensed that his helpful comment hadn't really helped at all.

"Mr Ebenezer Swingeford?" Mrs Hudson said.

"He owns this publishing house and a great many other things," said Belle. "Including a part share in the theatre. I have had the displeasure of his acquaintance once already this morning and I don't wish to suffer it again."

And yet Miss Belle looked longingly at the printing house window, and had her nose up against it, almost in the way Tim would press his nose to Miss Jagger's Dining Rooms window across the street.

"I *will* speak with him," Miss Belle said. She stamped her foot and went to the door to follow him in.

But right at that moment, Mr Fred fell over like a tree that was axed. Swooning and falling into the dirty gutter.

— 12 —

Mrs Hudson was the first to reach down to Fred. She moved with a swiftness that surprised her, dragging him up and out of the way of a coach-and-four that thundered past, the coachman shouting out curses. Fred fell against her and she tottered back and would have fallen if Belle hadn't held her.

"He's fainted," Belle cried. "Oh dear, the poor man. He did look rather ill. I shouldn't have made him come on this wild chase."

"He'll be all right," Mrs Hudson said.

Fred was standing on his feet, a little woozily, but he could walk.

Mrs Hudson looked up and down the street. There wasn't a single building she knew from her own time.

"Over there," Miss Belle said. "The Hen & Chickens Hotel."

She took Fred's other arm and stepped into the street and they weaved through the coaches and horses, making for an elegant four-storey Georgian building fronted with an ornate balcony. They walked Fred right through the front door and Belle turned left into a side room. A comfortable parlour, busy with men and women drinking and reading newspapers and letters, tables dotted around, comfortable nooks and crannies, booths with private tables. It was part parlour, part waiting room, part wine bar.

They swept through to a booth and dumped Fred down on the bench. A commotion all around at their entrance. "This gentleman has fainted in the street," Belle said.

The landlord, a great round Christmas pudding in human form with bushy whiskers, came rushing with a glass of rum and put it to Fred's lips. "My word, Miss Belle, he looks a proper fright. Stranger, is he?"

"A friend, visiting from afar, Mr Fezzwig."

"My son," Mrs Hudson said.

They looked to her. She noted the surprising ease with which the lie had popped from her mouth. It was important to have a cover story when you travelled, she remembered this. She had done the same with other people... people she couldn't quite remember. The girl with red hair. What was her name? And the young man with the funny moustache. He was called... Mitchell, was it? Damn this brain of hers.

"Do not be distressed, Madame," Mr Fezzwig said, reaching out and squeezing her elbow.

Her frustration at not being able to remember these damned names. He'd taken it for fear for her fainting son. Well, that would do. Until she could remember what she was here for, if they thought she needed help and pity, all the better.

Fred spluttered and opened his eyes. A flash of alarm at his surroundings. He wiped his mouth and his pale cheeks went a light shade of scarlet.

"There," Mr Fezzwig said, beaming. "That really has brought the colour back to your cheeks."

Not the rum, Mrs Hudson thought. The embarrassment. To faint in front of Belle. The boy was in love with her.

"I'm all right," he said. "It's nothing. Just the recent exertions of travel have taken it out of me."

Belle sat in the booth next to him and took his hand. He looked down at it in wonder.

"Whatever are you doing here, Tim?"

They all turned at the voice. A wiry man with a kind,

simple face and a top hat that was too big for him.

"I'm helping Miss Belle, father," Tim said. "Honest."

"Mr Cratchit," Belle said. "Don't be alarmed. Your son really was only here helping us."

"This man fainted," said the landlord. "In the street."

"I'm all right," said Fred.

Mr Cratchit patted his son's head and swept his hat off his own head, revealing a wiry mess of curls, and a receding widow's peak. "I do worry about my son, Miss Belle. There are unsavoury characters in the Froggery who would make young disciples of the boys and have them carry out all sorts of nefarious deeds. I want to protect my tiny Tim from that."

"As do I," Miss Belle said, reaching out to clasp Mr Cratchit's hand and pull him to sit beside her. There was ample space in the curved bench of the booth and they all found themselves sitting. "We are only here because my friend, Mr Fred, was taken ill and fainted in the street. Your son was passing and helped us. I believe he was escorting two guests from London to the printing house?"

The landlord put more glasses down before them and poured rum for them all. Mrs Hudson took one and felt it golden and warm. A relief.

"Why, yes," Mr Cratchit said, a little flustered to find himself press-ganged into this drinking party, looking about with unease to locate the thing he'd come for. "Those guests are talking with Mr Showell right this minute."

"It's Mr Charles Dickens and his business manager, isn't it?"

"I'm not supposed to say, Miss Belle. I oughtn't to, I really oughtn't. It's a delicate business matter."

"So he's here to arrange a publishing deal."

"I didn't say anything of that sort."

"I suppose it would be cheaper than publishing in London."

"It would, if that were what he was here for, and I cannot say if he is or he isn't."

"A monthly periodical, I'd guess. Not a book."

"Oh, you really mustn't prise it out of me, Miss Belle. That wouldn't do." He pushed the drink away and put his hat back on. "I really do have to get back to my desk. I only came in for…"

"Cratchit!"

A hoarse, hard as flint voice that sent a chill through the room, as if the caller had left the door open and brought in the winter air with him. Everyone shuddered, even though there was a roaring fire across the room.

Mr Cratchit shot up and almost knocked the table over. "Mr Swingeford, sir."

The man was a gruff old skinflint who might have been the most miserable looking pall-bearer in town, if he hadn't been wearing grey, head-to-toe.

"What on earth do you think you're doing?"

"I'm here to collect the mail, Mr Swingeford."

"You are here imbibing on my time."

"No, sir, honest, sir. I came for the mail and then saw my son here and enquired as to why he was here, concerned for my boy's welfare. Only it turns out he was here helping this young gentleman who fainted in the street right outside of the offices, Mr Swingeford, sir."

"Mr Swingeford," the landlord said, puffing out his chest.

Mrs Hudson couldn't be sure of the exact hierarchy involved here, whether Mr Swingeford, as a gentleman, outranked this mere tradesman, or if Mr Fezzwig being the landlord meant he was king of anyone who entered his domain. But there was a definite battle of wills here, both men stiffening like a pair of alley cats and trying to make themselves larger.

"I can confirm everything he says is true. Mr Cratchit is as honest as the day is long. There's no more honest and hard-working a man in the whole of Birmingham, I would wager, and he's never once taken a sip in here, more's the pity for my business, not even on Christmas Eve."

"Bah, Christmas Eve," Mr Swingeford snarled. "If I had my way…"

"Oh, do shut up, you miserable man." Mrs Hudson found that she was standing, and that those words had come from her. There it was again. Her lips running far ahead of her agonizingly slow mind. "Enough people have confirmed it for you. Now go away and find a crutch to kick or something."

Chuckles fizzed around the bar. Mr Swingeford's face went beetroot red. Mrs Hudson instinctively looked to his fists. She was quite sure that under his kid gloves, his knuckles would be white. He raised his cane as if it were a microphone that would amplify his words.

Mr Cratchit stumbled out of the booth and ran to the bar where he collected a bundle of letters. He scampered out of the place. His son watched him go with a look of quiet fury.

"And you, Miss Ruth," Mr Swingeford continued. "This is no place for a young lady. You will leave here at once."

Fred tried to raise himself but stumbled back. "Listen here, who do you think you are, ordering people around like that?"

A hiss flew around the drawing room as everyone sucked in a deep breath. There were a few delighted whoops. It was clear from the reverberation that Mr Swingeford was very much a man who could do exactly what he had done and no one would beg to differ.

"A young woman should not be in saloon bars unaccompanied," Mr Swingeford said.

"But I'm not unaccompanied," Belle said. "I'm with Mr Fred here and Mrs Hudson. They are relatives of mine, here to visit me for Christmas."

Mr Swingeford looked them up and down, first Fred and then Mrs Hudson. She felt his cold eyes take her in and a shiver danced up her spine.

"What relation are they to you? I was to understand that you were an orphan."

"Mrs Hudson is my aunt. Mr Fred here is her son. I think that makes him my cousin."

Mr Swingeford glared down now at Belle's hand, clasped on Fred's. She sensed his disapproval and drew her hand away.

"And when was this known to you?"

"Very recently," Mrs Hudson said. "We have been searching for our dear, long lost relation for years, and here, at last, we've found her."

Mr Swingeford looked them over each in turn, confounded by the easy lie. But he knew, Mrs Hudson could tell; he knew he was being lied to.

"I see you are bereaved, madam."

Mrs Hudson looked down at her black dress and cloak. "I'm a widow, yes."

"Recently?"

Mrs Hudson tried to remember. She'd had a husband. Once. What was his name? It had been so long. "No," she said, and she heard the thread of sadness in her voice. "It was a long time ago."

"And still in black. How very noble." Mr Swingeford turned from her and pointed his cane at Fred. "And what are your intentions?"

"My intentions?" Fred said.

"Towards the young lady here?"

"What? Are you her father?"

"Don't be impertinent. Miss Ruth is a ward."

"I'm unaware that I have ever been your ward, sir," Belle said. "Unless you are some mysterious benefactor of whom I've been ignorant."

"I am not your benefactor, no. But my investment in the Theatre Royal makes you a concern of mine."

"I am not one of the theatre's props," Belle said.

"No," Mr Swingeford sneered, grinning as if he were about to lay down a Royal Flush. "But as an unverified sitting tenant of the theatre, your position and the question of your propriety, weighs heavy on myself and the board of directors. And I do hope your relatives are not lodging with you. That would be most unseemly. The hotel is next door. Or even here, if they are poorer than they look."

He tipped his hat, turned and left.

The bar room resumed its hum of conversation, glasses chinking and the air warmed by a few noticeable degrees.

"Worst man in Birmingham," Mr Fezzwig said. "Ebenezer Swingeford. A horrible old mean-spirited skinflint tyrant. Even the dogs skulk out of his way when he walks the street."

"Ebenezer?" said Fred. "You're kidding."

"I am not, sir."

"I apologize for bringing so much drama to your establishment, Mr Fezzwig," Belle said, fiddling in her pouch and bringing out a coin.

The landlord took it. "It is your profession, dear Miss Belle. And though I am myself a mere amateur, I do rather enjoy a little drama from time to time."

Mr Fezzwig went back to his business behind the bar and Belle rose, looking about her in panic as if she wasn't quite sure she had everything. Like me, Mrs Hudson thought, so much these days she was looking all about her for that thing she had forgotten.

"I have little time," Belle said. "He will discover the lie. I am an orphan and he will look up the records. He knows as much, he needs only the legal proof. His sister, Mrs Jowett, who is on the board of governors of the orphanage, will attest to it."

"And what of it, Belle?" Mrs Hudson said. "Fiddlesticks to the old bully."

"I shall be turned out. Jobless and homeless on Christmas Eve." She got up and rushed out.

"Wait!" Fred cried.

But Belle was out of the door.

Fred stumbled to his feet and Mrs Hudson rose with him, downing the last sip of rum from her dainty glass.

"This is ridiculous," Fred cried, laughing manically and waving his arm out to indicate it all, nearly knocking Tim over if the boy hadn't ducked. "I don't believe this is happening."

Mrs Hudson pulled Fred closer and hissed, "This is what we're here for, I'm sure of it now. It's all something to do with Dickens."

"Is this all some bad dream?" Fred hissed. "Charles Dickens, Tiny Tim, Christmas Eve, Cratchit, Fezziwig? A horrible old miser called Ebenezer who's mean to everyone? And us: we're the ghosts of Christmas Yet to Come. What's going on?"

"I think we're about to see how Charles Dickens gets his ideas," Mrs Hudson said, leaning forward.

"You mean?"

"*A Christmas Carol* hasn't yet been written."

Fred gulped and swayed. "I don't think I can cope with this."

Mrs Hudson hutched up against him so he could put his hand on her shoulder. "Come on, Fred. We have to get Belle to help us."

"Help us with what?"

"To find out why we're here. It's something to do with Dickens. It absolutely has to be. But if she's more concerned with being thrown out onto the street, she won't be so inclined to spend time on us."

Fred shook her off. "Perhaps we're here to help *her*. Have you thought of that?"

He stumbled out of the door to the bright light of New Street.

Mrs Hudson looked around and shivered. All alone. The boy, Tim, looked up at her, a frown on his face. "Come along, boy. I think you shouldn't be here. Go home."

"I can't," said the boy. "I work at Showell's printing house."

She guided him out to New Street and the boy dashed across to J.W. Showell, Printers & Stationers. Charles Dickens was in there and he held the key to all of this, she was certain.

Looking up and down the street, she worked out that she was standing pretty much before the Odeon Cinema. A place she'd stood many times before. *Would* stand many times, a hundred years from now. She turned and followed Fred, a distant speck, limping down the street, chasing Belle, and wondered for a moment if that was her purpose: to bring these two young people together. She shook her head and dismissed it. No, it was all about Dickens, she was sure of it. If only she could remember.

She hurried on after Fred, fearing if she was left alone for a minute she might forget everything and be lost forever.

— 13 —

Bob Cratchit ran across New Street clutching the bundle of letters to his thumping breast, not caring if a coach-and-four hit him and ended his days. They were as good as ended anyways. Mr Swingeford had found cause to shout at him and Cratchit knew he was for the sack this very day. And on Christmas Eve too! How was he to break the news to his dear wife? He couldn't hide it for the duration of the one-day holiday, that would be impossible. Not with tiny Tim also there to see it.

That thought curdled his already soured heart. His poor son would be the only man working in the household.

Cratchit pushed through the door to Showell's and the bell chimed like it was announcing a funeral.

Mr Wilber, the foreman looked up from the counter desk, peering over his pince-nez spectacles, and back down at his ledger. Only he looked up again, startled at the sight of his assistant clerk.

"Are you all right, Cratchit? You look like you've seen a ghost."

"Not a ghost," said Cratchit, rushing to his desk and slicing open the mail with a silver letter opener. He had opened all the letters before realizing his hands were shaking. "It was Mr Swingeford. He caught me in the Hen & Chickens and thought I was a-drinking on company time."

"But I sent you to collect the mail, dear boy."

"That's what I told him, Mr Wilber. Only I don't think he believed me."

Mr Wilber tugged at his cravat and adjusted his vivid flowery scarlet waistcoat, suddenly needing to breathe a little easier. "Well, I'll certainly let him know it was the case."

But Mr Wilber gazed off into the distance and the look of horror on his face attested to the fact the he would not enjoy having to tell Mr Swingeford any sort of fact that might confront the old miser.

Cratchit could hear chatter from the rear office. The two gentlemen from London. Vitally important business. A contract that might secure their futures for a good few years, perhaps. Only that business now seemed no longer any concern of Bob Cratchit's. This business would continue without him.

"I'm so glad you didn't choose that other printers down the street," came one of the voices. Mr Dickens' voice, he thought. "Cornish's, was it? I don't want my work published by anything with the name 'Cheap Book Establishment'."

Cratchit wondered why Mr Swingeford wasn't here to discuss this business matter with the important guests. Did he deem it a trifling part of his wider portfolio?

Cratchit whispered to Mr Wilber at his side. "Has Mr Swingeford left this matter to old Mr Showell?"

Mr Wilber looked all around and shrugged at the mystery. "The very idea. You know as well as I do that Swingeford only kept the old chap on to keep the name above the shop front. Tradition and continuity, he said."

Yes, Cratchit thought. The very idea that Swingeford would leave business in the hands of the kindly old gentleman who'd built the place. And yet, he'd shown no inclination to rush back across the road. And what had he been doing in the Hen & Chickens, anyway?

"Well, wherever he is," Cratchit said to Mr Wilber, "he's in a cold mood for some reason and I rather fear will be looking to sack someone today. I rather fear it might be me."

"What was the matter with the…" Mr Wilber looked all around and behind just to make doubly, triply sure no one could overhear. "…old miser?"

"Who knows with that man?" Cratchit whispered. "Something or someone has slighted him and sent him in a terrible mood."

"When a man like that has his ego bruised, he goes on the prowl looking for someone to sack." Mr Wilber coughed and patted Cratchit on the back. "But I'm sure you'll be safe, Cratchit. Not to worry."

Cratchit felt quite sick and put a hand to his belly. He thought he might retch up the pudding his dear wife had left for his lunch. He was quite queasy. If this went on, he wouldn't even eat his Christmas dinner tomorrow either. "Just what is it about Christmas that makes Ebenezer Swingeford so utterly miserable and determined to take it out on everyone around him? It seems a thoroughly objectionable existence. He can't possibly enjoy his life, and all the money he makes doesn't make him any happier. In fact, as the years go by and his fortune increases, he seems more and more angry at everything in the world."

"Hmmm," Mr Wilber sighed. "His wife died in childbirth, I believe. And the child too. Twenty year since. At Christmas. The mockery of it. That's the story. He's always hated the season ever since, they say."

"Oh, I didn't know. How terrible for him." Cratchit felt quite guilty now on top of the queasiness.

The door opened and Tim came in. He stopped short, letting in the cold and seemed surprised to see them there, where they always were.

Cratchit sensed something behind and turned to see one of the London gentlemen standing in the door to the office.

"Oh, hello sir," he spluttered.

Mr Wilber also turned and jumped with a little yelp, covering his mouth as if he could cram back in all the words he'd said.

"Anything we can help you with, sir?" Cratchit asked.

The young gentleman just smiled and stepped into the shop, strolling around and taking in the surroundings, the shelves of publications and pamphlets and displays of printing processes. "I'm just taking a look over the premises. They are in there discussing business. Dreadfully dull."

"We didn't see you in the door there, sir," Mr Wilber said.

Cratchit wondered how much of their conversation the man had heard. This surely was the end of him.

"Not to worry," the young man said. "I didn't mean to loiter."

Cratchit had rather thought the older, larger gentleman would be Dickens, not this young chap with his unruly hair and bright eyes. He seemed barely old enough to be a successful author. And yet he was possibly about his own age: thirty years.

Tim skulked in and rounded the gentleman, with a such a sullen, sulking look about him that it proper pained Cratchit in his heart. "Not to fear, tiny Tim. We'll break for Christmas a little later, and it's the theatre show tonight."

"Oh and wait till you see my magic lantern show tonight, dear boy," Mr Wilber said. "This year it is no mere interlude for the play. Oh no. This year, my slides and animations shall take place throughout the show, on a scale never before seen."

He had talked about nothing else for weeks, thought Bob, so tiny Tim had undoubtedly heard of it. "Did you hear that, tiny Tim? What larks we'll have tonight, and Christmas Day tomorrow, come what may."

"I'm not so tiny, father," Tim said.

"No, you're a growing lad, that's true," Cratchit said. His son was no longer an innocent. The knitted brow of care was on his face. Life and its struggles had marked his boy. It was inevitable. And would be even more so if he were the sole breadwinner of the house.

"This boy is your son," Mr Dickens said.

"Yes, sir. My boy works here."

"Ah. He brought us from the station this morning, and brought us here too. I didn't know."

Cratchit wondered how Mr Dickens could know that Bob Cratchit was this boy's father, and why it mattered. Mr Dickens stared at Cratchit with a curious look, fascinated and amused at something. He'd almost definitely heard them gossiping about their master and would most likely tell him. Bob Cratchit would be for the sack. He was doomed.

Dickens reached out to the boy, as if to shake his hand. Puzzled, Tim held up his hands, black with ink. Dickens flinched and let out a surprised "Oh!" and stepped back.

This was the man who gave his son a half farthing, Cratchit thought. That was how the rich stayed rich. If you looked after the pennies, the pounds looked after themselves.

Tim bundled through the second door, his boots tramping through to the print room at the rear of the premises.

Bob Cratchit turned from the space where his son had stood. Perhaps in keeping the boy so close to him, he'd only hastened that loss of innocence.

Dickens thumbed a stack of anti-slavery pamphlets and hummed approvingly. "Very good," he said, rubbing his cheek. He picked up a pamphlet on the history of the Bull Ring. "Law, do they still bait bulls here?"

He'd said 'law', like the Cockneys said 'lord', Cratchit noticed.

"Certainly not," said Mr Wilber. "It was made illegal six years ago."

"They did bait a bull in Birmingham Heath four years ago," Cratchit said, and immediately thought he should have kept his mouth shut.

"How barbaric," Dickens said.

"We have the theatre now," said Mr Wilber. "To elevate the common man. You should see our Theatre Royal. Oh. Tonight! If you are staying, there's a charming Harlequinade. I shall be treading the boards myself."

Dickens grinned and examined Mr Wilber with new interest. "I know the theatre. In fact, I am due to see the performance."

"Mr Dickens! Really? What an honour!"

Mr Wilber's face had turned the colour of a great plum pudding and he looked ready to burst right out of his cravat.

"And you, Cratchit, is it? Are you also treading the old boards tonight?"

Again like a cockney, Cratchit thought. As if he'd come from low stock. Which sort of made sense. How could someone write of the poor so keenly, as he had with *Oliver Twist,* if he hadn't been among them up close in the dirt and grime for at least some part of his life? And yet he seemed keen not to get his hands dirty. Hadn't taken his gloves off. And he baulked at the sight of a young boy with black hands. As if there was something about a little ink that terrified him.

"Me, sir? Lord no, I'm far too shy a person to go onstage. I'll be firmly seated in the audience, sir."

"Yes, with your son, Tiny Tim, like you said."

There was something most decidedly odd about Mr Charles Dickens. He floated around the shop, only half in the moment, and with a very peculiar way about him. If Cratchit had met any others he might have been able to verify if this was the same with all authors or whether it was peculiar to Mr Dickens.

Dickens waved his arm to the window and the gloomy view of New Street outside. "I've noticed that so few people seem to be celebrating Christmas. Why is that?"

"I'm afraid there's not much call for it these days," said Cratchit.

"They celebrate Christmas in the country, where everything is much simpler, but there is simply no time for it in the modern town," said Mr Wilber. "We are a more sophisticated people than our bumbling country yokel cousins."

"How sad," said Dickens.

"Is it the same in London, sir?"

"I'm afraid it is. I wish it weren't."

The door swung open with such force that the bell clanged and almost fell from its hanging.

"Cratchit!" Mr Swingeford yelled. He pointed his cane as if it were a pistol and he might shoot poor Cratchit any second. "What was the meaning of your performance just now?"

"Nothing, sir, Mr Swingeford, sir. It was as explained to you by Mr Fezzwig, sir."

"That libatious buffoon. Well, I won't stand for it. Not on my time."

"Mr Swingeford," Mr Wilber muttered, "I sent Bob to fetch the post as he said."

"Get out, Cratchit. Get out now."

"What do you mean, sir?" Cratchit said. But he knew. The old miser had come to take out his earlier frustration. Whatever it was that had happened to him earlier today, Bob Cratchit was the man who was going to pay for it. He felt light, as if a trapdoor were opening under his feet and he was about to plummet, with only a noose around his neck to break his fall.

"Your services are no longer required."

"But, sir, it's Christmas."

"A poor excuse for picking my pocket."

At this moment, several people came rushing out from the back: Tiny Tim and Mr Showell along with Mr Forster, who filled the entire door frame.

"What is going on here?" Mr Showell shouted. "Oh, Mr Swingeford. It's you."

"Cratchit was seen drinking on the company's clock today."

"But I wasn't, sir."

"I have dispensed with his services forthwith."

"You can't do that."

Everyone turned to the young gentleman.

"Who on earth are you?" Swingeford said.

"I'm Charles Dickens."

Swingeford caught his breath, realizing this man was a client, an important client, not a mere customer.

"Are you telling me how to run my business, sir?"

"Certainly not, Mr Swingeford," Dickens said. He touched his twitching cheek again. "You may run your business however you see fit, even one that employs child labour. But I may also run mine. And I may do business with whomever I sense runs a moral business on sound Christian principles. Come, Forster. Let us take our business to Mr Cornish down the street. Perhaps he treats his workers better."

"But Charles," said Forster, "I've just concluded our deal with Mr Showell here."

"And now it's unconcluded."

"Now wait you," said Mr Showell, in his creaking old voice. "Cornish is far too small an establishment for your needs. And my colleague Mr Swingeford was a little hasty just now with Mr Cratchit. Of course we shall not sack him. Not on Christmas Eve. Not if it's true that he was not drinking."

"I sent him to collect the post, sir," said Mr Wilber.

"Humbug!" Swingeford cried, though he seemed more amused at the consternation he had caused than angered. *"Not at Christmas."*

"Not any time, if you want my custom."

Mr Swingeford smiled. It was a strange smile, as if he had never smiled in his life before and his facial muscles were not used to the contortion. "Mr Cratchit. I do accept your pleading, and Mr Wilber's reference."

Bob Cratchit felt the breath he didn't know he was holding leave his body in one almighty expiration of relief.

"You, boy," said Swingeford. "You must leave immediately."

"Mr Swingeford! I protest!" Mr Showell cried.

"Our new business partner objects to the use of child

labour. I will remedy that particular ill with immediate effect. Boy! Out!"

Tim looked at them all, each in turn, but no man said a word. He shrugged and slunk to the door and looked back as he went to the street. Cratchit feared his son might say something harsh to Mr Swingeford and burn all bridges between them, but the boy said nothing, merely cast back a look of utter spite. And the resentment was not aimed at his employer, Bob Cratchit saw quite clearly, but at his father.

— 14 —

Mrs Hudson rapped on the back door to the theatre, casting a wary glance over her shoulder at the shabby row of tenements. This morning it had seemed a place that threatened danger, but now the hum of activity, the clanking of machinery, the chatter and yelling of workers about their business made it seem so safe. Night would fall by four and then perhaps the danger would return, like a dark tide creeping in.

The door opened and Fred gave a flustered look of apology, at forgetting her, at leaving her behind. They went through to the lumber room where Belle lived. She was pacing the rug, biting a finger, her face flushed at the effort of running back.

"There's no time," she said. "I should run to Mrs Jowett and beg her to intercede, but there's no time."

Mrs Hudson went to her and hugged her, as much to stop her pacing up and down as anything. Fred slumped on the chaise longue.

"I'm doomed," said Belle. "Swingeford will turf me out on the streets. Perhaps he will even stop the performance. What am I to do?"

"I'll help you," said Fred.

She turned, surprised, as if her pet dog had offered help. "And what will you do, Fred Smith?"

"I don't know. Everything in my power."

And as he said the word *power*, he whimpered, as if he realized he had no power. With not a penny on him, he was poorer than Belle, poorer than every street urchin on New Street who might at least have a penny to their name. Fred Smith had nothing.

But Belle smiled and went to him. He stood and took her hands.

Mrs Hudson coughed.

Belle glanced back, looked at the rug, blushed and moved away.

"It's strange," she said. "I don't feel the strictures of propriety with you. Both of you. It's as if none of the rules of our society apply anymore. Perhaps because I see in you that they are gone."

She looked to them with a clear, honest gaze, longing for them to affirm it.

"They are," Fred said. "In my time."

"Careful," Mrs Hudson said.

"She knows. You know she knows."

"I've seen that time, Mrs Hudson. And more importantly, I've felt it."

"What did that feel like?" Fred asked.

"It felt like shackles had been taken from my limbs. It felt lighter."

Mrs Hudson stepped forward and placed herself between them. Fred slumped back down. It was vitally important that these two did not fall in love, that Fred did not interfere with this time. She knew it, it was a violent instinct that rose inside her, but she couldn't remember why it was important.

"Belle, my dear, tell me what will happen today. Tell me why you are so scared."

"Swingeford will go to his sister, Mrs Jowett, and she will tell him that you are not my family at all. She knows the truth. I was an orphan foundling, left on the steps of her own chapel. She placed me in the orphanage herself. She has taken care of me my whole life but she will not lie for me."

82

"Will she stand by while you are thrown out on the street?" Mrs Hudson asked.

"I have failed her. She will no longer intervene in my fortunes. She has done enough. She has said it many times. I am to make my own way in the world. I rather thought this might be that way." She looked around at the jumble of theatrical props and stage panels. "How could I think that the theatre could change anything?"

"And what of Mr Dickens?" Mrs Hudson asked. "He's crucial to this, I feel."

"Oh, he's going to review the play. I understand he is here to write a scathing, humorous review of our provincial theatre. The nation will laugh at us and he will be paid a few guineas. I had hoped to intercede and to persuade him to treat us fairly but it's hopeless."

"We're here to help you," Fred said. "I'm certain of it."

Mrs Hudson tutted and shook her head.

"The actors will be here soon," said Belle. "The star performer, Mr Aldridge will arrive at two. Any moment now. What am I to do?"

Mrs Hudson took her hands again. "Do nothing."

"How can I do nothing?"

"If that awful man comes and throws you out on the street, think about it then. Until he does, the show must go on."

"But he might cancel the show."

"And if he dares, let him. But until then, it carries on. And as for Mr Dickens; leave him to me."

"What will you do?"

"I think I know why he's really here." She tapped her nose.

Belle nodded and seemed to accept that Mrs Hudson knew what she was doing. She didn't really know anything, but Dickens was central to this, she was certain. She'd been seeking this moment in time all her life and it was all about Dickens coming to Birmingham, but that was all she could remember of it.

"I'll set up the theatre then," Belle said. She took one of the Carcel lamps and walked out.

They listened to her footsteps up the corridor. A door clanked as she bustled into the bowels of the building.

"You think that's the best thing?" Fred said. "Do nothing?"

"This thing we have, we need to avoid interfering. Messing up the past can... Oh, terrible things." She couldn't remember what they were, but she felt the dread of them. Some quite awful things had happened. Losing one's whole life, for instance. Losing everything, so that you were a stranger in your own life. Rather like this disease she had. Her memory disintegrating cell by cell every moment, till she was a stranger in her own life. Soon there would be nothing left of herself, nothing left of her memories, and she would be lost. And that was all you had to define yourself: your memories. That was all you had in the world.

"You've never used this to change the past?" Fred asked.

She shook her head. "I did once intervene to make sure my parents met for the first time. They had their first dance at Moseley Institute. A lovely dance night in... 1934. Benny Orphan and his Orchestra."

"That's..."

"What?"

"That's this week," Fred said. "You know. Back where I'm from. It's all confusing."

"Yes. Hard to get your head around. Especially a head as addled as mine."

"So you *have* intervened?"

"Only to make sure the past stayed exactly as it was. Someone was trying to threaten it, you see. I made sure it stayed the same. I don't remember the details now. I just remember that my parents always told me they fell in love at that dance. If it didn't happen, I wouldn't be here. In a way."

"So doing nothing is always best?"

"Yes it is."

"I can't believe that. I can't see all this, this terrible poverty and privation, all the things that are wrong here — I can't see all this and do nothing."

"It's Dickens," she said, distracted. "The reason we're here is something to do with Dickens. I know it. I just wish I could remember why."

"Well, perhaps that's why you're here. But I know I'm here for something to do with Belle."

Of course he thought that. He was in love with her. He'd been in love with her since the moment he'd clapped eyes on her. It was obvious. And she with him. Mrs Hudson felt she should stop it, but wasn't that also interfering?

"Well, let's go and help her, then," she said, and added with a wry smile, "The show must go on."

— 15 —

There was nothing he could do.

Dickens watched the boy skulk out of the shop. It was heartrending. He had seen quite clearly the father-son rift that played out before his eyes, like a Greek tragedy performed on the stage. And his own part in it did not escape him. His baulking at the use of child labour had led to the boy being thrown out. There was nothing he could say. The awful old miser had taken him at his word and given him what he demanded. Charles Dickens was well and truly hoist on his own petard. Or rather, quite tragically, the boy Tim Cratchit had been hoist on Dickens' petard.

A family torn asunder, and at Christmas too. All he could do was make amends in some way. He caught Forster's warning glare and lowered his eyes. The only thing to do now was to let this deal be done so that no more harm came to the likes of the Cratchits.

Mr Swingeford clapped his hands and took them all by surprise. "Well, I'll not sit here idly and talk business over tea. I prefer to walk. Gentlemen?" He ushered them to the door.

"I like to walk," said Charles. "A fine idea."

They trudged out to the cold street, teeming with life, and the incessant hum of manufacture. It was almost as he'd written about in *Pickwick* years ago, when he'd exaggerated it, of course. The hum of labour resounding from every house, the whirl of wheels and noise of machinery, the din of hammers, the dead heavy clanking of engines from every quarter. It was almost like the ceaseless roar of London.

"Since I am to impress upon you the capabilities of this town, as that is why you are here, let me show you what this town is capable of." Swingeford strode into the street and crossed to the other side.

They walked up a while, weaving their way between the promenading townsfolk, dressed in the finest fashions, Dickens noted.

"There is a great deal of the Greek about the architecture," Forster said.

"The Greek Revival is the fashion, I am told," said Swingeford. "But you may note it is that hour of the day when the fashionable elite of Birmingham take their afternoon stroll and promenade to observe the art works."

Dickens looked all around for the art works but could only see the great Gothic facade of the grammar school and the view down the street marked Peck Lane, which plummeted down to something that was clearly not a fashionable street in the Greek revival style. He stared hypnotized. Down there was grime and dirt and squalor: the fetid horror of the poverty that pursued him in his nightmares.

"I see there are shabby slums just within spitting distance of this grand boulevard," he noted drily.

"Ha. The Froggery," Swingeford sneered. "It will soon be gone. A new railway station is planned and I am to be a major stakeholder in its creation. A grand, central station. It will wipe all of that off the face of the earth."

"Grand, and central, Charles," said Forster. "You were only saying this morning how that's what this place needs."

"Indeed."

"But that's not what I wanted to show you." Swingeford pointed across New Street at the building opposite with his cane.

He had crossed the street purely so they could take in the

full majestic sweep of the building Dickens hadn't noticed in the gloom this morning.

It had three storeys; the ground and first floor fronted with Doric pillars, and on top of those sat four statues. Above them, a giant hoarding of Greek letters carved into the stone.

ΠΑΝΤΕΧΝΗΘΗΚΑ

Dickens squinted. "What on earth is that?"

"The home of Birmingham art works."

"But what does it say?"

"Pantecknicker," said Swingeford.

"I don't think it does," said Dickens. "There are more syllables in it for a start."

"It says Pantechnetheca," said Forster.

"Ah, the benefits of a classical education," Dickens joked.

"Pantecknicker. That's what I said."

"But what does it mean?"

"I don't think it means anything," said Forster. "Nothing I recognize."

"It's Greek," said Swingeford, sneering, as if these men were yokels from the Black Country. "Come, let's go inside and ye shall wonder."

He crossed back over. Dickens gave Forster a sour look.

"Let's play along, Charles," Forster said. "You can pretend, can't you?"

He didn't wait for an answer. Dickens followed him across the street and entered the grand building to find a palatial showroom that was more like a museum. The art works were displayed on stands or in glass cases around the great hall of a building, and reverent gentlemen and ladies walked awestruck among them. But for the evidence of the counters and the clear indication that the artworks were being wrapped up and purchased, one would not know that this was a shop at all.

"Here you will find all manner of valuable manufactured articles with a concentration of goods from the local area,"

Swingeford said, as if it were his own museum and he were its sole benefactor. "They once scoffed at the idea that the manufactures might be seen as arts, but we have proved them wrong."

"I thought the arts were pursued entirely for their own sake," Dickens said.

"They may be that," said Swingeford.

"But these are produced for profit."

"The Brummagem article was once a term of abuse but has now become a thing admirable as a work of art."

The ridiculous effrontery of it, Dickens thought, trying not to laugh out loud. They could call it a 'depository for the arts' and that meant that Birmingham wares belonged within the brackets of the arts.

"I suspect you think me a country bumpkin from the provinces," Swingeford said. "But this is a city of manufacture that is putting London in the shade. I see your capital producing nought but disease and immigrants."

Dickens stiffened and felt Forster squeeze his arm. His friend feared he might punch the old miser and it must have shown in his face because Swingeford cackled with malicious glee.

"You bring your business to Birmingham because you suspect you can get it on the cheap," he said. "But beware this city's reputation of itself. A Birmingham art-work is becoming renowned around the world."

"Art-works?" Dickens said. "You mean trinkets and baubles and machine parts?"

"Yes, that I do. And all come to the Pantecknicker to see them on display."

Dickens shook Forster's hand off and stroked his spasming cheek. That wretched rheumatism striking him at the most inopportune moments.

"Oh, how now, dear brother? What have we here?"

They turned and bowed to the elderly lady who sidled up to them.

"Gentlemen," Swingeford said, with a hint of discomfort, "allow me to introduce my dear sister, Mrs Jowett. Mr Forster and Mr Dickens."

"Mr Dickens? The author?" Mrs Jowett asked.

"Mr John Huffam, please," Forster hissed. "He is travelling incognito."

"Oh, I see," said Mrs Jowett. She held out her gloved hand and both gentlemen kissed it. She looked all around, as if she'd forgotten something, as if something else entirely was on her mind.

"I rather believe our mutual friend might be ashamed of coming to do honest business in this backwater," Swingeford growled.

"Not at all," said Forster. "We merely thought it a necessary precaution. Everywhere Charles goes he is mobbed. The poor fellow has no privacy."

"So this is almost like a holiday for you," Mrs Jowett said.

"You might say that," Dickens answered. Distracted as she was, she was altogether more agreeable than her wretched brother and he sensed a charitable soul.

She lowered her voice and took his hand. "Mr Dickens, I did so admire *Oliver Twist* and your bold choice to present a novel with a child protagonist."

"I hadn't fully thought that it had not been done before," Dickens said, looking modestly at his shoes.

"A child cannot be a main character," Swingeford said. "Why, they have no intelligence, no character at all. A child's soul is barely formed until they come of age at 21, and even then their experience of life is not worthy of examination."

"I beg to differ," Dickens said through gritted teeth. "Go out on that street and you'll find children whose experience of life is nothing but want and need. They are cast half-formed into the Battle of Life that privileged old men are protected from, they struggle in squalor, with shame and hunger, and they bear the brunt of man's ignorance. Why, I could walk through that Froggery you so despise and in a half hour find ten score children who have more experience of the world than every man who sits in Sir Robert Peel's parliament right now."

"Hear hear," said Mrs Jowett. "Well said."

"Humbug," said Swingeford. "Now, if you gentlemen would excuse me for a few moments, there is a pressing family matter I wish to discuss with my sister. Please do explore the art-works to your content."

He took Mrs Jowett's arm and led her off.

"Charles, I'm sorry," Forster said.

"How can I enter into business with that 'fine old English gentleman', that *gammon,* that *Tory?"*

"Because that's the way of the world now, Charles."

"Never, I won't accept it."

"They are the government now. Their locomotive rides through this land and nought will stop it, I fear."

"And it rides over the backs of all of us."

"Aye, I fear it does at that."

"But while it does there's money to be made from it? Is that it? The country's done for!"

Forster sighed. "Charles, it is my job to make sure you make money. You are approaching bankruptcy. Your periodical, your art, will not find its way into the world without investment by the likes of Mr Swingeford."

"I think I'd rather go find my way in that slum."

Forster let out a benign chuckle. "You wouldn't last a day, Charles, you're a man who's never seen dirt and grime up close at all."

Dickens gasped, an icicle piercing his heart. His cheek spasmed again. The smile fell from Forster's face when Charles turned a glare on him of such ferocity that he seemed to fear for his life.

"You know nothing of the dirt and grime and hard work I might have seen, John. You know *nothing* of my life."

Dickens stormed off to the window that looked out onto the street. He wanted to walk out and go hide in that hotel room, or walk a hundred miles or all the way back to London, but he was trapped. Trapped in this absurd trading post masquerading as an art gallery. Trapped in a business charade with this vile old miser. Trapped in his worst nightmare.

No, not the worst. Young Master Green reaching out for him in his dreams. Those pleading eyes. *Don't leave me here in this hell. Save me from this.* Always that boy's eyes haunting him, and waking with the guilt that he would gladly stamp on his face to escape the dirt of that place.

He would grin and do business with that vile miser so he didn't fall back into the dirt.

A bustling behind him. He put on a fake, sickly smile and turned to Mrs Jowett and the snake she called a brother. A manservant struggled behind her carrying a pile of boxes tucked under both arms and piled right up to his chin.

"Mr... ahem, Huffam," Mrs Jowett said. "I understand you are to attend the Harlequinade at our Theatre Royal today. There is a special young lady who has been a charitable case of mine her whole life who is largely responsible."

The girl who'd chased him down New Street. Pretty, with dark eyes. She had said she'd written the play. "How charming," Dickens said.

Mrs Jowett gazed out at the street, as if someone were calling her name. Charles wondered what tragedy had recently befallen her. It was the unmistakable distraction of a woman in deep shock. She squeezed Dickens' hand, like a mourner at a funeral. He bowed and she bustled out with her manservant tottering behind, bearing the full weight of her generosity.

Swingeford seemed in an even blacker mood than before, if that was possible in one so thoroughly and utterly disagreeable, and Dickens wondered at the family matter he'd discussed with his sister. Yes, he was quite certain now: whatever it was they'd discussed, it was quite tragic.

— 16 —

Tim Cratchit dashed across New Street and scuttled into Peck Lane, taking the tumble down to the Froggery, away from fancy New Street with its toffs walking up and down in their fine clothes. Fury burned in his chest and in his fists. The impotent fury of rejection. Blast Swingeford and blast the man who couldn't be called Dickens. No, *Dickens*. He *was* Dickens. No more lies. Blast Dickens. And blast father too. Blast them all!

He shuddered against the bitter cold and shoved his black fingers into his pockets as he walked, his breath a cloud before him. It was going to snow. Sometimes you could tell, like you could taste it in the air.

He passed the new synagogue and the crooked lane that was actually called The Froggery, even though everyone called the whole neighbourhood hereabouts the same name, which was curious, as if the area had only started with that single crooked street and grown outwards till it covered a few acres.

He trudged down the hill and crossed Queen Street, looking right to spy the back of the theatre through the murk at the top there. He was going there with his pa tonight: the stupid Harlequinade for the poor children. He spat as he crossed the street and hurried on down to where Peck Lane and Pinfold Street emptied out. The bottom of the world. The bottom of the midden. And there, right at the bottom of it all, a chapel and a prison.

He stood by the door of the Connexion chapel. His mother would be in there, washing the floors and cleaning out the chamber pots for Mrs Jowett. And when she was done with that she'd trudge home to the Cratchit hovel and do the same again for all of them.

He fingered his collar and felt the frayed edge where it was torn. Slogger Pike had ripped it and his mother would sigh and patiently stitch it tonight, her poor eyes straining by the candlelight. Tomorrow would be Christmas and they would eat a goose the size of a pigeon with some scraps of vegetables scrounged from the market and all pronounce it a feast fit for a king.

He choked and gagged on the ball of pain lodged in his throat.

Damn Swingeford and Dickens and damn his father, and damn himself too for being a Cratchit. He'd rather burn down their house than sing *I Saw Three Ships* again and say *God bless us, every one.*

Across the street, the brooding presence of the Dungeon, with the spikes above the gate and the roof tiles all hanging off, holes and rafters exposed. An old prison, long abandoned. Slogger Pike and his gang were in there. It belonged to them, until such time as the toffs bothered to come down this way and raze it to the ground.

Slogger Pike had murdered the moneylender Marley eight years ago this Christmas Eve. Everyone said so. The old money lender had his skull beaten in and no one mourned him. Not a single person. No one had told the police anything and they couldn't pin it on Slogger Pike. They said Marley's face had been smashed in so brutally his jaw had detached from his skull and flopped down onto his chest. A horrible sight, the housemaid had said. The story had spread all over the Froggery within an hour. And still they talked about it.

Eight years ago tonight.

As Tim Cratchit was being born. The strange coincidence of it all: Tim had taken his first breath as Marley breathed his last.

He tried to imagine the Slogger Pike he knew doing that to a man. Could he be so brutal? Or had he let the rumours spread just so people would think he'd do that to them too if he wanted?

Slogger Pike answered to no man, they said. Whereas Bob Cratchit slogged his guts out for men like Swingeford and crept around like a kicked dog all his life. In this world, one needed to be like Mr Swingeford, or like Slogger Pike. Though they were at opposite ends of society, they were the same. They took what they wanted and damn and blast and hang everyone else.

He thought he could still smell the stench of Slogger Pike's saveloy breath. *You find out what you can about that money, you hear? You tell me everything.* He dug into his pocket and pulled out the shiny half farthing. He could walk right across the street and tell Slogger Pike all about the business deal. The wad of money. Pike expected it. But he didn't have to tell him that the money was in the drawer in the hotel room. He could say the fat man from London had handed the money to Swingeford and it was all now locked safely away. He could say Swingeford had walked across the street to deposit the cash at Atwood & Spooner's bank.

It would be the easiest lie in the world. He looked up at the roundel window of the chapel tower, high above, a crick in his neck. It would be the whitest lie too. A good lie.

His mother was inside. He could knock this door and she would hustle him inside if Mrs Jowett was away and feed him some scraps from her kitchen, fold him in her warm embrace.

He stepped into the gutter, crossed the street to the Dungeon and rapped on the great wooden door.

— 17 —

There was a sound rap against the theatre's back door and Mrs Hudson went to answer it to find it half open. The broad figure of Mr Fezzwig, the landlord of the Hen & Chickens Hotel, stood there, brandishing his cane. This was how gentlemen knocked a door, she thought, by rapping on it with their cane.

"Oh, hello, Mr Fezziwig."

"Fezzwig, my dear. Mrs Hudson, isn't it?"

"That's right. Belle is engaged in preparing the stage for this afternoon's performance."

Mr Fezzwig held out his arms. "To whit, I am here."

A startled moment before she realized. "Oh, you're part of the cast?"

"A minor star of the Harlequinade for the past eight years," he purred.

"Come in, come in." She stepped aside for his massive frame.

Another voice called. Footsteps running. "Hilly ho!"

A gentleman in a vivid red flowery waistcoat and sleek white hair that poked out from under his top hat.

"Mr Wilber. Well met," said Fezzwig. "Allow me to introduce Mrs Hudson. She is the long lost aunt of our dear Miss Belle."

Mr Wilber bowed and swept his hat off his head. "An

honour, madam. And what a fortunate turn of events. A long lost aunt!"

"Sadly, without a fortune to bestow," Mrs Hudson smiled. "Alas, this is not one of Mr Charles Dickens' novels."

The two men roared with laughter.

Another half dozen men and a few women came running up to the door. A happy band of amateur actors. Fezzwig introduced them all to her and to Fred in a blur of greetings — there was Mrs Magwitch, Master Pocket, Miss Peggotty, Mr Heep and Mr Jarndyce and a few others whose names she didn't catch. They filed inside and through to the stage area, all lit up and golden.

"Oh, I say!" Fezzwig roared. "It stirs my heart every time I see it. Such grandeur."

Belle rushed to greet them all with delight, her careworn frown disappearing. She looked so beautiful and radiant, so happy. Mrs Hudson looked to Fred and it was there all over his face. He saw it too. He was in love with her. It was impossible not to be. Everyone here was a little bit in love with her.

Mrs Hudson walked to the edge of the stage to look out at the vast auditorium, rows of plush crimson seats, the gilded boxes that lined the upper tier, elegant filigree decoration along the columns and the cut glass chandeliers hanging from the ornate ceiling.

Was it right to intervene and deny Fred that love? Deny Belle too? Who was she to decide they shouldn't be together? Perhaps this was why Fred had been called here. Mrs Hudson was here for Dickens, she was sure, but what was that to do with Fred Smith? Perhaps he had his own purpose and it was Belle who'd called to him through a hundred years.

And who was to say that there was any purpose to any of this? This gift, this curse, might all be just a random accident, a timeslip, a cosmic joke. A wormhole opened up and swallowed some poor victim who found themselves one of Time's laughingstocks.

Fred came to her side and looked out at the auditorium. "It's rather grand, isn't it?"

"The same in your time?" she whispered.

"Not quite as grand as this. Imagine being able to live here."

"And then imagine being cast out," she said.

Fred frowned and looked back at Belle surrounded by her excited amateur cast. They were already going through their parts and strolling the boards, making last minute adjustments to the performance they had no doubt rehearsed already.

"I'm sorry. I didn't mean that. Everything will be all right. I'm sure of it."

Other voices called from the back of the auditorium. The front of house was opening.

"Mr Aldridge will be here any moment now!" Belle announced.

There was a squeal of excitement amongst the entire cast and they marched up one of the aisles and through to the front of house. Mrs Hudson and Fred followed, through a ballroom space, a bar to one side and a coffee house to the other, both of which were opening for business.

Belle threw open the doors to New Street and the cast piled out.

A coach pulled up and two people emerged. A black man dressed in the finest clothes leapt out and gave his arm to a white woman who stepped down and remained on his arm.

For an instant, Mrs Hudson thought he might be her servant, but she dismissed the thought. He was too well dressed, too sure of himself, too regal. He was the centre of attention and he knew it.

"Mr Aldridge!" Belle cried, rushing to greet him.

"Miss Ruth! I am here!" he said in a rich, American accent.

Ira Aldridge greeted Belle and the cast, but he was also greeting the street, as if he might take the entirety of New Street into his embrace, and it seemed the entire street reacted to his presence. A buzz of energy crackled about him. Everyone turned from what they were doing and rushed to greet him.

"Mr Aldridge!" ladies cried.

"It's Ira Aldridge!" gentlemen called.

"The African Roscius!"

Ira Aldridge leapt up to the coachman's seat and clambered effortlessly onto the roof of the coach, arms aloft on his makeshift stage. The entire street applauded, as if the curtain had just opened on his greatest performance.

A throng formed around the theatre in seconds and the street was blocked. The coaches and carts that could not get past did not mind. The drivers stood on their mounts and grinned from ear to ear. Passengers in those carriages stuck their heads out and craned to get a better view. Even the horses seemed to nod their heads and flick their manes in approval.

"Dear people of Birmingham," he called in a deep, sonorous voice. "The African Roscius has returned to the town that forged his fame! It was fourteen years ago almost to the day that I first trod the boards right here. I gave you *The Slave* and *Othello* and you, the good people of this fine town, took me to your hearts!"

"Bravo!" came the cries.

"And today I return, to wish you all the greetings of the season!"

"Happy Christmas!" they cried.

"Good tidings!"

"But I've not merely come to wish you season's greetings, good people of Birmingham!" Ira Aldridge continued. "I have come to tread the boards once more at the Theatre Royal for the grand Christmas Harlequinade, today at four!"

The street erupted, hats were thrown into the air and it seemed that the Christmas spirit had well and truly landed on New Street with a colossal bump.

Across the street, Mrs Hudson spied two figures watching

the scene: Charles Dickens and his business manager, the large chap, John Forster.

Again, she was startled that it wasn't the Dickens she expected at all. But of course not. This was 1842, and the Dickens in her head was much later. This was the young man. He didn't have the wiry goatee and the careworn face marked with a criss-cross of wrinkles like an old paper bag. This wasn't the Dickens of popular imagination, the Dickens on the ten pound note — not at all — this was a young man with a smooth face, lively blue eyes and long hair, sleek and black, that flowed around his collar. He was just starting out in the world but he had already made his name, and already thought he had failed and his star had waned, his work was done. How odd that this Charles Dickens hadn't yet written *A Christmas Carol*, or *Great Expectations, Hard Times, A Tale of Two Cities, Bleak House, David Copperfield*. All of these were yet to tumble from his mind onto the page.

She edged around the crowd as Ira Aldridge jumped from the coach and was mobbed by his adoring public. She hurried over the street, pushing through the fringe of the mob.

"Mr Dickens. How lovely to meet you."

Forster stepped in front of her. "Now, now, madam, let's not continue that nonsense—"

But Charles Dickens shrugged him off. "How delightful to make your acquaintance."

"Mrs Hudson."

Charles Dickens took her in, but he couldn't help looking over her shoulder to the scene across the street. There was a sickly grin. It was jealousy, plain and simple.

"And you're here to witness Mr Aldridge. How lucky for you. Such a star. Getting all the attention."

"Yes, quite."

"His fame burns so bright, and he will be the talk of the town tonight when he steps on stage."

"Law, really? I'd no idea his fame extended beyond the London stage."

Dickens' voice was thick, as if he had a speech impediment of some kind — as if he had just finished eating cake and was yet to wash it down. And while he spoke in a formal manner, was there just a trace of cockney about it?

"Oh yes," Mrs Hudson said. "He's quite the star here, as you can see. Worshipped. Adored. Eclipsing all others."

Dickens' sickly grin became a sneer.

"You'll be seeing the performance this afternoon, I hear?"

"Well, yes, I'm to write a review."

"Wouldn't it be so much better for you to come and meet with Mr Aldridge and the cast, and the very talented lady who runs the place?"

"I'm afraid that wouldn't be seemly," Dickens said. "A reviewer needs to maintain a degree of autonomy, you see. It wouldn't do for a theatre critic to let it be known he was present. With my fame, that has proved far too difficult a task."

The fat man with him sighed at this.

"Oh, nonsense!" said Mrs Hudson. "I imagine everyone would be thrilled to meet the famous author. I imagine most people don't even know you're here in our town. They might go as wild as they have for Mr Aldridge here. Of course, it might be that you wish to remain in obscurity?"

"No, not at all," said Dickens. "There's no reason at all to skulk around pretending I'm not here."

"Charles. I mean, John," Forster hissed. "We agreed!"

"Oh, nonsense," Dickens said. "Come, Mrs Hudson. You must introduce me to Mr Aldridge and all your theatre friends right this minute."

He was already crossing the street. Forster groaned in despair. Mrs Hudson gave him her best smile and hurried after the author.

— 18 —

Mrs Hudson followed Dickens through the mob surrounding Ira Aldridge.

"Charles Dickens," the author said as he greeted him warmly with a handshake. "How very pleased I am to meet you, Mr Aldridge."

And it was as if he'd let off a grenade in the street. The mob, already at hysteria pitch, howled with delight.

"Dickens!"

"It's Charles Dickens!"

"Here! In Birmingham!"

"Dear Boz!"

"My niece said it was so. She saw him at the station this morning. I didn't believe her!"

Dickens waved to the crowd and climbed up on the coach to a roar of acclaim.

John Forster held his face in his palm.

"How wonderful it is to be here in this fine town again!" he cried. "Like Mr Aldridge, I have been here many times before. You might remember how fondly I wrote of it in *The Pickwick Papers?*"

"Yes!"

"Bravo!"

"Well said!"

"And may I say how wonderful it is to see that the people

102

of this fine town still observe the season and that there is a veritable buzz of festivity about the place."

New Street crackled with applause and then there were cries of delight as snowflakes began to drift down from the leaden sky.

"Oh, and it appears it might be a white Christmas!" he cried.

The air danced around him, as if on cue, a delightful stage effect.

"We must revive the old Christmas customs," he cried, "and let them not fall into disrepair. Let this season be one where we reach out to each other and give the best of ourselves!"

The crowd applauded heartily and everyone stood an inch taller and made plans to get a Christmas wreath for their door within the hour.

Fred leaned close to Mrs Hudson and murmured, "I feel like I've walked into a Christmas card."

"And may I say how delighted I am that the Theatre Royal is to perform a show on Christmas Eve for the poor children of the parish. How fine and noble it is. God bless us every one!"

The applause rang out and echoed all the way down New Street, from the pillars of the Town Hall to the spire of St Martin in the Bull Ring.

Mrs Hudson watched the effect his words had on those who gazed up at him. In particular she noted the joy on Belle's face. And when he'd finished his speech and went into the theatre with the mob of the cast, she felt her work was done. Whatever it was she was here to do, perhaps she'd done it.

John Forster tutted and shook his head. "There's no containing him," he said. "No use. No use at all."

"He's adored," said Mrs Hudson.

"And that adoration is like air to him. He can't live without it."

"Come inside, Mr Forster. I fear he may be occupied for some time yet."

She couldn't help chuckling as she walked in. The crowd outside the theatre dispersed and went about its way on New Street with a lighter step and full of Christmas spirit.

Mrs Hudson breezed through the ballroom space of the Theatre Royal's vast foyer, with the Shakespeare Rooms tavern and the coffee house on either side already doing brisk business.

They went through the auditorium and joined the cast on the stage in the warm limelight, all fussing over Ira Aldridge and Charles Dickens. It seemed the colourful nature of the cast had been turned up a few notches. Mrs Hudson could see that they were acting up for him as they brought out their costumes and sashayed under the lights — acting *Dickensian*. Unless everyone really was like this and Dickens might have been more of a realist than she thought.

Forster seemed to read her thought. "They all want to be in his next book."

Mr Fezzwig tottered around on stilts and everyone whooped with delight to see such an enormous man stalking the stage. He had a great green fur-lined robe that came down to the floor to hide the stilts. He was a gentle great roaring giant.

Mr Wilber insisted on giving a sneak preview of his magic lantern effects.

"Oh," Dickens cried. "I do love a good magic lantern show."

"Mr Wilber is quite the enthusiast," said Belle. "He relishes the chance of using it on the stage every Christmas. For the poor children of the Froggery, it is the only opportunity they get to see a magic lantern show."

A ghastly vision appeared on the great white backdrop curtain, and everyone stepped back, shocked.

The black silhouette of a coach-and-four that moved and grew bigger, riding towards them. It looked like it might burst right through the curtain.

It loomed bigger and bigger till they saw the coach driver's face was a hideous grinning skull.

"Bravo!" said Dickens. "Astonishing!"

Mr Wilber came from behind the curtain and bowed to their applause. "We must show Mr Dickens the Ghost!" he said.

"Oh yes! Do!"

"It's perfectly horrid!"

"What is it?" Ira Aldridge asked.

"Of course," said Mr Wilber. "You haven't seen it yet. The Ghost's costume is horribly macabre!"

"There's a Ghost?" Dickens asked. "I thought this was a Harlequinade?"

"It is," said Belle. "Every year we stage a Harlequinade, of sorts, and every year we write it in a different way."

"But you have young lovers, a bullying father trying to marry off the young lady, a comical servant?"

"Some of those things, yes. But I have a ghost who transforms the mean father and makes him mend his ways by showing him his past, his present and his future."

Dickens stroked his chin. "Interesting. Pause you, isn't that rather like my story in *The Pickwick Papers?*" He looked to John Forster.

"Which story is that, Charles?"

"You know. The tale of Gabriel Grub, visited by goblins who show him his past and future."

"Oh yes," said Forster. "Quite similar."

"I have meant no attempt to copy your work, Mr Dickens. I assure you my play, as trivial as it is, was original and came from my own imagination."

"Of course," said Charles, forcing a smile. "I meant no accusation. There are only so many stories we can tell. I'm sure yours is quite unlike mine."

Mr Wilber came running out from backstage with what looked like a horse collar. "This is such an ingenious device.

105

Miss Belle here designed it herself."

He placed the collar over his head so it sat on his shoulders. Fiddling with the contraption, he snapped it tight so it created a false lower half of his face.

"I say," said Dickens. "That looks wonderful."

Mr Wilber took a bandage and tied it under the contraption's chin, knotting it on top of his head.

"The idea," said Belle, "is that the false jaw sits over the real jaw and when you untie the knot on top of the head, the false jaw flops down."

Mr Wilber pulled at the knot on top of his head, the bandage fell loose and his jaw flopped down to his chest.

Everyone howled at the grisly effect.

"Oh, it's horrible!"

The ladies turned away and squealed. The men chuckled with delight. It was the most gruesome sight. Mr Wilber's real jaw was hidden and it looked like his mouth had fallen open in a grisly red abomination.

"Stop it!" Mrs Aldridge cried, covering her eyes and burying her face in her husband's shoulder. He bellowed a hearty laugh.

Mr Wilber took the contraption off, his silver hair matted with sweat.

"Inspired by the death of Marley," Mr Fezzwig said. "God rest his soul."

"Marley? Who's that?" Dickens asked.

"Oh, most terrible affair," said Mr Wilber. "Eight years to this day, wasn't it?"

"Indeed it was," said Mr Fezzwig. "I remember it exactly, as it was the very night I first trod these boards, in the Christmas Eve Harlequinade of 1834."

"Old Marley was a moneylender round these parts," Mr Wilber said. "Brutally murdered in his own home on Christmas Eve. Just like that." He held up the ghastly contraption and flapped the jaw.

"Take it away!" one of the other ladies cried.

"And here's the irony," Fezzwig said. "The man who did it walks free but now resides in the old prison."

"Almost as if he's cocking a snook at the law."

"No one knows that it was him."

"Everyone knows that it was him."

"Slocombe Pike. A ghastly, vile creature. A pestilence on the poor people of the Froggery."

"Well," said Belle, "it is to be hoped that our performance today will give those poor people some respite from their situation."

"Hear hear!" cried Mr Fezzwig.

"That is the awesome power of the theatre," Dickens said, clapping his hands. He turned and spun in the limelight, holding out his arms as if to embrace the theatre. "I almost took to the stage myself, you know? I had an audition with the Covent Garden theatre but on the appointed day I was laid up with a terrible cold and an inflammation of the face. I chose the life of a man of letters instead. But oh, the magic of the stage!"

He was struck with a sudden idea.

"One of you ladies," he said. "Your pocket handkerchief, if I may?"

He went to Mrs Aldridge and she took out a purple silk handkerchief tastefully embroidered. Dickens took it, bowed and held it up for all to see. He pushed it into his fist, smiling archly, prodding it till it disappeared entirely. He waved his free hand over his fist, swirling an aura of magic.

"My dear lady," he said, "I'm afraid your pocket handkerchief has gone. And is now…"

He smacked his fist and fanned out his hands and there, he held a paper cone full of coloured beans.

"… transformed by the power of magic into… a posy of comfits!"

He presented the cone to Mrs Aldridge. Everyone cooed with delight.

"Oh! Sweetmeats!"

"Comfits!"

Mrs Aldridge ate one. "They're real!"

She offered them around and everyone took one.

"Sugarplums!"

Applause rang out. Dickens bowed.

"A magician! As well as a great author!"

"'Tis a mere frippery," Dickens said. "I bought a conjurer's kit from Hamley's of High Holborn and I aim to perform a magic show for my son's birthday in the new year."

Mr Fezziwig stepped forward and gripped Dickens' arm with sudden vehemence. "Oh, Mr Dickens! You ought to be in our play! Your magic would so delight the children!"

"Oh, yes!" they cried.

"What a capital idea!"

"Oh, do!"

Belle held up a hand to shush them and drew Dickens away. "No, you mustn't bully Mr Dickens into performing for us. He is here to review the play for a periodical and we mustn't compromise him."

Mrs Hudson caught the speck of disappointment in his eye.

"It is true," he said, "I am supposed to maintain a level of professional detachment. Even to be here, talking to you all..."

Forster took his elbow.

"But I shall be delighted to attend your pantomime," Dickens announced.

"It is also a mere frippery," said Belle. "A simple entertainment for the children."

"What could be grander and more noble an undertaking at this time?" Dickens said.

The cast broke out into warm applause, with cries of "Hear hear," and "Well said," and "Very good!"

"I shall return and take my seat and be glad of the entertainment."

John Forster took out his pocket watch.

108

"Now, my dear thespians, I fear my manager has business for me to attend to. Much as I would love to stay and talk of theatre with you good people."

"No!" they cried. "Go!"

Mrs Hudson saw they would have railroaded him out of there if he had stayed a moment longer. The great author had other business to attend to — in *their* town! — and he should be about it this instant. They agreed whole-heartedly, even though it would mean his leaving.

Charles Dickens strode off the stage and up the aisle, Forster pushing him in case he changed his mind, the entire cast waving him away.

"Now, good friends," Belle said, clapping her hands. "We need to go through our entrances and exits one last time, and for the benefit of Mr Aldridge, take him through the staging."

Mrs Hudson and Fred edged away to the wings and watched the bustle of stagecraft for a minute. But then... something curious. One by one, the cast stopped listening to Belle and stared out at the auditorium.

Belle noticed and followed their gaze.

Mrs Hudson looked too as the theatre fell silent.

Standing in the aisle was a shadowy figure in a top hat. Ebenezer Swingeford swept the hat from his head, and cast a cold, impenetrable gaze on them.

"Miss Ruth," he said, with a leering kind of smile. "I must talk with you on a matter of grave importance."

— 19 —

Belle excused herself and instructed the cast to continue with the last minute preparations. Mr Fezzwig took command and Belle asked Mr Swingeford to accompany her to her 'drawing room'. As she did so she looked to Mrs Hudson, and so did Swingeford.

"Yes, of course," said Mrs Hudson. A man could not go to a young lady's drawing room alone. And Mrs Hudson was her guardian. Though she did wonder at Belle's earlier comment that she didn't quite count as a 'lady'. Mrs Hudson wondered at the rules of social engagement for working class women. Was it the same or were they mere beasts of burden and no more needed a chaperone than a cat or a dog?

"And you also, sir," Swingeford said, looking to Fred.

"Oh, yes, all right," said Fred with the air of a boy in his first week of work suddenly called to the boss's office.

Belle led them backstage and down the passage to the lumber room at the rear of the theatre. She stroked her dress out as she sat and Mrs Hudson noticed her straight back and proud bearing. She was not to be intimidated, even if she was to be thrown out of her home.

Swingeford looked askance at the untidiness of it as if he wasn't sure where to sit. Belle waved him to the other chaise longue.

"I'm afraid I wasn't expecting company. I can send out for

tea."

"No need," said Swingeford. "I don't care for tea."

He sat, perched on the edge of the chaise longue and stared at a point over Belle's shoulder. Mrs Hudson craned to see what took his attention. A box frame in the corner of the room, curtained off. She pondered what it was and realized it was a sleeping compartment. A bed in a box that was, in effect, Belle's bedroom. It was the kind of 'bedroom' most people in the country had. The idea of a room all of its own, devoted solely to sleeping, was one of unimaginable wealth. Most people in the country lived in one- or two-room hovels with their entire family.

"This is where you live, is it?" Swingeford said.

"Mr Swingeford, if this regards my domicile here, I can assure you that it has not been a problem for the existing committee members. I am acting as unofficial caretaker and largely unpaid manager of the theatre."

"That is not an ideal arrangement and is certainly to be frowned upon."

"Then I suggest you might propose it to the committee."

"I hope there will be no need for that."

Belle, Mrs Hudson and Fred all exchanged a puzzled glance. Was there a glimmer of humanity in the man?

He cracked a smile. And crack was the most suitable word, as it gave the impression that his face had indeed cracked, so long had it been set in a grimace.

"I had the pleasure of my sister's company today," Swingeford said.

"Yes," said Belle, "I was there."

"Not this morning. This afternoon. We talked of the matter of your recent good fortune."

"My good fortune?"

"Your reconciliation with your long-lost relatives."

This was it. Mrs Jowett would have told him the truth. Belle closed her eyes for a moment, a woman before a firing squad. Fred shuffled uneasily.

"My sister confirmed your story."

"Oh?" said Belle.

She couldn't hide her surprise and Mrs Hudson wondered if she too looked amazed. Fred coughed and covered his mouth with his fist. Why would Mrs Jowett have confirmed the hasty story they'd made up? It was clearly a lie. Had she chosen to protect Belle from this man?

"It is most curious," said Swingeford. "All your life she has referred to you as an orphan. She put you in the city orphanage herself, having found you on the chapel step all those years ago. And now she agrees with this story regarding your family. Why is that?"

"It's not a story, Mr Swingeford," Fred said.

"Yes," said Mrs Hudson. "Why would you doubt it?"

Swingeford bowed his head almost to hide his cunning smile. He knew it was all a lie. "I am glad your legal guardian is here, Miss Belle. In a way, it is most fortunate. I can now say what I couldn't say this morning."

"I'm not sure I understand," said Belle.

"I have a proposal to make."

"A business proposal?"

Swingeford frowned and seemed to think about this. He seemed unsure. He tilted his head as if considering the merits of how it might be a business proposal, and how it might not. "I suppose that all depends on how one might look at it. Business... yes."

"You know I have no controlling stake in the theatre, Mr Swingeford. I am not on the board at all. You have a share. I do not. As I say, I am merely the theatre's caretaker and live-in manager."

"This is an issue that has been overlooked by the committee."

"I think it has been very much in their best interests."

"And that should change, in due course. Yes, it shall."

What was he getting at? His new investment in the theatre seemed to spell the end for Belle's independence, but he had a proposal for her. It seemed to hint at some hope.

"Mr Swingeford," Mrs Hudson said. "You were to make a proposal?"

"Ah, yes. My proposal." He looked around the room as if he might have mislaid his business proposal or it had been secreted somewhere in a game of hide-and-seek.

"Yes," said Belle, "what is the nature of this business?"

"I mean to offer you a hand."

"A hand?" said Belle.

"That is to say… yes, perhaps it is a business matter. An agreement of mutual benefit. A merger, or more accurately, by the letter of the law, an acquisition. Yes, an acquisition, why not? Custom does look upon it as that, it has to be said. The weight of tradition bears out the analogy."

"Mr Swingeford," said Belle. "I do not follow."

Mrs Hudson groaned as she realized that Swingeford's business proposal was…

"A proposal?" said Fred.

"I mean marriage," said Swingeford.

Fred laughed. A short, sharp bark of amusement. But on catching Belle's stricken face, he turned pale. His mouth sank into a crooked snarl, like he'd had a stroke.

"Marriage?" said Belle. "You are offering marriage?"

"Yes, isn't that obvious?" said Swingeford.

"No," said Fred. "That can't happen."

"And what concern is it of yours, cousin? Do you mean to make your own proposal?"

"What? No," he said.

Too forcibly, as if the idea was horrifying.

Belle gasped, as if that firing squad had responded to the command to fire.

"It seems to me that I only need ask permission from you, Mrs Hudson, to call on Miss Ruth again and pursue my interest."

"You want to marry her?" Mrs Hudson said.

"I am prepared to overlook our difference in social

113

standing. Since your appearance today, Mrs Hudson, it is obvious that you are of a class that is tolerable to me and I need not fear too much the stigma of marrying beneath me."

"This can't be," said Fred.

Belle wrung her hands on her lap, looking all about the room for an escape hatch.

"Once your bank accounts have been studied, ancestral lineage inspected and a dowry agreed upon we might announce the engagement."

Belle shot up with a cry. She snatched her cloak and ran from the room.

"She is overwrought," said Swingeford. "That is understandable. Her fortunes have changed beyond recognition this day."

He rose and took up his top hat and cane. "Mrs Hudson, Master Hudson. I bid you good day."

— 20 —

Belle ran. She ran along the backstage passage, she ran along the stage, ignoring the calls of her cast members, the only family she had in the world, she ran through the auditorium and through the ballroom and out through the doors to New Street where the snow was falling so thick, a beaded curtain, that she couldn't see the dome of St Philip's church at the top of Bennett's Hill, above the old post office.

She ran up New Street towards the looming pillars of the Town Hall, and passed a roast chestnut seller, the blast of warm air and the sweet, earthy smell so comforting that she almost halted to join the huddle of people surrounding his brazier.

She hurried on till Christ Church loomed on her right and she crossed the street, the snow already settling on the dirt. She skirted the edge of the church and the pokey little shops set into the surrounding wall — Carrs brew house, Freeman's pantry, Jones, Smith, Wakeham and Jones again.

She rounded the base of the church and came to the little square where Ann Street wrapped an arm around the church as if to shield it from the competitive imposing grandeur of the Town Hall.

A cluster of carol singers on the steps of the church chimed *Good King Wenceslas* and rattled a bucket of coins for the poor. In the square, a gang of boys threw snowballs around the gas lamp. The sky was dark, night falling fast, only the flurry of snow lighting the air.

The boys scampered around the square, snowflakes dancing around them. From the door of the White Lion pub, a gang of men peeped out, clutching tankards, laughing and egging on the boys with cries of "Tallyho!"

Belle halted and took it in.

There seemed to be a cheeriness about it all. Everyone was grinning and in good spirits. Had it been the effect of Dickens' speech? Everyone ignored Christmas. Too busy for it in the big towns like this. A cumbersome holiday. They frowned and scowled in the city.

And yet this afternoon seemed different. The first time she'd sensed a magic in the air. The spirit of the season. As it used to be, so they said.

Was it one man's speech — a few little words reverberating on the air — that could change life for the better, go out and make people smile and love their neighbour? Could a few mere words on the air change people's hearts? As if his words had taken flight and fluttered all the way down New Street, sprinkling magical fairy dust on even the people who hadn't heard them. Or could it be that the people who'd heard his words carried them and spread them, like a common cold, a virus for good.

A gentleman with a lady on his arm edged around her and climbed the steps to the church. Clad in the finest clothes, the woman younger than the man so you might mistake her for his daughter, but the way he held his arm out for her to hang onto, like a prince with a hawk, showing off his property, it was obvious she was his wife.

Belle watched them climb the steps and enter the church, the dull echo of movement from inside reverberating around the vast white emptiness. She saw herself on Swingeford's arm, perhaps this same day next Christmas.

She turned from the sight and looked south to the mouth of Pinfold Street that tumbled all the way down to the

116

Froggery. Could the magic bring a little happiness there too, or would it only work its spell on New Street, where the privileged promenaded?

She retreated from the square, an imposter, and skulked away from the carol singers and snowball fighting boys. She trudged into Pinfold Street, as if the Froggery were calling her down into its dark heart, as if the joy of the season wasn't hers to live. She retreated from the warmth and the circle of light into the shadows.

A building loomed before her, half obscured by the night blizzard. She pulled her cloak tighter about her and shivered at the familiar outline of the place.

The orphanage.

This dark building was the repository of all her memories. She had spent her entire childhood here, until they had thrown her out on the street at the age of fourteen to make her own way in the world. A hard, cruel place, were beatings and gruel were dispensed with glee by stern-faced, cold hearted matriarchs demanding thanks to God but showing not one morsel of Christian charity. Even the detached condescension of Mrs Jowett had seemed like a mother's love after that.

Isabelle Ruth had been formed here. A foundling girl given two forenames — the names of the nuns who had found her dumped on the steps of a chapel in the Froggery. Even there, where desperate mothers raised their ragbag of offspring on meagre rations of bread and dripping, there was no mother or father that wanted this girl.

And now a man wanted her.

The worst man in Birmingham. And twice her age too.

Could the words of an author have melted something in the heart of a mean old man like Swingeford? Was that even possible for an awful old miser like that?

His proposal was a business proposition, nothing more, and he had stated it with all the heart of a hostile takeover bid. *An acquisition,* he'd said. He was to acquire her. And yet he would require her to make a deposit, a dowry, for the privilege, after which he would own her, have rights to her, promising to pay on demand the sum of comfort for the rest of her days.

All she would have to do was live with him, listen to him, every day, have his hands on her every night, be owned by him, acquired, invaded.

His awful dead hand on her. Passionless. Like falling into one's own grave.

Why hadn't Fred intervened? she wondered. All he had done was laugh when Swingeford proposed. She didn't know why that hurt her so much, but she had wanted this boy, this man who was a stranger before this day but whom she felt like she'd known her whole life — she had wanted him to intervene, to protect her, to refuse Swingeford's proposal for her. Why had she wanted him to do that?

But he had laughed.

She looked down Pinfold Street to the Froggery in the darkness, only little pinpricks of light down there — a few oil lamps to light the slum, and there, the lamp that Mrs Jowett placed in the roundel window of the chapel tower. Was it that or was she imagining it because she wanted to see it?

Back up the other way, the glow from the gas lamps of New Street and the faint air of a cheery Christmas carol.

She stood frozen, unable to make a decision.

One way darkness and freedom, the other way lightness and death.

— 21 —

Mrs Hudson and Fred rushed out after Belle, passing the actors on stage.

"What is going on?" Mr Fezzwig shouted.

"She went that way!" Mr Wilber called, pointing through the auditorium to the rear stalls.

She climbed down the side stairs and rushed through to the front of the building. So slow. She was old. Fred might have run on ahead and caught her already.

They came through the ballroom at the front of house and burst out onto New Street to find the snow was falling thick now, snowflakes dancing in the frigid air. She looked up and down the street but the blizzard made it difficult to make her out.

"I'll go up," Fred said. "You go that way."

She nodded and was marching down the street in an instant, following her footsteps of this morning when they'd chased Dickens to the printing house. She passed it on the other side with no sign of Belle and came to the Hen and Chickens Hotel. She popped her head through the door but Belle wasn't in there. In truth, Belle could be in any shop, bank, pub or store on the street, and there was no way Mrs Hudson could search them all. But something told her the girl would run, to be as far away as possible from the tragedy that had just happened.

At the end of New Street, she came to the junction with High Street. On the left it ran straight along. She could see no one that wore a cloak like her own. On the right the street dropped down to the Bull Ring market. She could make out the outline of St Martin's, Nelson's statue standing before it, just as it was in her own time. Nothing else was the same though.

Allin's old curiosity shop called out her. In the window it said *Multum in Parvo*. What was that in English? She'd studied Latin, she remembered. A great deal in a small space. She thought of her own shop. *Pastimes*. Yes, that was it. She'd been trying to remember the name all afternoon. Names were the worst. They were constantly eluding her. She stumbled on down the hill along the row of shops and came to the Bull Ring, a jumble of tented stalls, costermongers and street hawkers trading their wares in a cacophony of shouts and calls. The sweet smell of baked potatoes masked for a delicious moment the stench of the street. It was worse than an open sewer. How did anyone live in such filth?

They didn't, she thought. They died in it. They scratched out a mean existence and they died, mostly very young.

A grubby girl in rags held out her bony hands, pleading, gaunt, hollow eyes.

Mrs Hudson recoiled, shamefaced. She had nothing to give her. No money. She owned nothing. Even her fine clothes were the borrowed rags of a theatre cast-off.

It was hopeless.

She came to the Nelson Hotel right next to Nelson's statue and rested on the railings that guarded the war hero.

What was she here for?

Belle. Yes. That was it. The girl had run off and they needed to find her.

A small army of women were filling baskets with chestnuts, potatoes, onions, apples, plums from the various market stalls. Mrs Hudson jostled her way through looking for…

Oh, what was it again?

She came to an old crone standing in the gutter clutching bundles of rosemary and sage, and she was caught by the sweet, earthy scents.

It transported her to a memory. The scent of Christmas.

Her mother and father on Christmas Eve. Decorating the tree and pouring Smoking Bishop. They always let her have a little glass, even as a girl. They took turns in reading aloud *A Christmas Carol.* She would listen to them, lying on the rug, the open fire crackling. The glow of tinsel on the tree. Her stocking hung on the mantelpiece.

Such a beautiful, warm, safe feeling.

The darkness outside and listening for the sound of a sleigh flying through the night sky, somewhere between her parents' words. Dickens' words.

She couldn't see her parents' faces anymore. What did they look like again? But she could hear them reading about Tiny Tim and Fred Cratchit and Marley and Scrooge. Their faces had gone. How long before their voices faded too? How long before every memory was gone? Would she even know them next Christmas?

"Are you all right, my dear?"

"I'm sorry?"

The lady selling rosemary. "You're looking quite lost."

"Oh," said Mrs Hudson, glancing around. "I don't think I am."

"Where are you off to tonight, my dear? Home's not far I hope. In this." She shook her shawl and snow sprayed off her.

Where was home? Mrs Hudson had no idea. Where had she come from? Oh, that feeling again. She clenched her fists. It would come, it would come, just a little time.

She'd been looking for someone. Who was it now?

In fact, where on earth was she?

"You really do look lost, my dear."

It came. A phrase like a flash of a knife blade, clean and pure. "The Birmingham & Midland Institute," she said.

121

"That's where I'm going."

The herb seller crinkled her face up. "I don't know of any such building, my dear."

"Are you sure? I think I'm supposed to go there."

"Never heard of it."

She retreated, backing away from her.

"Don't go, lady. I'll call a policeman to help you."

"It's all right. I'm quite all right."

She turned and marched up the hill, not sure where she was heading. Nothing looked familiar. She glanced back at Nelson's statue and the church behind it. St Martin in the Bull Ring. That was clear enough. But looking up the hill it was all different. No Rotunda, no great bronze bull.

She came to the top of the hill. A sign said New Street but it didn't look like it at all. The Hen & Chickens Hotel on one side and, oh, that was the old King Edwards school. Knocked down when she was a baby, but she'd seen so many photographs of New Street with it there. It seemed to be the only building she knew.

She trudged along the street. A print shop on the other side. Showell's. That was familiar. Hadn't she been there before? It was important.

Dickens. Yes. Charles Dickens. She'd followed him up this street earlier today. And there was a girl. A pretty girl in a cloak, just like the one she wore.

She halted and checked her reflection in a sweet shop window. An old woman staring back at her. Was the young woman herself? Was it a memory from long ago? She looked about her at the ladies and gentlemen on the street. She was in a Dickensian Christmas card. It couldn't be herself as a young woman.

No, that was right. It had been earlier today. She'd followed Charles Dickens up the street.

She banged her fist on her forehead. This stupid brain of hers! Why couldn't it remember anything?

From a pocket sewn into the cloak, she fished out a diary.

Yes, that always told her what she was doing. She edged under the glow of a gaslamp and leafed through the pages. It was Christmas Eve, yes. The diary was printed for 2019 but her scribbled note said *It's Christmas Eve 1842. You need to find Dickens. He is the key to all this.*

She was here to help Dickens. He was a young man. Yes, that was right. He was a young man who was a little surly and mean, and he said something beastly about his wife. So why would she be helping him? He would write some wonderful books, and they were books that changed society, forced Victorians to look at themselves and how they treated their poor. There was that. Perhaps that was what she was meant to be doing.

It was all so confusing.

If only her mind wasn't so scrambled.

Why hadn't she written it down in this blasted diary? What was the point of writing the appointment if she didn't know what it was for?

She was sure she had to go back to her own time and do something very important there. At the edge of her mind, just out of reach, there was some urgent thing to be done. Only she couldn't remember what it was.

Perhaps if she left now she would remember it. She could force herself to leave and go back to her own time, and then she'd remember what it was she had to do.

She walked on up New Street, sensing that the upper part of the street would hold the answers. She had come from that direction earlier today when she'd chased Dickens.

She crossed Lower Temple Street to the Shakespeare Tavern on the corner, and just up the road the portico that said *Theatre Royal.*

Yes! It flooded back to her. Belle, the theatre, Fred, all of it. She was looking for Belle. That was it. Fred had gone the other way, up the street.

She wanted to cry with relief. Each time she blanked out like this it seemed longer and longer for the memories to

123

return. One day, they just wouldn't come back at all and she would be lost. It was inevitable, and then she would be caught in a living hell.

Caught in a place like this.

Livid horror seared her heart. To be trapped here, penniless, having to scrape a meagre living on the streets, selling clumps of herbs or something. Dying in the cold.

She stood on the corner of Lower Temple Street. Down there was where she'd come from. The mangled chrome dome of New Street Station, like a crumpled hub cap in the gutter. It was there, if she thought hard enough.

A coach-and-four thundered down the street from the direction of the Town Hall, Parthenon-style pillars just visible through the blur of snow.

She had to go home, while she could still think clearly, while she still had some memory left. She had no idea why she was here to help Dickens. Fred wanted her to help Belle.

The carriage thundered towards her, its wheels spraying slush into the gutter.

The placard outside the theatre announced the Christmas Harlequinade at four today. She was stuck here in this trivial matter of a theatre and a pantomime. She laughed at the word. *Pantomime.* The very definition of a frivolous activity that meant nothing.

No. She would leave Fred and Belle to whatever Fate or Time had in store for them.

A gust of wind smacked a flurry of ice into her face and she tottered, stumbling blindly into the gutter as the carriage roared down on her.

— 22 —

Fred watched Mrs Hudson set off down New Street and wondered if he ought to let her loose on her own. It was a dangerous place and not the city either of them knew. He recognized almost nothing. He could make out the outline of St Philip's dome up there, which was something you just couldn't see from here in his time as New Street was lined with tall Victorian buildings. And up at the top of the street, the Town Hall stood guard with its Parthenon pillars. He'd attended concerts there all his life. Had Belle said it was a new building? To think of it as something new, when in his life it was the oldest building on New Street: the one constant of the city centre that had stood while all around it changed.

Mrs Hudson disappeared in the pavement crowd. She was adrift. Alone in a Birmingham she didn't recognize. And so was he.

He pushed on up the street. Nothing for it now. The important thing was to find Belle.

On the opposite side of the street stood the portico of the Society of Artists. Yes, that was still there too in his own time. He passed a chestnut seller and got a hot blast of heat and fragrance that made his belly roar. He'd eaten nothing today. He was starving,

Only he wasn't. There really were people here who were starving.

125

He came up to the top of New Street and was knocked back by the force of what was there. Or what wasn't.

There was no Council House. Instead, there was a great ugly church squatting where Victoria Square should be, and a mean row of houses that almost touched the corner of the Town Hall and spilled out to a little square where a street lamp sat. It was a village square, nothing like the great civic square he knew, guarded by Queen Victoria's statue.

Carol singers huddled in the cold at the steps of the church and a gaggle of boys threw snowballs.

The street sign said Ann Street. Could there ever have been a time when the Council House hadn't stood here? He was drawn to the first shop in the row. Suffield's Pharmacy. Coloured bottles of liquid glowing in the window. The building was topped with battlements.

He looked all around but there was no sign of Belle.

If he found her now, he would tell her how he felt. He definitely would.

The carol singers rattled a tin. He shrugged and indicated his empty pockets. Did his costume look like that of a rich gentleman? It was painfully thin and he could have done with a greatcoat, the cold was so bitter.

The mouth of the church invited him. Would she be in there? He didn't think so, but then, he didn't know her, not really, not at all. For all he knew she might be in there praying devoutly.

He retreated along the curve of the church wall, shops inlaid. Across the road, the mouth of Pinfold Street, dark and foreboding.

He turned from it, about to move on, when he thought he saw something. The outline of a dark hooded figure. The Ghost of Christmas yet to Come stepped right out of the pages of Dickens' book.

No. It was Belle.

He ran across the street, snow on his boots.

"Belle!"

The hooded figure turned and a face peered out of the murk. "Belle. Is it you?"

She looked away as he ran to her and he knew she'd not wanted to be found. How stupid of him to run her to ground.

"I'm sorry," he said. "We were worried for you."

"You needn't worry after me, Fred. There is nothing to be done."

This was the moment. He should tell her how he felt. He should tell her he was in love with her and had been from the moment he'd seen her. But his tongue cleaved to the roof of his mouth. They didn't belong together. He wasn't supposed to be here. This was all a bad dream and he would wake any moment and she would be gone — a desperate ideal he'd created in his unconscious mind: a ghost of a dream.

"You don't have to marry him," he said.

"Don't I? What do you know about that?"

"You're a free woman. You can do what you like."

She scoffed. Like he was a silly boy.

"You think I know nothing of the world," he said.

"You know nothing of my world."

"I know my world is safer. I know the average age of mortality in London is 27. If you're working class, it's only 22."

"But a life of privilege lies before me."

"We all breathe the same air. Typhus is no respecter of class."

She looked him up and down and seemed amused. "Tell me about your time. What does it offer to a woman like me?"

She pointed to the square and they walked out of the shadows towards the church and the carol singers.

"What does it offer? Well, for one thing, women over the age of 21 have the vote. There's true equality at last. Oh, and there are aeroplanes, actual flying machines, and waterworks and sewage systems, motor cars and electricity, even indoor plumbing in some houses and medicine. So many diseases have been eradicated. A brave new world. An industrial

127

revolution has reached its peak and transformed society and mechanized everything."

"Including war?"

They came to the church steps and halted. The icy blast of challenge in her voice. He nodded and looked at his snow-covered boots. "Yes, there's still a great deal of that, alas."

"When you came here, you were bleeding." She touched his forehead where the scar still glowed livid just under the brim of his top hat. "Was it some kind of war?"

"Of a sort. A riot. A street battle. A political thing."

"Like the Chartists? Or Peterloo?"

"Yes, something like that. Men fighting over their beliefs."

"So not much has changed a hundred years from now."

He turned from her and clasped the railings, a man in prison, doubting himself. Was it really a better time? That dreadful Oswald Mosley and fighting fascists in the street. Perhaps it was better for her here.

"Are there still men like Swingeford?" she asked. "Men who wish to hoard all the money in the world and see everyone else go to hell?"

He nodded, all hope leaving him. "Yes, of course there are, but there is progress."

She didn't respond. He turned to find her gazing at him. Was he expected to say something? He could tell her he loved her, like he'd said he would.

She grimaced and turned away, digging in the folds of her cloak. She took out a coin and dropped it into the carol singers' tin. And she was walking away. "We must return."

He followed her down New Street. She crossed at the Society of Artists' portico and he caught her up, trudging beside her down to the theatre. There was an urgency to her step. She was keen to get back to the theatre and, perhaps, to Swingeford. A carriage came roaring past and on down New Street.

"Mrs Hudson?" Belle said.

Fred looked up from his sulking.

128

"Mrs Hudson!" Belle yelled.

She was there on the street corner, just by the theatre, about to step into the road in front of the carriage.

"Stop!" Fred cried.

The carriage hurtled towards her, spraying slush into the gutter. A flurry of snow blinded him and it seemed she was lost in a snow cloud just as the carriage reached her.

— 23 —

Mrs Hudson stepped back and the coach-and-four roared past with an unearthly clatter, splattering slush up her cloak. She turned down Lower Temple Street, blinking, half snowblind, certain that the New Street Station of 2019 would be there when she reached the bottom of the hill.

A clockmaker's window. She caught her reflection against the display of gleaming carriage clocks and paused, hypnotized, just for a moment, but pushed on down the hill.

"Mrs Hudson!" Fred yelled.

She froze. Caught.

Fred and Belle on the corner, rushing to her. Fred came and grabbed a hold of her arms. "I thought you'd gone under that coach. What are you doing?"

Mrs Hudson didn't answer. She couldn't tell him what was really on her mind. It suddenly felt like the worst betrayal.

Belle came and stood behind Fred. He looked over her shoulder at the row of drab buildings where New Street Station should be. "Don't go."

"What do you mean?"

"You want to go back. I can tell."

"Look at this," she said.

He looked around at it and smiled. "Yes. It's amazing."

"You call this amazing?"

"I do. I've just been up to Victoria Square."

Belle frowned. Of course she did. Why would the square be named after a young queen who'd only just taken the throne?

"The Town Hall is the only thing I recognize," Fred said. "There's no Council House. The Library isn't even there behind it."

"That old thing," said Mrs Hudson. "It's been and gone."

"What? That beautiful building?"

"They replace it in 1965 with a new building. A big, ugly brutal thing."

She sighed and shrugged. What was the point of telling him that too had been knocked down and a new big, futuristic glass building was going up in its place. Building and bulldozing, building and bulldozing, always and forever.

"Is it because of this war you mentioned?" Fred asked.

He murmured it but Belle heard and clutched her cloak tighter around her.

"The library? No. It survived the war. It just didn't survive the town planners. Fred, you ought to go back to 1934. It's safer there."

"But there's a bloody great war coming."

"Yes and it will be terrible. But this city will survive it. And there's a better world to be built after it."

He shrugged, lost for words.

Belle gazed on him, curious to know what he would do.

"Don't romanticize this," said Mrs Hudson. "Every generation thinks what has the world come to? It was better in the good old days. But it's nonsense. Look at this. Children and women begging in an open sewer. Life is hard and brutal here."

He bowed his head and swallowed and looked back at Belle, and Mrs Hudson could see she was what kept him here. She was worth staying for. He was in love and it was hopeless.

She took his hand. "Ignore me, Fred, I'm just an old woman. Be amazed if you like. I'm the last person to deny anyone that sense of wonder."

"I don't know if I *can* go back," he said.

"There's always that danger."

"How do you control it?"

"I suppose you have to have something to go back for."

"I don't think I have anything."

"Then perhaps there's something keeping you here."

Belle shuffled and half turned away.

"You'll work it out," Mrs Hudson said.

"I don't think I can do this without you."

There it was, the deep need of another. Something she hadn't felt in a long time. Or something she'd forgotten.

"Very well," she said.

"You're staying?" he asked, unable to hide his smile.

"I think I have something to do there, though I'm damned if I know what."

Fred took her elbow and they walked back up the hill to the corner. Belle linked arms with the old lady and pulled her into the theatre.

She wondered if she would ever get home again.

— 24 —

Emily Cratchit hovered on the chapel doorstep, shivering in the icy draught, trying to catch sight of a coach or carriage through the snowfall. They so rarely came down the Froggery way that you could wait for ages. Sometimes it was best to send a boy up to New Street to get one, but she couldn't even see any boys.

Her poor Tim was out there in this, out there somewhere. Bob had sent word about his sacking and she'd nipped out when Mrs Jowett was on her shopping expedition and run home, but he wasn't there. The poor boy must be distraught.

Five shillings a week lost. Which put an unearthly strain on Bob's fifteen shillings and her own eight. How would they manage in the cold winter months beyond Christmas?

She shivered and pulled her shawl closer about her. A light from the glum window of the Dungeon across the street. There was a right bunch of Not Rights squatting in there, made you fearful of your safety on a dark night like this.

The sound of a horse coming down Pinfold Street and the swishing of wheels on snow came through the gloom and she stepped forward and raised her arm. But it was a drayman's cart. Damn this cold and damn this whole day.

Last year Mrs Jowett had let her off a full hour early. "Go be with your family," she'd said, "and a Merry Christmas to you all." Emily had rushed home to Bread Street through the dingy lanes of the Froggery. It had been light still, she remembered, or was it just that the moon had been big and bright in the sky, almost a full moon, casting a spooky, spectral light over the snow. It made her shiver with fear and quicken her step to get home and light the stove, get a warm fire going to dispel any ghosts that might take it into their heads to come and haunt the Cratchit household.

Tonight was different. It was the last quarter, the moon a solid half-a-sixpence hanging above the faint outline of the Town Hall up there at the top of the hill, and Mrs Jowett needed her to stay on a little longer.

She retreated to the door, to feel at least a little warmth from the hallway on her back. A last quarter moon meant release, letting go, forgiveness. But how could you forgive a man like Swingeford, bullying your husband and sacking your son on Christmas Eve, and now lord knows where he'd got to? And that was this woman's brother.

Though that wasn't her fault. You couldn't blame her for having a monster for a brother, no. But it had to affect everyone around. Mrs Jowett had been in fine spirits this morning, and then that odious, stingy, hard, unfeeling brother had called and, well, whatever it was he'd said had broken Mrs Jowett's heart. She'd been all ajitter ever since, shaking she was. She'd barely been able to rise from the couch to make her annual trip to the stores to buy presents. And when she'd returned she was even worse. Billy the manservant had said she'd met her brother again at the Greek shop and they'd Had Words.

"I dain't hear what they was, but I know when two people are Having Words, and they Had Words."

He'd claimed he'd not heard the substance of these Words, but she'd pushed him till he looked over both shoulders, leaned close and told her, "Old Swingeford asked about Miss Ruth's long-lost relations who'm visiting."

"Relations? She don't have no relations. She's an orphan."

"That's what he said. But Mrs Jowett said she knew about

them and it was true. She was an orphan but that dain't mean she dain't have no long lost relations."

"But it can't be true. I've known her near on since Tim was born and there's never been any talk of relations."

"Well, they're here. And Swingeford seemed in a proper mard about it."

Emily pondered how strange it was. Mrs Jowett had agreed to a lie. What was she up to?

And now Mrs Jowett was all flighty and distracted. Was it something to do with money? She had the look of a woman who knows the bailiff is coming but who tries to put on a smile for the sake of the children. Weren't they all like that: putting on a false smile, pretending all was jolly, while the likes of Ebenezer Swingeford hammered at the door demanding every last penny, every single thing you had. That was what it felt like in these dark times and no mistake.

Another carriage, this one coming down Peck Lane. It sounded more hopeful. She rushed out to the corner and waved it down. A hansom cab, the driver perched on the rear. It would have to do.

"What ho, cabman!" she called. "Passage to New Street. Theatre Royal."

He tipped his hat and pulled up right outside, the horse breathing great clouds of steam.

"Wait there!" She rushed back inside and through the hallway to the drawing room where Mrs Jowett sat in an armchair, gazing into the fire with a sad, forlorn look about her. "I've a cab, Mrs Jowett. Only a hansom."

The old lady stood up too fast, juddered and swayed, but took up her walking stick and headed for the door.

"He's right outside, Mrs Jowett. You'll be at the theatre in two shakes of a lamb's tail."

Mrs Jowett halted and grasped Emily's hand. "I need you a little longer, my dear."

"Of course, Mrs Jowett. I'll help you into the cab."

"Come with me. Ride alongside me. See me to the

theatre."

Emily's heart sank. There was no escape just yet. "Why, yes, Mrs Jowett."

She guided the old lady out to the street, urging her to watch her step in the snow, and walked her to the cab, opening the folding door and taking the lady's weight as she climbed aboard. When she was in and settled, Emily ran round to the other side, looking both ways up and down the street in case a carriage or cart was coming, silent on the snow.

A pair of eyes at the window of the Dungeon.

A ghost face staring at her. She held its gaze for a moment. Then it was gone.

Shivering, she climbed into the cab and sat beside Mrs Jowett. The driver cracked his whip and turned the cab around the corner and cantered up Pinfold Street.

Mrs Jowett watched the buildings pass, the whole higgledy-piggledy row of shanty houses and jerry-built tenements constructed back to back without drainage. But she didn't seem to even see it, any of it.

She took hold of Emily's hand again and she felt that impulse to pull them away. Her ugly red raw hands against Mrs Jowett's white silk gloves. They were horny hands. That was all you could call them. Dear simple Bob would hold them and kiss her fingers and she would cringe from him, they were so shameful. Who could love those hands? That was the simple soul her husband was, and wasn't she lucky to have that. Always a jolly countenance to see them through.

And didn't the likes of Swingeford take advantage of that.

And didn't the likes of his sister take advantage as well.

The hansom climbed the last bit of the hill past the old orphanage, and the horse slowed, fighting to pull them the final few yards, its hooves slipping in the snow, snorting, skittering. The cabman cracked his whip on the poor beast's flanks. It whimpered and pulled them the last yard and into the light of the square where the Town Hall stood and Christ Church.

She would be glad when this day was over. Mrs Jowett had been such a needy presence and Mrs Cratchit feared she would never escape her. Her dear Bob and tiny Tim would be at the theatre for the Harlequin, as always. It was her place to be at home, preparing the house for the holiday. Or at the market getting the last scraps of vegetables to scrape together some kind of feast.

They sailed down the gentle slope of New Street to the Theatre Royal and pulled up. She leapt out and let Mrs Jowett lean on her to clamber to the pavement. The old lady looked up at the welcoming lights of the theatre as if it were her scaffold.

"Come just a little more and see me inside. I need your arm to rest on."

Emily Cratchit shuddered. She wasn't dressed for such a place as the theatre. Even if it was just the annual show for the poor children, her hands were red and her dress stained with scrubbing floors, her shawl threadbare, her bonnet dull and grey. If only she could have worn her Sunday best.

"Ma'am, I'm not dressed for this. It's the first-class entrance. I'm not even dressed for the side entrance round the corner."

"I need you just a while longer," she wheedled, and it was like a child.

Mrs Jowett paid the cab driver and thanked him and he sped off. Emily watched him go with a sinking heart. Now she would have to walk home. Of course, it hadn't occurred to Mrs Jowett to get the driver to take her back. Her class just didn't think of things like that.

Emily offered Mrs Jowett her arm and they shuffled into the theatre.

How the rich could last without the poor to see to their every little need, she didn't like to think. They wouldn't last two days left to their own devices, she was certain of that. They barely got through that single day of Christmas without the likes of her to dress them, feed them, see to their every need. By Boxing Day, the relief to have servants again was a thing to behold.

Inside, the ballroom was all golden and shining and all the most fashionable people had gathered. It must be what the Assembly Rooms looked like. She lowered her head instinctively and curled in on herself, so much that she didn't see Mr Swingeford approach. She was looking at his boots when he spoke.

"Dear sister. So long we do not see each other and today we meet three times."

Mrs Jowett didn't smile. "And they say good things come in threes."

"I'm here to see Miss Ruth. Have you seen her?"

"I imagine she'll be behind stage making preparations for the performance. Why so much interest in her today, brother?"

"The main thing that interests me most today is you," he said.

Emily Cratchit longed to interrupt and make her excuses to leave, but she was stuck having to watch this conversation.

"You don't normally take any interest in my affairs, brother," Mrs Jowett said.

"I'm most interested as to why you have concurred with Miss Ruth's story."

Emily stole a glance at him. He was smiling but it was the smile of a crocodile. Oh, he was such a mean, vicious old miser. His only delight seemed to be other people's misery.

"What story?" Mrs Jowett asked, unable to conceal her contempt.

"That these people who've come from afar are her long lost aunt and cousin."

"Why do you say that's a story?"

"Because you know more than anyone she is an orphan. She was abandoned on the steps of your own chapel. That's why you took an interest in her. That's why you took her fortune in hand when she graduated from the orphanage. You are hiding something, dear sister."

Mrs Jowett waved a dismissive silk-gloved hand and looked around the ballroom for more interesting company. "What concern is it of yours? She is nothing to you anyway."

"Oh, on the contrary, sister. I have asked for her hand in marriage."

Emily let out a little shriek, like she'd seen a rat. She tried to hold it in but it popped right out of her mouth and there was nothing she could do about it.

Mrs Jowett turned quite pale and let out a low moan. She put her gloved hand to her mouth. A fist to cover a scream. But she didn't scream. She swallowed and said, "What have you done?"

"I have assured her of a certain future, of comfort and happiness."

"She's young enough to be your daughter."

"Nonsense. She is young and beautiful, despite her lower social status. She is strong and will breed well, to provide me with succession."

"She will not. She is most unsuitable."

"I think I shall be the decider of what is suitable," Swingeford said.

Mrs Jowett stammered and said, "And do you think it's suitable that she is having an affair with a gentleman from this theatre?"

"What?"

Emily stared now and her mouth fell open. She couldn't help it. Everything that came out of the mouths of these two was shocking. Why would the old lady lie like that? Miss Ruth was the model of virtue.

"Yes, with Mr Aldridge," said Mrs Jowett.

"The blackamoor actor from America?"

"The very same."

"You lie."

She slapped him. It happened seemingly before Mrs Jowett knew it herself. Swingeford did nothing, but his grey face turned a shade of purple. "She has made a fool of you, brother."

Swingeford gripped his cane and for a moment it looked like he was going to strike his sister, but he turned and stormed off through the crowd.

Mrs Jowett raised her chin and gathered herself, a strange satisfied smile on her face.

Why would she say such a nasty lie about dear Miss Ruth, whom she'd always shown kindness to? Well, a certain kind of kindness. Not that of a mother, like Emily treated her own children. You loved them and your heart bled for the poor little mites, always fighting to keep Death from the door, always wanting the very best for them even when you couldn't provide it. Worried sick every night that you were losing them. Her poor tiny Tim out on the streets mixing with all sorts of bad ruffians. He might join that criminal gang who ran pitch-and-toss games across the street and live in a dungeon, but she'd fight to stop that from happening.

"Mrs Jowett?" Emily said.

The old lady couldn't hear her, still watching her brother's head move through the crowd.

"Mrs Jowett, ma'am?"

"Yes? What is it?"

"If you're finished with me, ma'am?"

"What? Oh, yes. You may go."

"Thank you, ma'am. Merry Christmas."

Mrs Jowett looked to her as if Emily Cratchit had wished her ill health all her remaining days. "I don't think it is," she said. "I don't think it can be."

"Yes, ma'am. Well, I'll be going then."

Mrs Jowett tottered and grabbed Emily's arm. "No."

"Ma'am, what is it?"

The old lady whimpered, hit by a fresh bolt of agony, and the whimper became a low moan, just like she'd made this morning after her brother had departed. What was this invisible power he had to inflict pain on his sister?

"Ma'am, is everything all right?" As the words left her mouth, she knew how stupid they sounded.

"Nothing is all right," Mrs Jowett groaned, gripping her tightly. "Emily. Take me back home. I feel ever so…"

She slumped against her and Emily took her weight and walked her back out through the ballroom throng, muttering *excuse mes* and *if you pleases* till she reached the door and plunged into the cold night.

A boy loitering before the theatre, ragged, looking for trade. She recognized him. He ran errands for John Jobbins the baker round the corner on Lower Temple Street.

"You, boy, call me a cab."

The boy jumped to attention and ran out to the street to wave down a cab. He was back in moments calling, "Here, miss. Got one for you." He was holding out his palm.

Emily grabbed Mrs Jowett's purse. "Help her into it, boy."

The boy took her. He was so small it seemed impossible that he could hold her, but she leaned against him and he took the weight and walked her out to the muddy street, her skirts swishing in the slush.

The cab was pulled up in the middle of the street. The cabman jumped down and helped to load the old lady aboard. Emily took out a sixpence and pressed it into the boy's hand.

"Now, boy, I need you to take a message to a man inside the theatre. You know my husband, Mr Bob Cratchit, yes? He'll be in the stalls tonight with my son, Tim."

"I know him, miss."

"You tell him that I've had to be called to Mrs Jowett. She's taken ill and I need to send for the doctor. Tell him I'll be home later tonight as soon as I can."

He ran off into the theatre and Emily climbed up next to Mrs Jowett. She was quite faint, slumped against her, moaning.

"Driver. The Connexion chapel rectory on Peck Lane and Dudley Street. Thank you."

They set off up New Street with a jolt and he turned down

Pinfold Street at the top and descended into the Froggery, exactly the way they'd come only minutes before.

As the cab descended, the cold air full in their faces, she wondered if she might have sent a message to Miss Ruth to warn her of what she'd heard. But no. It was nothing to do with the likes of her. So much lying and deceit and hurt, and all of it coming between her and her family and their Christmas.

The cab clattered down the dark street and she looked to the right as they passed Well Street. Her home on Bread Street tantalizingly out of sight. They passed it in a flash and she clutched her shawl about her. The snow was creeping through her boots and her toes were numb. She might have been home right now lighting the fire and warming the house for Christmas. The cab rattled on down the hill and came to the chapel, opposite the Dungeon. It was just a few dark streets to home with the snow to light the way, but it might as well be a hundred miles.

— 25 —

Mrs Hudson allowed Belle to take her deep into the bowels of the theatre, her mind still racing. She had almost given in. Almost escaped. But she was stuck here now. She had to see this through. Whatever it was.

She followed Belle, bustling around the theatre, checking on the auditorium that was filling now, and Fred followed, sullen and shy. It appeared the audience entered through three different doors, from different streets: the toffs entered from the front of house and took up the boxes; the middle classes came in from a bar on Lower Temple Street and took seats in the upper circle; the poor children of the Froggery streamed in from Ethel Street and filled the stalls.

Through a peephole at the side of stage, she spied Bob Cratchit and his son Tim taking their seats, both smiling, even the boy. It was true. This was the one night of the year they could forget their troubles.

They went backstage, down a passageway, off which were the dressing rooms. Dickens had returned, eager to perform his magic tricks. Belle had slotted him in as a distraction in one throwaway scene. The long-suffering Forster watched him put on his make-up and kicked his heels.

She linked arms with Fred and squeezed his hand. "Cheer up, Fred. The show must go on."

He forced a smile, pretending all was well. Perhaps he was

just happy to hang around and help Belle like he said. It appeared he hadn't made any overtures to her, and this was probably good. Mrs Hudson would step in and prevent it if she had to. Who was to say that Belle shouldn't marry Swingeford? That was most likely what was destined to happen if they hadn't crashed this party.

If Fred distracted her from that, the outcome could lead to tragedy.

She tried to remember the name of the girl whose life had been wiped out due to something like this: a girl who'd gone to the past with a boy, and he'd made a change. Yes, he'd saved someone's life, prevented a murder, and they'd returned to the present and the girl had discovered her whole life wiped out.

What was her name again? It was important. Rachel! That was it. Rachel was the living proof that blundering into the past and changing things led to tragedy. And there had been others too. She couldn't remember their names, but she had a vague sense of a small band of other figures in the shadows beyond Rachel, just out of reach.

Let Fred be disappointed in love, she thought. It was for the best.

Belle asked Fred to go in the men's dressing rooms and tell them it was ten minutes to curtain. Dickens and Aldridge had their own and the rest of the men shared a large room.

Belle and Mrs Hudson entered the women's dressing room, a poky cupboard where three women squeezed around each other like a contortionist's act.

"Ladies, we have ten minutes," Belle said, clapping her hands excitedly. "Break a leg."

Before they could answer, a shout came from outside, a voice raging, a great banging clattering down the passage.

Belle ran out and Mrs Hudson followed.

It was Swingeford. He stormed down the passage, banging his cane on every door, shouting, "This play will not happen! I will not sanction such licentiousness in this theatre! I forbid

144

it!"

The actors piled out to see.

"Mr Swingeford," Belle cried. "What is the meaning of this?"

"You!" he yelled. "How dare you even question me? It is your disgusting behaviour that shall see this theatre closed, tonight and forever!"

Fred stepped between Swingeford and Belle. "Who do you think you're shouting at, you old tyrant?"

"This theatre is closed! Closed, I say! This performance is cancelled!"

Dickens pushed forward. He was in a shirt open at the neck, his face plastered with foundation, eyes painted black. "Mr Swingeford, you cannot mean that. What is this? There are two hundred or more children out there waiting for this show to begin. You cannot cancel this!"

"I can do what I like."

"Mr Swingeford," said Belle. "I beg you. There is one good day in the year at least when these children can laugh and feel some warmth from their fellow men. All year round it is nothing but a brutish struggle for these poor children. You would rob them of this one day of hope?"

"Are there no orphanages? And the Union workhouses? They are still in operation?"

"Indeed they are," said Dickens. "I wish they were not."

"Then let them provide that relief. Why should this theatre give free tickets to the idle poor when others pay for their entertainment?"

"Because others can afford it," said Belle. "The board of trustees have always allowed this charity."

"That shall change. I'll see to it."

"What is it you want?" Belle asked. "Why do you do this?"

"I have been informed of your despicable behaviour."

"What?" Belle said. "What have I done?"

"You have been involved in a sinful liaison with…" He turned, searching the faces all crowded around and pointed at

145

Ira Aldridge. "With… *that.*"

There was a collective gasp.

"That's rubbish!" Fred shouted.

"What are you saying?" Belle asked. "Who said this?"

"How dare you!" Ira Aldridge yelled. He pushed his way through the crowd, bearing a wooden sword.

His wife pulled him back. "No, Ira! Don't!"

"I'll run him through for this calumny!"

"Don't deny it!" Swingeford said, brandishing his cane, but looking a little relieved that Mrs Aldridge was able to hold her husband back.

"Take it back!" Aldridge cried. 'Take it back!"

"No future wife of mine shall sully herself in such activity," Swingeford said, trying to look down his nose at Ira Aldridge with as much condescension as he could muster. "Nor shall she cheapen my name."

"It is not your name that is at risk," said Belle. "It is *my* name."

"The theatre has made you wilful and debauched. You have spent too much time here and not enough at chapel. I will see to correct that."

Belle put her hands on her hips, shaking with anger. "Why do you invest in a theatre if you think it so disrespectable?"

"It is an investment, nothing more."

It was obvious, Mrs Hudson thought. He had bought a controlling share in the theatre purely to corner Belle, to trap her in this snare. His smug smirk attested to it. "Mr Swingeford. It is clear to everyone that this is nonsense. Miss Belle here isn't involved in any way with Mr Aldridge, nor any other man here."

"Tell me who said this lie!" Aldridge screamed. "I'll sue them!"

Swingeford backed away to a spot where he was safely out of the reach of Ira Aldridge's wooden sword. Mrs Aldridge stood before her husband and turned to Swingeford, fire blazing in her eyes. "Who is maligning my husband? I demand to know!"

Swingeford cast her a look of utter contempt, from her feet to her bonnet, as if to question how she even dare talk to the likes of him.

"Mr Swingeford," said Mrs Hudson. "The very idea is preposterous. Mr Aldridge arrived here by coach not two hours ago, with his lady wife, and hasn't been in Birmingham for years."

"Whoever told you this is a liar," Fred said.

"How dare you?" said Swingeford. "My sister is not a liar. She is a Christian woman of fine upstanding character."

"Your sister?" Belle said. She put her hand to her breast, wounded.

"And yet she's lied to you," said Fred.

"Perhaps not a lie," Mrs Hudson said. "Perhaps she believes it to be the truth, with all her heart, but she has simply mistaken something for the truth. An effect of age, perhaps?"

Mr Fezzwig said, "My dear mother swears there is a ghost living in her larder who steals her cheese. A cheese-eating ghost. It is nonsense, but she believes in her own truth."

"Could it be that your sister is confused?" Mrs Hudson asked.

"Why, you said so yourself this very morning, Mr Swingeford," said Belle.

"That I did. Yes." He looked from one to the other, a rat cornered, looking for a way out.

"Everyone here will attest to this girl's virtue," Mrs Hudson said. "And as I've said, Mr Aldridge arrived two hours ago for the first time in years, and neither he nor Miss Ruth have been out of anyone's sight since then."

She thought of the moment Ruth had run away. Yes, she'd been out of sight then, but she stared Swingeford down and dared him to doubt her.

"You have clearly maligned the poor girl, and Mr Aldridge," said Dickens. "You must apologize at once."

"Apologize?" Swingeford said, looking around at the two score faces accusing him and feeling much less sure of himself.

"I accept your apology," Belle said, putting a hand on his arm. "And now, Mr Swingeford, if it pleases you, we shall prepare for the show."

"I demand we have this out with my sister, this instant."

"Certainly, Mr Swingeford. I would be delighted of your company, and your dear sister's, and we may discuss the matter and..." she added pointedly, "other matters that have arisen today. But let it be after the show. I beg you."

Swingeford put his gloved hand on hers and raised his chin in as haughty a manner as he could muster. "Tonight at nine, I shall expect to see you at Mrs Jowett's."

"Thank you," Belle said.

Swingeford marched out with his nose in the air, pushing Fred out of the way.

The cast watched him go and their eyes all turned on Belle, curious at the scene they had just witnessed.

"Why did you agree to meet him?" Fred asked.

Belle looked to Mrs Hudson. "Because the show must go on. If he would stop it from happening, think of all those children who'd be so disappointed. I couldn't send them to their cold beds tonight without a little Christmas cheer."

"You can't marry him," Fred said.

The actors gasped.

"Marry him?"

"He's proposed?"

"That awful old man?"

"Yes," said Belle, closing her eyes at the thought. "He has proposed to me this night."

"What a dreadful old bully," Dickens said. "You absolutely should not give in to him."

"It appears I have little choice."

"It's monstrous," said Mr Wilber.

"He thinks he can buy a woman like a railway stock," said Mr Fezzwig.

"Aren't all marriages business partnerships?" Forster asked.

"So speaks our eminent bachelor," Dickens snapped.

"That's rather cruel," said Forster. "And I resent it from someone who is so unhappily married."

"I'm not unhappily married!" Dickens laughed, a little too forcefully.

"You referred to your wife as the Donkey this morning."

"It's my pet name for her. And a husband may let off a little steam now and then without his love being called into question. If you ever married you would know it, John. I dearly hope you one day get to feel that frustration."

"Yes," said Mr Fezzwig. "Why should you escape the misery?" He let out such a bellow of a laugh that everyone joined in. It was all a joke.

Belle smiled to cover her pain. "I have given Mr Swingeford permission only to court me," she said. "It matters not if I eventually refuse his offer of marriage. I still have that card to play. It is the only thing left to me."

"And are you going to refuse?" Fred asked.

Belle said nothing.

Fred shook his head and stormed off.

They all watched him go and shuffled uncomfortably.

"I think Mr Fred might be harbouring feelings for you, dear Miss Belle," said Mr Wilber. "I have seen it in his eyes."

"Don't be silly," said Belle.

"Most definitely," said Mr Fezzwig. "It's obvious to a blind beggar."

"And he's angry with you," said Mrs Aldridge.

Ira agreed. "The rage of Othello. Jealousy."

"He can't be angry with me," Belle said. "He has made no feelings known to me. Swingeford has at least done that. Now, ladies and gentlemen. It is time."

She clapped her hands and the cast scrambled back to their dressing rooms to grab their props and don the last accessories of their costumes, and in twenty seconds they were filing to the stage.

— 26 —

Bob Cratchit pushed through to the auditorium with Tim at his side, a fatherly hand on his shoulder. He couldn't call him 'tiny' anymore, he reminded himself. He feared those days were over now. A little bit of his child's innocence lost. He was growing up and growing away.

The gilded grandeur of the place took his breath away and he gasped in wonder.

"Look at it, t… Tim. What opulence. What majesty!"

They piled in and took seats in the stalls as close to the stage and as near to the centre of the row as they could get, the poor children of the Froggery and their parents piling in with an unruly scramble for seats. Up in the boxes, the toffs looked down on them with paternal smiles.

An orchestra struck up a dainty ditty and the children stamped their feet along with it and clapped too, it was such a joy to see them so happy, laughing, giddy with glee. You never saw them like this any other day of the year.

But Tim wasn't so happy.

Bob patted his son's knee and gave him a consoling smile to gee him up. The poor boy was probably still fretting on the unfortunate events of the afternoon, getting sacked by Swingeford. Probably still distraught. That five shillings was a loss and the house would feel the pinch and no mistake. But something would turn up. Tim would get a position

150

somewhere else. After Christmas.

"Don't think on it, Tim. Put it behind you. It's Christmas."

They would enjoy the Harlequinade and walk home in the snow, father and son, where Mrs Cratchit would have the fire roaring and the house warm and the festivities could truly begin.

The curtain opened and the crowd let out such a thunder of applause, most of it from the children in the stalls. The toffs upstairs clapped politely. It must be a very different experience when the theatre wasn't full of children from the Froggery. Not as jolly, that was certain.

The first scene was a comedy slapstick routine with a young gentleman and his clumsy servant. It was a good job there was very little in the way of dialogue because nothing could be heard over the screams of joy. It was as if the children had been bottling up all their laughs for this one moment.

Then, when they'd got it all out, on came the beautiful young lady, the poor heroine of the story — and wasn't that Miss Belle herself playing the part? — and her evil miser of a father, played by Mr Wilber was forcing her into marrying a mysterious African prince, played by Ira Aldridge. Only Miss Belle wasn't remotely in love with him. But that didn't matter to the father because this African prince had a Mountain of Money, and that was the Most Important Thing in the World. Mr Wilber was such a convincing old miser and, oh! wasn't he impersonating Mr Swingeford? He had his walk and the way he clutched his cane and the way he said "Bah!" and "Humbug!" whenever anyone said something nice to him.

Bob craned his neck to see if Swingeford was in one of the gilded boxes but he couldn't find him. He nudged Tim. "Oh, if Mr Wilber doesn't watch out, he might be getting the sack from old Swingeford himself, eh?"

Tim forced a smile. He really was out of sorts. But never mind, he'd be quite back to himself again after a good old

Christmas Day with the family. Tomorrow would be a fresh start for all of them.

A boy came along the row and Bob moved his knees aside to let him pass, but he stopped and said, "Mr Cratchit, sir?"

"Yes, boy," Cratchit said, surprised.

"I've a message from your wife. Mrs Cratchit."

"What is it?" Bob felt the colour run from his cheeks and his heart thumped in his chest.

"Mrs Jowett was taken ill at the theatre tonight. I helped her into a cab myself. Mrs Cratchit says she has to take her home and get the doctor. So she might be late home tonight. She said I was to come and find you and let you know, sir."

"Thank you, boy," Cratchit said.

The boy hovered. Cratchit dug in his waistcoat pocket and pulled out a penny. The boy slunk off, disappointed.

At least it wasn't Emily who was ill. For a moment he'd been quite taken aback and feared the worst. The thought of his dear Emily suffering was too much to bear. And yet, one day it would happen. One day, hopefully in the far future, many years from now, either he or his wife would have to watch their beloved take their last breath and slip away into the unknown. The thought was terrifying.

No, he thought. It was nothing so dramatic. All he could hope was that this wouldn't ruin their Christmas. They were to wrap the presents for the children tonight and there was so much to prepare for their special day. It seemed rather unfair that Mrs Jowett should fall ill on the only holiday they had as a family, but it couldn't be helped.

He caught Tim's look of concern.

"We'll stay. It's all right. There's nothing we can do. Ma will be home later. We'll have our Christmas as a family, don't you fear, t... Tim. It'll be the best Christmas ever, you wait and see."

He put his mind back to the show and shoved away his dark thoughts.

The young gentleman and the beautiful young lady had

run away together and were now engaged in a series of picaresque adventures. And here they encountered a mysterious magician, Mr Bongo the Great, who performed magic tricks.

And wait, wasn't that... why, it was surely Mr Dickens! A hum of recognition fluttered around the theatre, mostly in the balconies as the children wouldn't have recognized the great author. The same whispered words a breeze flying all around the place.

"Is that Dickens?"

"Why, it *is* Dickens!"

"Dear Boz, on the stage!"

And he was a delightful magician. He pulled a rabbit from a top hat, he made the boy disappear, only to bring him back again in a puff of smoke, and he took a little ragged girl from the audience to great applause and merriment and turned her into a dove that flew into the rafters. He apologized to her poor mother and suggested that she might now feed the birds every day just in case one of them was her daughter, and the audience howled with laughter.

But Tim didn't seem at all interested in the show or Mr Dickens' magic performance. He kept looking up at the boxes, more interested in the society ladies and gents. Mr Forster was up there watching the show. Yes, wasn't Mr Dickens supposed to be there with him, writing a review on the play? And there he was on the stage, performing in it. A proper turn up for the books.

Tim fidgeted and stood.

"Where are you going, Tim, my son?"

"To the Necessary."

"You'll miss the show, Tim."

"I have to go, father."

"Go on then."

And off he scampered along the row.

Fancy needing to go to the Necessary. It was such a plush, luxurious place to be that you ought to relish every single moment of it. Just to be lucky enough to sit here and take in all this. Not just Mr Dickens' conjuring — the whole place was an act of magic. And Mr Wilber's magic lantern projections were indeed a triumph. The boys and girls *oohed* and *aahed* with such reverence. And the adults too. No one had ever seen anything like it. Ghostly backdrops of exotic locations that shimmered and melted, and ghosts and ghouls that flew about the stage. A horse and carriage rode towards everyone in silhouette and it seemed like it would ride right off the stage and crush the entire audience. They screamed and ducked, till it filled the screen all black and disappeared to great and relieved laughter.

And now the young lovers encountered a friendly giant played by Mr Fezzwig from the Hen and Chickens Hotel. He must have been twenty feet tall, tottering around on stilts. Only you couldn't see the stilts under his great green robe. The children cried out in amazement. A real giant. Some of them were even crying. But Fezzwig beamed a great smile and gave out such a jolly laugh and then delved a hand into a giant sack and threw sweets into the audience. The children scrambled for them, and those that were crying very quickly stopped to try to catch the sweets with the rest. He threw so many that there can't have been a single child in the theatre who didn't get at least a couple.

And Tim had missed it.

Where had the boy got to? He looked all around him but couldn't see him in the aisles making his way back to his seat. Was he lost?

Bob wondered if he'd run off. He'd been sulking all day, since Swingeford had turfed him out. Understandable. But there was something else. His son was sullen, sulking, angry — a closed fist. Was this the way of the world? Was this how his son turned from boy to man? It wasn't what he'd hoped. He didn't want to see his son turn into one of those angry young men. The kind of men who fell under the spell of Slogger Pike. But there was little he could do. He was losing control. He was watching it happen, like a tragedy unfolding on the stage and he couldn't stand and shout from his seat and warn the actors under the limelight that disaster was upon them.

He got up from his seat and edged along the row, and out through the exit door, out from the warmth and laughter and into the cold corridor. There was a Water Closet there and he entered and called "Tim?" His voice echoed back to him. The Necessary was empty.

He skirted along the passageway that emptied him out to the rear of the New Royal Hotel, out into the harsh cold and a pristine snowdrift that coated the alley. Pristine but for a set of footprints that went halfway up the alley and mysteriously stopped mid-way.

In the dark gloom he tried to see if his son was loitering there, or out there at the end of the alley where the gas lamps from Ethel Street glowed and the street was a golden blaze of snow.

Something fell from the building to the side. A bump and a scuffle. A boy jumping from a window.

"Tim?"

The figure turned, frozen, his face hidden in shadow.

"Tim? Is that you?"

The boy ran. It was Tim, there was no doubt about it. Cratchit ran after him, up the dark alley to that chink of white light. The boy reached the end of the alley, looked back once more and dodged out of sight.

Cratchit came to the alley's mouth, skidding on the slippery snow.

His son, Tim, scampering off, looked back once more, clutching something to his chest, his face lit by a gaslamp at the foot of Ethel Street, the last lamp before the dark shadow of the Froggery.

A man loomed out of the shadows and put a hand on Tim's shoulder. A leering face notorious in the Froggery. A face you crossed the street to avoid.

Slogger Pike.

They ran off together into the darkness.

Bob Cratchit stood frozen in mute horror and knew one thing for certain.

This Christmas he had lost his only son.

— 27 —

Belle took her final bow with the entire cast and the curtain closed a last time. The applause thundered on. The breathless ecstasy of triumph plummeted in her heart, a skylark falling, and she realized, before the applause had even petered out, that she must now face Swingeford and Mrs Jowett's bizarre accusation.

And Swingeford's marriage proposal.

The applause behind the curtain died and the rumble of a thousand exiting feet came under the chatter of the children talking excitedly as they left.

"A triumph!" said Mr Fezzwig.

"The best ever!" said Mr Wilber.

The cast hugged each other on the stage.

"The reviews shall call it so," said Ira Aldridge.

Everyone looked to Dickens.

"Well, I can't very well write a review of my own show now, can I?" he said. "That would be most unethical."

They roared with laughter.

"Mr Dickens," Belle said. "I do apologize if you have foregone a lucrative commission."

"Nonsense," he said. "I wouldn't have missed this for the world."

"Besides," said Forster, "we came here for far more lucrative business."

Mr Wilber tapped his nose. "We're not allowed to talk about that."

"Yes, Mr Huffam," Fezzwig said.

They roared with laughter some more.

"It was folly to presume that we might ever come here incognito," Dickens said.

"Well, that can hardly be blamed on me," said Forster.

This was the best of it, Belle thought, this post-performance bliss, the camaraderie of it, the overwhelming emotion that this bond could never be broken, this happy band of players.

She looked out to the wings where Mrs Hudson and Fred stood. Both of them beaming. Belle held their gaze for a while and the voices faded. Fred, when he smiled, gave her such a look that made her feel... oh, all light and her knees gave way a little and her belly flipped over. And then her heart was doused with such sorrow that he wasn't interested in her and had shown her nothing.

And what was he even? A ghost from Christmas yet to come. A spirit who would disappear with the morning dew. A vision her imagination had conjured. Nothing more.

Mr Fezzwig grabbed her and kissed both her cheeks. "You are a genius, my girl!"

The curtain was rising, revealing an empty auditorium, only the hubbub from the Shakespeare Rooms and the coffee house at the front, and the Theatre Tavern on Lower Temple Street to the side.

She was the first to see him.

A solitary figure stood on the stage, coming from the side. Belle realized one audience member had stayed. She didn't recognize him at first, his face so haunted.

It was Bob Cratchit. His shoulders hunched, clutching his top hat.

The cast ceased their chatter as they too became aware of the presence. All of them detecting a malevolent strain that infected the air.

"Why, Mr Cratchit. What is it?" Belle asked.

The look on his face, like he'd seen a ghost and almost passed on to the other side himself with the shock of it. She knew that look. It always came with bad news. It always came with the sense of life changing for the worse, forever after.

"I'm afraid something awful has happened," Bob Cratchit said.

He didn't say it to her. He looked to Dickens and Forster.

"Sirs," Cratchit said, swallowing hard. "You wouldn't happen to have kept the money for your business transaction in your hotel room today, would you?"

Dickens and Forster shared a glance.

"Well, yes," said Forster. "What of it?"

"And you wouldn't have happened to let my son, young Tim, see you do that, would you?"

Forster's mouth fell open.

"What is this?" Dickens asked.

"I fear… that's to say, I suspect, though I can't be certain, that there might have been a robbery."

"Good God!"

"How do you know?"

"That is to say, I fear that it might be my son that's responsible."

"What's the meaning of this?"

"Your son has robbed me?" Dickens said.

Cratchit looked at the floor. Tears dropped to the stage. "My Tiny Tim," he cried. "The shame of it."

"What in God's name has happened?" Forster roared.

"He's run away," said Cratchit. "He's run away and he's with Slogger Pike now. Oh, my poor tiny Tim."

"Never mind your poor tiny Tim. What about our money?"

Forster leapt forward and took hold of Cratchit, shaking him till his teeth rattled, and it all exploded. Belle found that she was between them, pushing Cratchit away, and Ira and Fred were holding Forster back. Everyone was shouting all at

159

once.

"Slogger Pike took him," Cratchit yelled in despair. "They ran to the Froggery, where they know no police constable will follow."

"Forster!" Dickens yelled. "Please contain yourself! Can't you see the man is distraught?"

"*He's* distraught? He'll be distraught when he's in prison right along with his son!"

"Mr Forster," Belle said, lowering her voice and speaking calmly, deliberately. "Please remember where you are."

It had the desired effect. Forster came to himself and lowered his face, embarrassed, and muttered an apology.

"Now, Mr Cratchit, please tell us what has happened."

Bob Cratchit tugged at his shirt and straightened his cravat. "My Tim was ever so distracted during the show, and I thought it was due to his losing his employment today, when Mr Swingeford sacked him."

"Sacked him," Mrs Aldridge muttered. "At Christmas."

"And I noticed he was looking at Mr Forster up there in the box an awful lot of the time. Not that the show wasn't wonderful. You were all quite brilliant and engrossing to the entire audience... all except my Tim. And when he excused himself to attend the Necessary, I had a bad feeling. I can't explain it. Like when you know something awful is happening. I went to find him. He wasn't in the Necessary. So I went outside. He jumped down from a window at the rear of the hotel and ran away. I saw him under a gaslamp, clutching something to his breast. And I saw Slogger Pike take him. They ran off into the Froggery together. My son and that awful man."

"Have you ever seen him about this man before," Dickens asked.

"No, sir, never! Not my Tim. He's a good boy."

"He's a thief," said Forster.

"I've tried ever so hard with the lad," Cratchit said. "I really have. It's just with times as hard as they are, I know he feels it something terrible. The shame of our reduced circumstances. I know his employment at Showell's made him feel better about things, like he was contributing to our family. When he lost that, I feared something awful would happen, but not this."

Dickens and Forster shuffled their feet and looked at the stage. "I'm very sorry," said Dickens. "I feel as if I'm to blame."

"Not you, sir. You're not to blame. I'm his father. Perhaps I didn't raise him right."

"I'm going to the hotel to check on this," Forster said, "and then to the police."

"I beg you," Cratchit pleaded. "Please don't report this to the police."

"Mr Cratchit," Forster said, astounded. "A serious amount of money has been stolen."

"I beg you. Give me a chance to retrieve the money."

"We can't do that," Forster said. "A robbery has been committed."

"Let me make it right. Let me save my boy. If the police are involved, it's the end for him. He'll go to prison, or perhaps even be transported."

"That is what happens to common thieves," said Forster.

"I don't want to lose my boy. Let me pluck him out of the depths. Let me save his soul."

"I'm afraid what needs to be saved is Mr Dickens' business and his livelihood," Forster said, strolling the stage and tucking his thumbs into his waistcoat like a lawyer making his case. "His family rely on that. If that deal is concluded, it is also your family, Mr Cratchit, that benefits, and yours Mr Wilber."

"There is that," said Wilber. "But as welcome as it may be, I do say Showell's printing house will carry on without your money, Mr Forster, Mr Dickens. There. I've said it."

Dickens turned away and walked to the edge of the stage, biting his thumb, the crude magician now turned Hamlet.

161

"So it's Tiny Tim that's at stake," said Belle.

"He will surely hang for it," said Ira Aldridge.

The women all gasped and clutched their throats.

"They wouldn't hang a child," Forster protested. "He'll merely go to prison."

"Not my boy," said Cratchit. "He's a good boy. Just so hurt and angry."

Dickens turned and spoke. "Little wonder having to work for that man."

"Pah! *Any* man," said Forster, pointing an accusing finger at Dickens. *"You* make your living from these printing houses that print your stories, Charles, and every one of them employs children to sweat and toil for you. Their labour is on your hands. You can't pretend that your hands are clean."

"I'm opposed to that. I supported the Child Labour Reform."

"While you engage them in labour. You can't wash your hands of it."

Dickens looked at his hands and wiped them on his coat, even though they weren't dirty, Belle noticed.

"Mr Dickens, sir," said Cratchit, rushing to the author and grasping those hands. "I know you want your money back. It's an awful lot of money. But I just want my son. He's dearer to me than all the money in the world."

Dickens pulled his hands from Cratchit's grasp, smiling with embarrassment and nodding, looking around at all their faces. "I'll help," he said.

"Charles!" Forster yelled. "I simply protest!"

"The first link in the chain happens in childhood. We're talking about an innocent child. A child who hasn't done a single wrong before in his life. Led astray, perhaps even threatened and bullied into this by a villain worse than my Bill Sykes, if the stories are to be believed."

"This is not one of your fictions, Charles."

"What's the point of my fictions if a real, living Oliver Twist needs my help and I turn away and let a real, living Bill

Sykes take him! What kind of man am I if I let that happen?"

"I'll help," said Fred.

Everyone turned to the young stranger. He stepped forward into the stage's limelight glow, a little self-consciously, and patted Cratchit on the shoulder.

"I also," said Fezzwig. "Let me get a chance to wallop that Slogger Pike good and proper. I'll do it, I tell you. I'll do it for us all!"

"And I'll be by your side," said Mr Wilber.

"All for one and one for all," said Ira Aldridge, grinning.

"We'll all help, Mr Cratchit," Belle said. "How could we not, tonight of all nights?"

Bob Cratchit burst into tears. He fell to his knees and clasped his hands in prayer. "Thank you, thank you, thank you. God bless you, every one."

"Come on!" Fezzwig bellowed, snatching up one of his stilts and brandishing it like a cudgel. "Let's do it!"

"Wait," said Fred. "Not so fast. There's no point rushing to a knife fight only armed with knives."

"I have this broom," Ira Aldridge cried, brandishing it as if it were a spear.

Yes, Fred was right, Belle thought. They were going into the Froggery, to the Dungeon, to face Slogger Pike and his gang. "Unless we're going to clean the place for them, I don't think that's going to be much use."

"What do you suggest we take?" asked Fezzwig. "A cannon?"

"I'm speaking figuratively," said Fred. "We're running to their manor. They have the edge. Let's give ourselves the edge."

"What can we possibly have that will give us the edge?" asked Mr Wilber, taking off his broken jaw contraption.

"Fred is right," said Belle, smiling. "Fools rush in. But we need a plan."

— 28 —

Mrs Hudson linked arms with Dickens as the troupe walked down the Froggery streets choked up with a dingy mist. She held onto him and he supported her as her boots slid on the icy ground, but there was enough dirt and gravel to make it not so treacherous, and he was young and strong enough to hold her as they walked.

There were no gas lamps in this part of town. The black house fronts with their white-topped roofs served as street lighting. The sky was black and gloomy, all the chimneys emitting a thick smog, but snow floated in the gelid air.

Belle and Fred walked together ahead and Mrs Hudson wondered if they were becoming closer. She checked the warmth in her heart. She was supposed to be preventing them getting together, but she couldn't find any reason for it. There was nothing in her pocket diary to guide her so who knew if it was right or not?

Forster huffed and puffed behind them, and Cratchit, Fezzwig, Mr Wilber and Ira Aldridge brought up the rear with their props. Everyone carried a lantern, lighting the way through the dark streets, a candlelit procession.

"What an awful place," Forster complained. "There no Christmas cheer, not in these mean streets."

"Nonsense," said Dickens. "Listen to that. Even in this slum, the poor take a little comfort of the season."

They passed a squalid tavern from which came the unmistakable chime of a carol sung low and out of tune, but with a feeling that could not be denied.

Forster said, "This isn't like one of your tours through the rookeries in London, where you hire a constable and go wander the streets to observe the lower side of life."

Dickens didn't seem to hear him. He groaned and muttered, "Why didn't I—?" He put his fist to his mouth and Mrs Hudson felt him shudder at the violent thought that racked his body.

"What are you thinking on?" she asked, squeezing his hand in hers.

"Oh, nothing. There was an old woman at the station this morning. I just wondered where she is right now, and if she's warm and cared for. I might have given her something. A little something, just to make a difference."

"You're a good man, Charles Dickens."

"No, I don't think I am," he said with such sadness and so matter-of-factly that she knew it wasn't false modesty. "I'm envious, cynical, greedy, selfish. Here I am, worried about money, so I put a wall around myself and defend my castle. And they make me blame the poorest of us for this. As if these poor wretches are taking money from me."

"Well, they are," said Forster. "They actually *did* take your money."

"And the vicious gang of robber barons that sit in parliament right now took money from everyone here. That's the cause of this. This Slogger Pike may be a vile thief and even a murderer but his work is child's play compared to Sir Robert Peel."

"You can't blame the government for poverty," said Forster.

"I certainly can, when they rob us all. And I refuse to succumb to their cynicism. They brutalize us with their callousness. It infects us, till we are as ruthless and uncaring as they are. See how they turn us into monsters."

They passed wretched hovels, their broken window patched with rags and paper. Noxious smells came from the cellars, sometimes a blast of something sweet; fruit and sweet sellers concocting their wares.

They dodged slops emptying from windows, passed boys barefoot playing in the snow. In a basement hovel, they caught briefly the sight of children huddled in bed, their mother reading them a story. Negotiating the winding lanes of the slum, they passed melancholy pawn shops. Rats ran across the street and sometimes it seemed that cellars were teeming with them, squeaking their vile symphony.

"How amazing is it," said Dickens, "that misery lives side by side with wanton excess." He hooked his thumb back towards New Street and its stores where the rich promenaded. "Poor Master Green," he said.

"Who?" Mrs Hudson asked.

"Someone I remember. Someone I left behind once. You don't know the dirt that was on these hands."

Mrs Hudson squeezed his hands extra hard and whispered, "Warren's Blacking Warehouse."

He looked to her with amazement. "But how do you know about that? No one knows about that. Only my father and mother and they never talk of it. They pretend it never happened."

She lowered her voice so that Forster wouldn't hear. "The whole world will know about it one day, Charles. I've seen it. Your past and the future. You know that, don't you?"

They walked on, just the sound of their feet crumping in the snow, and she thought he wasn't going to respond.

"Yes," he said. "I see it. You have the same power. You're a ghost."

"The living are ghosts to a ghost. It's all about which end of the telescope you're looking through."

"My shame will come out one day?" he asked.

"Not shame. No one will judge you for it. The world will see why you have such compassion for the poor, for those

166

who can't defend themselves, for the children who are crushed by men like Swingeford."

"By men like me."

"We all play our part if we don't try to stop it," she said. "It takes a brave person to know it and change."

And even as she said it, she wondered why it mattered. She was intervening. They would help this band of players save Tim Cratchit. Dickens was intervening too. But what did it matter? What did it have to do with her? Dickens was just some writer whose stories her parents read to her when she was a child, and she couldn't even remember her parents' faces anymore. The memories all fading.

Dickens fell silent. They followed Belle and Fred ahead and she wondered what they were talking about as they wound their way through more streets, turning this way and that.

Belle looked back to make sure they were following, and turned into a dark void between an alehouse and a chapel. The grass was hard with frost and uneven. Mrs Hudson struggled and Dickens helped her over the rough ground. They came out to a grey space, a vast white sheet of snow, dotted with stone tablets.

A spectral place.

She squinted in the gloom, trying to work it out.

A graveyard.

Their lanterns lit up the gravestones, casting shadows across the gloomy snow.

"It always gives me a terrible sense of dread, this place." Belle said. "I don't know why."

She pressed on, and Mrs Hudson noticed Fred held her hand as they tramped through the snow towards a cluster of dark buildings.

"The chapel is just ahead," said Belle, "and the Dungeon is opposite. All along this row are the chapel's almshouses. There are rooms for thirty-five fallen women here."

"Wonderful," said Dickens. "Such a noble enterprise."

"Alas, Mr Swingeford revealed this very morning that he's going to knock it all down. They're building a railway station here, something more grand and central."

"Ah," said Forster, huffing and puffing with the exertion. "You were only saying this morning that that is what this town needs."

"Quite," said Dickens.

"All of this will be gone soon," said Belle. "A giant station here. The largest building in the city, Swingeford said. Imagine it."

Mrs Hudson and Fred shared a secret glance. They'd seen it. Mrs Hudson had seen it in three of its guises — the Victorian glass-roofed station, the concrete station under a shopping centre, and the Grand Central mall — and as it was now before it had ever been dreamed up. She looked around her at the grim tenements and the crooked gravestones and tried to imagine which part of New Street Station this was. Perhaps where she'd stood last night — this morning? — with the giant Christmas tree in the atrium.

Belle pushed through the rear gate of the rectory building, Mrs Jowett's residence, lighting the way through a backyard with her lantern, and they gathered at a door. The tradesman's entrance. She knocked at a brass knocker whose face was a lion's head.

"Shall we sing a carol?" said Mr Fezzwig. "We do rather look like a bunch of carol singers."

Steps came to the door and Mrs Cratchit answered. "Miss Belle, it's you. I wondered what was going on." Her eyes fell on the troupe of players behind. "Oh my! Whatever is the matter?"

Bob Cratchit stepped forward. "Dear Emily. It's about our Timothy."

Stark fear wrote it itself on Emily Cratchit's face.

Belle smiled and said, "It's all right. We've come to help him."

The troupe piled into the kitchen, so many of them, Belle thought, even though the kitchen was rather large: Mrs Hudson and Fred, Mr Fezzwig, Mr Wilber and Ira Aldridge, Dickens and Forster.

Bob Cratchit tried to calm his wife, but as he listed all that had happened — her son was missing, and a thief, and he was with Slogger Pike in the Dungeon across the street — the horror of it grew on the poor woman's face.

"It'll all turn out for the best," Bob said.

"We're going to save your son, Mrs Cratchit," said Dickens. "I promise you."

"And if you don't mind me asking," Emily Cratchit said. "Who are you?"

"This is Mr Charles Dickens," said Bob proudly.

"The author? The *Oliver Twist* man?"

"'Tis I," said Dickens.

"He's the important gentleman from London I couldn't name," said Bob.

"Charles Dickens. Here," said Emily, slumping at the kitchen table. "Is this a dream? I fear I'm seeing things and this is all a dream."

"Alas," said Dickens, "It's all quite real. Your son is in danger but we intend to save him."

"Where is Mrs Jowett?" Belle asked.

169

"What?" said Emily, confused, as if it were the most irrelevant, stupid question in the whole world to ask at this moment. "I don't care about that. I care about my Tim and my family. That's all I care about."

She shrieked and put her fist to her mouth.

Belle took a chair and held her hands. "I know that, Emily, but it's important, please. I beg you."

"My son's important. My family's important."

Bob Cratchit came forward and hugged his wife.

"Emily, my dear, it's all right. All of these nice people have come here expressly to help Tim. They're going to rescue him. They've promised me. But Miss Belle and Mr Aldridge here also really need to know what's happening with Mrs Jowett. Can you help them?"

Emily gathered herself, sniffling, wiping her nose on the back of her hand. Bob Cratchit produced a handkerchief, which she screwed up into her fist.

"I'm sorry," she said. "Mrs Jowett was taken ill. The doctor is with her in the drawing room She's been in an awful state all day, flittering about. Her brother upset her terrible when he visited this morning. She went out to shop for her Christmas gifts and seemed better, but then later was struck again at the theatre. It was dreadful. That's why I'm here instead of at home. I fear it's the palsy. Terrible thing."

"She made a terrible accusation," said Ira Aldridge.

Emily Cratchit wrung her hands and looked at the floor. "Indeed she did, Mr Aldridge. I heard her say it with my own ears."

"Why would she tell such a lie?" Belle asked.

"I don't know, Miss. But even as the words left her mouth, I could tell that..." Emily Cratchit lowered her voice, "... she was lying, and I could tell that she knew it was a lie. The only one who believed it was Mr Swingeford."

"But why?" Ira asked. "Why would this woman lie about such a thing? And would she not think I would sue her?"

Emily shrugged. "Perhaps she's ill. Perhaps it's more than

the palsy. There's some awful game she's playing with her brother and they seem to delight in spiting each other."

"Yes," said Belle, "it seemed that way this morning. Something was going on between them, something from the distant past."

"But I don't care about that anymore. She's never shown any kind of care for others that I know of. It's all right living in a chapel but…" She shook her head and grimaced, holding her words in.

Fred said, "So Swingeford proposes to you, Belle, and his sister tells him you're having an affair with Mr Aldridge. She seems desperate to destroy his marriage to you."

"She has almost destroyed mine in the process," said Ira Aldridge.

"It is a terrible calumny," said Dickens, "and she ought to be confronted with it. One can't go around telling such lies."

"You'll get little sense out of her," said Emily. "I don't know that she might ever recover."

"You're dealing with a mad woman," said Fred. "It's obvious."

"Well," said Belle. "We'll deal with her later. For now, though, we came for another reason."

"Yes," said Dickens, "it's time to put our plan into action. May we see the tower?"

"The tower?" Emily asked.

"It looks down on the Dungeon," said Belle.

"Yes, of course. Let me show you right up."

She went with Dickens, Fred and her husband, each taking their lanterns, plus the heaviest of the sacks that Fred had carried over his shoulder. The others listened to them creep up the stairs till their footsteps faded.

Mr Wilber, Mr Fezzwig and Ira Aldridge each put a heavy sack on the table.

"I feel we should prepare for this," said Fezzwig.

"Prepare?" asked Mr Wilber.

"I feel this might be the most important role I have ever

undertaken."

Emily Cratchit returned alone. "Mr Dickens, here. I must be in a dream."

"A Midwinter Night's Dream," said Mr Wilber.

No one laughed.

"He starred in our Harlequinade tonight, you know, Mr Dickens" said Mr Fezzwig. "He acted alongside me."

"He's always been a frustrated actor," said Forster.

"The theatre's loss is literature's gain," said Mr Wilber.

Belle stood. "Gentlemen," she said. "It's time."

They reached for the sacks on the table and began to unpack them.

— 30 —

Tim Cratchit had run through the dark streets, all the way down the hill to the Dungeon, so fast it seemed like he was Jack falling and breaking his crown. Except he hadn't gone up the hill to fetch a pail of water, he'd gone to steal a load of money. And he hadn't fallen with no Jill; he'd fallen in with Slogger Pike. There was no crown broken, but everything else was in pieces on the floor and would never be mended again.

He'd broken it all. He was a criminal now, an outlaw. He was on this side of the divide in society, forever despised by respectable people.

As soon as they had reached the Dungeon, Slogger Pike had said, "Gimme the chinks," which didn't make sense, as the money was all in papers, not coins.

Tim handed over the wad of money and Pike flipped through it and leered, chuckling with delight. It was more money than Tim had ever seen and it seemed more money than Slogger Pike had ever seen too.

Pike gave a special knock at the great wooden gate that was taller than two men and someone heaved a wooden block away on the other side.

They pushed through to a cramped courtyard, stone steps leading up on both sides to a wall-walk against the parapet. It was like a castle. Upstairs at the back was the old guard house where Pike and his gang of boys lived, though there were cells too and Tim wondered if he would sleep in one tonight.

He would wake on Christmas Day — his birthday — a thief in a cell.

By the light of a few lanterns, Tim was introduced to Pike's gang, mostly a bundle of ruffian boys from the Froggery, boys he'd seen around the streets; pickpockets and scavengers, boys with no shoes and no family. This was their family. And this was his family now.

He thought of his dear mother at home now preparing the house for Christmas. She would be distraught. He dearly wanted to be with her, but there was no walking away from this. Might Slogger Pike let him go, now that he'd handed over the money? Surely he'd be happy with that? But then, to walk out of this place without the money… he could never go back to his mother's warm embrace. The die had been cast.

He remembered Charles Dickens' magic spell this morning. *My name will cause untold calamity should you say it three times.* Tim tried to work out if he'd said his name three times. He surely must have.

Pike put the wad of money in a cupboard in the corner, perhaps the cupboard that had once contained the keys to the cells. He didn't lock it. There was no lock. And who would steal from him, the man who'd murdered Jacob Marley so brutally?

There was a girl named Polly, and it was clear she was Pike's sweetheart. He sent her out to Miss Jagger's Dining Rooms with a pound note to open an account. She returned a half hour later with a tray of warm pies and puddings.

"You should have seen me," she said, laughing. "No one dared stop me. I walked as bold as brass down Peck Lane with the tray on my head, like an Arab girl."

"You're Pike's wench," Slogger Pike said. "Everyone knows that."

"That copper, Donaghy, gave me the evil eye, but I laughed in his face."

"Damn the peelers!" Pike yelled. "It's us against them, Tim. But they're too scared to come down here and make a fight of it."

"Kick one of them and they all get a limp!" one of the boys shouted.

The phrase was taken up with glee and they sang it in a tuneless chant, punching their fists in the air.

Kick one of them and they all get a limp!
Kick one of them and they all get a limp!
Kick one of them and they all get a limp!

They devoured the hot food and one of the boys cried, "We've never eaten so well!"

"You stick with Slogger Pike. You'll eat like princes the rest of your days."

They devoured every last crumb, licked their fingers and settled back, bellies swollen.

"That's a proper Christmas feast, and no mistake," Polly said.

Tim had to admit, he'd never felt so full. Much as his parents scrimped and scraped, even their Christmas meal was nothing to compare to this.

Pike pulled the girl close to him and gave her a greasy kiss, slobbering like a St Bernard dog. The girl laughed and let him tongue her cheek. Her eyes were on Tim. He turned his face away, bewildered. It was that secret language the adults talked — those unsaid words he didn't understand.

Then something banged the great door.

The sound boomed all about the Dungeon. Everyone jumped and stilled their voices.

As Polly was about to speak, "What was—" there came another great boom.

And then a third.

As if an artillery regiment had fired three great cannon shots at the door.

Pike rushed to the window to take a peek at the courtyard. The boys crowded beside and behind him. He yanked the guard room door open and ran round the wall-walk to the spiked parapet that overlooked the street. Polly and the boys

175

followed and so did Tim. They peered over the battlements to see who had knocked so loud.

There was no one at the great wooden gate below, but a cloaked, black figure stood across the street in front of the chapel. A woman's form, her features hidden by a hood.

How had she knocked so loud, and from the other side of the street?

She held a lantern at her knee, so it cast a pool of light at her feet.

"It's a girl," said Polly.

"Who are ya?" Pike called.

The voice came across the snowy expanse. A young woman's voice, innocent and frail. Familiar, though he couldn't place it. "I'm the daughter of Jacob Marley."

Silence. Slogger Pike didn't know what to say to that and seemed dumbfounded.

Polly, gripped her shawl about her and looked proper spooked.

"What do you want?"

"Justice!" she cried in a low moan that resonated on the wind.

Tim felt like a spider was crawling up his neck. He reached to scratch it, and it sent out a multitude of little spiders scurrying all over his skin.

"Are you codding me?" Pike said with a malicious laugh.

The laugh said that people didn't last very long for codding Slogger Pike.

No answer came. The black figure stood silent.

"Settle her, Slogger," said the oldest boy.

"Shut up," Pike snarled.

The boys exchanged doubtful looks. Maybe they'd never seen their leader so uncertain. They'd never seen him challenged.

"You better clear off, or I'll settle ya, see."

The figure raised a hand and pointed a finger at him, accusing.

Slogger Pike bellowed a laugh and it was joined by four or five more. All the boys and all the men in his gang.

"Jacob Marley demands justice," the ghost cried.

"Ha! That old story," said Pike. "No one could ever prove I did that!"

"Jacob Marley can prove it."

"He's dead, you old witch, and he ain't coming back to tell anyone anythink."

"He's told me what you did."

More laughter.

"What you gabbin on about?" Pike yelled.

"Till he gets justice, he's doomed to wander through the world. He's looking for you, Slocombe Pike. He's looking for you!"

More laughter, less riotous than before, because Pike himself was not laughing. The laughter died down, unsure of itself.

"Marley knows what you did to him."

"Pah! Now off with yer. Or I cut you up like a Christmas goose."

"You will be visited by three ghosts tonight."

"What?" said Pike, with such genuine *why me?* amazement that Tim thought he heard the child in the man.

Something familiar about this. *Three ghosts shall visit.* Where had he heard that?

"Three ghosts that come for your soul, Slocombe Pike."

The figure raised the lantern so it lit her face in the shadow of the hood, revealing a pretty face, a young face, but ghostly and eerie, lit like that.

It was Miss Belle.

It wasn't a ghost or a witch at all. What was she doing? He searched the faces of the other boys and of Slogger and none of them recognized her, that was clear.

Of course. *Three ghosts shall visit.* That had been part of the play tonight, just as he'd left. He hadn't been listening to most of it, but that was what Mr Wilber's character had

177

shouted from the stage. *Three ghosts shall visit tonight.*

It angried up Slogger Pike's blood. "I've had enough of this," he snarled. "Do her, boys."

Tim felt a knot of fear rise in his throat and he wanted to be sick. Miss Belle against these ruffians. He hated to think what they might do to her.

Tim and Polly watched Pike and the boys run down the stone steps and across the central courtyard. Pike heaved the wooden beam off the gate and ran out.

Miss Belle was still there, the same dark figure in the same cloak, pointing a finger at them.

Pike skidded to a halt. "What?"

Why had she not run from him?

And also, there was something not right about her. Her face hidden again, but her hand had aged. The finger pointing at Pike was not the finger of a young lady, it was the old wrinkled finger of a witch. She raised the lantern to her face again and revealed her aged face.

"What is this, you hag?"

Pike made fists and rushed towards her. He was going to hammer the old lady.

Then a blinding beam of light shot at them. It was as if an accusing angel had torn the night sky apart and pointed a blaze of light from Heaven at them.

They halted, shielding their eyes, blinking, blinded for the moment.

And then something loomed out of the darkness behind her.

It came from behind the chapel tower.

A monstrous presence thumping out of the black night.

They all stared.

A great shape.

Something gigantic.

A great figure in a robe.

A giant!

It strode towards them from the black night, roaring, "Fee

fie fo fum!"

An ogre, a demon, a colossus.

Tim watched aghast from the parapet, only half aware that Polly had gripped his arm and was squeezing for dear life.

Pike and the boys scattered in the snow below, dashing back into the Dungeon's courtyard.

The giant stumbled after them. It was coming across the street, level with the parapet, coming right for Tim!

Polly screamed and fled. Tim followed her, darting around the wall-walk to the rear of the Dungeon. They met Pike and the boys scrambling up the stone steps to the guard room. Tim glanced back in terror.

A giant coming for them! And they'd left the gate wide open.

The hem of its great robe came to the gate and Tim looked up to the spiked parapet wall where the giant's great ogreish face peeped over the battlements.

It roared, and it seemed like it roared with the force of a great trumpet.

Pike, Polly and a dozen boys all somehow tumbled through the door at once, and Tim followed.

Pike slammed the heavy door shut with a clang and peered through the grille.

The shaft of light swept the courtyard, searching, and it sent a shiver right through Tim. What if Miss Belle really was a witch and had summoned these ghosts? But now he thought about it, the light really was shining from the tower of the chapel across the street, as if the chapel tower had turned into a lighthouse.

A voice came booming from the courtyard. "Slocombe Pike!"

A man's voice, deep and sonorous. Not Miss Belle's voice, and not the voice of that awful giant.

"Come out and fight, Slocombe Pike!"

American, it sounded.

"Go and get him, Slogger," Polly said.

Pike gave a little whimper and looked around for a weapon. He grabbed a cudgel, opened the guard room door and stepped out.

Tim crept out behind him. The others were all whimpering in the corner.

Standing in the centre of the courtyard in a pool of light was a pirate, brandishing a silver sword. An African pirate!

"Which spirit are you?" Pike yelled, unable to hide the quiver of fear in his voice.

"I am the ghost of Black Caesar!"

The infamous pirate of the Caribbean! There he stood, but twenty feet away.

Tim's mother had read him grisly stories of Black Caesar's exploits in a penny dreadful and said if he didn't sleep, Black Caesar would come for him in the night and drag him away to serve as cabin boy on his pirate ship. And here he was in the flesh, finally come to steal Tim Cratchit away, just as his mother had promised!

"Get gone!" Pike yelled. He gave his cudgel a practice swipe.

Black Caesar flashed his silver sword around his head. It was a great big scimitar like a Turk's. "You won't! You're a coward! I know the secrets of your heart. You cannot face a man in honest combat. All your life you've been a snivelling little chicken-hearted yellow belly!"

Pike's whimpering grew a little louder. He looked back to his boys and saw that he'd lost them. Polly put a crucifix to her lips and was praying.

"Hush, wench!" Pike growled.

"Lord save us from these spirits!" Polly wailed. "I'll be good. I'll be good the rest of my days, please, God, I promise!"

It set off a wailing and a crying that spread through the boys — the youngest first, till it went right through to the oldest — and soon Slogger Pike was the unhappy nursemaid to a gaggle of screaming babies.

He roared with rage, spittle flecking his rough chin and, brandishing the club with a scream that was more encouragement than bravery, set off down the stone steps to face the pirate.

The beam of light moved from Black Caesar and flashed across to Pike coming down the steps. It hit his face and he recoiled, blinded for a moment, before pushing on to reach the courtyard below.

The light went out, but Tim could still see blobs of blue and yellow floating in his vision.

Black Caesar was gone, leaving only the eerie snow to light the scene. Pike stood alone in the courtyard, looking around bewildered for his foe, the gate still wide open.

The giant had gone, Tim thought, and now Black Caesar had vanished. That left one more ghost to come.

"That's right, run, Black Caesar! I ain't afraid of you!" Pike yelled into the night.

He had but barely said it when the light flared again and shot out from the chapel tower. Pike recoiled and covered his eyes.

In the second before the beam of light hit Slogger Pike, Tim thought he caught sight of something. Up in the roundel window of the chapel, a round disc as the light hit it, a mirror perhaps, and the face of a young man with long hair. Just for a moment. And then the beam of light had blazed forth.

Pike was muttering to himself now. Was he praying like Polly, begging angels to intercede and save him from these ghosts?

The boys found bravery from somewhere and all came to the door, spilling out onto the wall-walk.

Slogger Pike went to the steps and took one step down when there came an unearthly clank of chains.

But not from below.

The sound came from their right. Tim turned.

Standing on the wall-walk was a dark shadow. The beam of light crawled along the courtyard and up to their level and illuminated the figure in the corner.

They all stared in horror.

Oh what a ghastly sight!

An old man pointed a finger — pointed a finger at Slocombe Pike. He had a bandage under his chin, tied at his crown. He undid it and his jaw flopped right down onto his chest, his obscene gaping mouth and all his teeth falling open.

It was Jacob Marley's ghost!

Pike screamed. The boys screamed. Polly screamed.

Then they scampered, like a pack of rats, fighting their way down the steps.

And suddenly, there were ghosts flying all around the courtyard!

Tim found his feet take him not to the stairs to follow them but to the guard house. He darted in, ran to the cupboard, grabbed the wad of money, shoved it in his pocket and ran for his life. Let the ghosts take him to Satan himself, if they must, but even if it was too late for them, he would try to clear his conscience and at least go to Hell knowing he had tried to give the money back.

The boys had shoved, jostled and fallen their way down the stone steps and scrambled across the courtyard and out of the gate.

Slogger Pike ran into the night shouting, "Get away from me, Marley!"

His howling faded off into the dark with Polly's scream.

"Tiny Tim!" Marley's ghost called, reaching out for him.

Tim dodged his grasping hand and ran for the steps. He stumbled and missed and found himself falling.

He hit the snow in the courtyard and his ankle cracked, a sharp jolt of agony shooting through his leg.

Figures came through the open gate: the giant, though now he was a normal-sized man dragging a long train of robe; Black Caesar, grinning a bright smile; the cloaked woman — yes it was Miss Belle — and another cloaked woman who was old. Wasn't it Mrs Hudson?

Tim looked back up at the top of the stairs, where Jacob Marley's ghost pulled his jaw right up over his head and revealed himself to be Mr Wilber.

And then another woman came running into the courtyard, faster than them all, holding out her arms. She reached him first and he was in his mother's warm embrace once more.

— 31 —

Fred watched from the roundel window as the troupe retreated to the safety of the chapel, going round the rear to the tradesmen's entrance.

"What a flare that was!" Dickens cried, putting the mirror down and clapping his hands for joy.

Bob Cratchit ran for the stairs and was bolting down them in a flash. Dickens scampered after him, chuckling and hooting with delight.

Fred cast a glance back at the Dungeon — its great gate wide open, a routed castle, its army fled — and took the two lanterns with him to light his way down the spiral stairs. He could already hear them piling excitedly into the kitchen.

He skipped the last few steps to the hallway and pulled up at the sight of a gentleman with a top hat and a leather bag coming out of the drawing room, closing the door quietly behind him.

"Ah, you must be one of the relatives come for Christmas. I can hear the festivities."

"Yes," said Fred, feeling suddenly woozy, as if on the verge of swooning, the ground unsteady beneath him, like the hallway had become a ship's deck.

"Mrs Jowett is suffering cramps and spasms," said the doctor. "It is not, in my professional opinion, the palsy. She is rather overwrought and of a weak constitution. I have recommended a good deal of rest. I'm glad to know that she has her family round her. Merry Christmas."

He put his top hat on his head and scurried out.

Fred put his palm to the wall and edged down the passageway that led to the kitchen. He pulled himself together as he entered and searched for Belle. She turned in the mob of faces and swept the hood from her face. He started with shock.

Grey haired and aged.

It was Mrs Hudson.

Fred laughed. He'd been fooled, just like Slogger Pike had been fooled.

Belle came through the crowd, patting shoulders, congratulating them all, and her eyes found his across the room. For a moment she stared, and the moment felt like an age. Their gaze burned up the whole room and no one saw it, and he knew he was madly, utterly, desperately in love with this woman and could not leave her.

Her earnest gaze broke into a friendly smile, the kind she'd give anyone in this room, but he'd seen it, in that moment that lasted an age — he'd seen her love for him too. She pushed through and came to him, the fire of victory burning in her eyes and in the excitement, he pulled her into an embrace and kissed her full on the lips. She pulled back, shocked, and he saw his mistake.

"I'm sorry," he said.

Belle smiled and looked at the sprig of mistletoe hanging from the beam above. "Don't be sorry." She squeezed his hand and he knew she didn't mind, but there was decorum to think of. She'd probably had enough scandal for one day.

Mrs Hudson saw and frowned. Just why was she so against this thing between Belle and him?

Dickens was sounding off on how tricky it was to negotiate the light. "My arms are aching with holding that mirror and angling it just so."

"It worked like a charm!" said Bob Cratchit.

"Who would have thought," said Ira Aldridge, "that three lanterns aimed at a mirror could create a light to equal Saul's on the road to Damascus?"

"A devastating effect!" Mr Fezzwig cried. "Well done, Mr Dickens, Mr Fred and you too, Cratchit!"

"Mr Fezzwig, you scared the bejeebers out of me when you came walking on your stilts!" said Ira. "And shouting *Fee Fie Fo Fum* as well."

"A little improvisation," Fezzwig said modestly. "Not too much?"

"No! Perfect!"

"Your pirate was a triumph, Mr Aldridge," Fezzwig said. "And your ghost of Jacob Marley sent shivers down my spine, Mr Wilber. Oh and Belle, you were awesome in your gravitas."

"The swap with Mrs Hudson," said Forster. "I believe none of them saw it."

"A simple case of misdirection," said Dickens. "That is the basis of all magic."

Tim cried out in pain, sitting on the kitchen table where his mother had dropped him after carrying him in.

"Your ankle is broken, my tiny Tim," she said.

"Not a break," said Tim, bravely. "But it hurts to touch."

"A sprain," said Forster, "by the look of it. You'll have to rest it for a month or so."

Tim reached inside his jacket pocket and took out an envelope — a thick wad of money the size of a book. He held it out to Forster. "Here you are, sir. This belongs to you."

"How strange," said Dickens. "This is how we began this morning."

"I'm so very sorry, sir," said Tim. "I don't know what came over me."

Forster shuffled and harrumphed and pocketed the money, patting his heart. "It's all right, boy. We'll say no more about it."

"Am I to go to prison now?" Tim asked.

Emily hugged her son so tight that he let out a little yelp.

"No, boy," said Dickens. "I think you've seen enough of prison. The money is returned so there's no harm done."

"Slogger Pike spent a little of it," said Tim. "A pound, I believe. Although most of it was placed on account at Miss Jagger's Dining Rooms."

"I'm sure we can get that back," said Bob Cratchit.

"A pound is a small price to pay for saving a good boy from a life of crime," said Dickens. "Isn't that right, Forster?"

"I believe it is, yes, Charles."

Fezzwig went to the scullery and came back with a broom. "We need to fashion a crutch for this boy. This will do, I think."

He got Tim to lie down flat on the kitchen table and placed the broom against him to measure how much he needed to take off so it was just the right height for him. He scored a mark with his thumbnail.

"Do you have a saw, Mrs Cratchit?"

"No, I don't think so. There's an axe in the scullery."

Fezzwig took the broom out to the scullery. They heard three careful strikes of iron on wood and he came back with the broom in two. "That's done the trick! It will do for now. I'm sure Mrs Jowett can spare a broom."

"It's the least she can spare, the old witch," said Ira.

Everyone fell silent and Ira turned, aware of a presence behind him.

Mrs Jowett stood in the door, leaning on a walking stick, a Carcel lamp in her other hand illuminating her face, old, sick and sour. "What is all this noise? Who are all these people?"

Emily Cratchit, beaming a bright smile, announced, "Oh, Mrs Jowett, I'm so glad to see you're well again. I'll be off now, late as it is. I'm going home with my son and my husband. So, I wish you a Merry Christmas."

"We'll come with you," Mr Fezzwig said.

"Yes," said Mr Wilber.

They looked to Ira Aldridge, who was staring at Mrs

Jowett, arms folded.

"Mrs Jowett," said Belle. "I believe you owe Mr Aldridge an apology."

Mrs Jowett gazed on the actor, and it seemed her face was hard as flint and she would not move. Then she crumpled, her lip quivering, her eyes on the floor.

"How can you ever forgive me?" she moaned. "Such an awful lie. I apologize from the bottom of my heart for the hurt and shame I've caused. But if you only knew why…"

"What possible reason could you have?" said Ira.

Mrs Jowett shook her head, slumped into a chair at the table, placing the lamp before her and held her face in her hands. "A wicked, awful, terrible thing to say. Please forgive me. I shall come this minute to your wife and tell her it was a lie. This very second. I shall beg her forgiveness."

Ira Aldridge stepped back, as if he feared this old woman and her vehemence. "That won't be necessary," he said. "Perhaps tomorrow."

"Christmas Day," Mrs Jowett said, a little wistfully. "Perhaps we might meet at Christ Church for the morning service."

Ira bowed his head. "Certainly. Christmas morn," he said.

Emily Cratchit threw on her coat and pulled Tim off the table. "We'll be going. Goodbye to you all. I can't thank you enough for saving my boy."

Mr Fezzwig and Mr Wilber picked up their sacks containing their clothes and the terrible false jaw contraption and each took one of the stilts.

"May I walk with you, gentlemen?" Ira Aldridge called.

"Certainly, sir!" they replied.

"You're most welcome," said Emily Cratchit.

"I must return to my dear wife at the New Royal Hotel," Ira said. "But it is only up the hill."

"Perhaps we'll stop off at the Rose and Crown on Bread Street for a celebratory drink?" said Bob Cratchit.

"Capital idea!" said Mr Fezzwig.

"Well, it is Christmas," said Ira Aldridge. "I suppose I can send a boy to fetch my wife so she can join us in a wassail."

"As long as it isn't this boy," Bob Cratchit said, patting Tim's head. "He won't get very far on that leg."

They all went out to the hallway, leaving Mrs Jowett at the kitchen table. Emily Cratchit hugged every last one of them: Dickens, Forster, Belle, Mrs Hudson and Fred.

"Come on," said Bob Cratchit to Tim. "You can't walk in this." He picked up the boy and heaved him up onto his shoulder, but he was too heavy.

"Let us help," said Mr Fezzwig.

"If Tim doesn't mind being carried by a couple of ghosts," said Mr Wilber.

They each gave a shoulder and Tim sat on their crossed arms. Emily and Bob carried the sacks. Mr Fezzwig and Mr Wilber each used a stilt as an effective staff to negotiate the snowy ground.

They called out a hearty *Merry Christmas* and walked off up Pinfold Street, holding tiny Tim up high.

Mrs Hudson, Fred, Belle, Dickens and Forster watched them go.

"What a charming sight," said Dickens. "If it doesn't look like the Holy family, and the three wise men."

They all involuntarily gazed at the Dungeon across the white street.

Forster chuckled. "That evil Pike chap was as scared as a lamb!"

"Did you see them run?" said Charles.

"It was the best production ever!" said Forster.

"Tonight's Harlequinade excepted of course," said Fred.

A carriage came down the hill and passed the merry band on their way into the night. It came to the chapel and the driver, wrapped up so thick he must have been wearing half a dozen coats, pulled up, his horses clouded in steam.

The carriage door swung open and Ebenezer Swingeford stepped out.

— 32 —

Fred bristled at the sight of the old miser, come to demand an explanation. The triumph of the theatre performance and the rescue of tiny Tim soured at the memory of Belle agreeing to meet him here to discuss Mrs Jowett's slur against her. And 'other matters', he'd said.

His proposal of marriage.

Poor Belle had only allowed herself to be bullied into it so the show could go ahead.

Fred stepped in front of Belle as Swingeford entered the hall, but Swingeford merely cast a withering look of scorn on them all and headed for the drawing room.

"Mrs Jowett is in the kitchen," said Mrs Hudson.

"The kitchen?" said Swingeford.

"Yes. You'll find her there."

His scornful gaze went from the drawing room door to the door across the hall that led to the servants' quarters, and he examined each of their faces — Fred's, Mrs Hudson's, Dickens', Forster's, Belle's — as if they might be playing a joke on him.

Mrs Hudson let out an exasperated sigh and flounced off through the door to the kitchen. Fred took Belle's elbow and guided her forward, making sure he was between her and the old miser. Dickens and Forster followed and Swingeford could stay in the hall all night if he cared to.

Mrs Jowett was still at the kitchen table, the Carcel lamp gurgling before her, its sickly glow lighting up her face so she looked like a ghost.

She barely acknowledged them as they entered, but she looked up at her brother and sighed and nodded with grim determination, as if this was a moment she had long dreaded.

Mrs Hudson sat at Mrs Jowett's side and put her hand on her arm.

Fred ushered Belle to a seat at the table and did the same, sitting beside her and placing a supportive hand on her arm.

Swingeford stayed standing over them, his cane behind his back. "So it wasn't that Aldridge beggar. It was this man. You are the man at the theatre who intends to usurp me."

"I am not a crown, to be fought over by warring princes," said Belle.

"I do mean to usurp you," said Fred. "I'll do everything I can to stop you marrying her."

"How dare you be so impertinent? And you, her cousin."

"He is not her cousin," said Mrs Jowett.

"But you said he was. You confirmed it."

"I have told so many lies today," she sighed. "If the Lord take me tonight, I fear I might go to Hell."

"It's true," said Belle. "Mr Smith and Mrs Hudson are no long-lost relations of mine."

"I thought as much," Swingeford said. "But why did you confirm their lie, sister?"

"Because I too shall do everything in my power to stop you marrying her."

"This is abominable," Swingeford said. "And it shall make me all the more determined to make it so."

Mrs Jowett gave a sad smile. "Oh no, Ebenezer, you truly won't. It has come to this. It has come to this."

Swingeford stared.

Everyone stared. Had Mrs Jowett truly gone mad?

She rose from her seat and picked up the lamp. "The answer lies behind the chapel."

She walked out through the scullery to the rear door and for a moment, no one moved, unsure if they were to follow or not.

Belle rose and Fred went with her. The others tramped out to the cold night behind them, following Mrs Jowett's figure, black against the snow and the lamplight before her.

Fred glanced behind to see Dickens and Forster had both taken a lantern to light the way. They walked through the snow-covered graveyard, a grim procession.

Mrs Jowett stopped at what seemed like an overgrown, empty patch of grass, clumps of weeds and briars poking through the blanket of snow.

Fred saw that it was not empty, but there was a little gravestone, moss-covered, a modest, squat little thing, smaller than a milestone in a hedgerow.

"What humbug is this?" Swingeford said.

Mrs Jowett held her lamp aloft and pointed at the grave. "There is why I told such an awful lie. There is why I've sought to sunder your marriage proposal."

Dickens knelt down and wiped snow from the gravestone, revealing the inscription:

Susannah Bell
And Child
Died 1822

How curious, Fred thought. Mrs Hudson had said her name was Susannah too.

Swingeford let out a little snort of disgust. "You think you can appeal to my sentimentality. I do not look backward into the past. I look to the future, always, my gaze set firmly on the horizon, on tomorrow. Those who dwell in the past are prisoners to fate."

"You fear the world too much," Mrs Jowett said. "All your other hopes have merged into the hope of being beyond the chance of its sordid reproach."

"Who is this?" Mrs Hudson asked.

"There lies the poor woman Ebenezer Swingeford abandoned," said Mrs Jowett. "The poor girl he ruined."

"I would have married her," Swingeford said, "But it was not the right time. It conflicted with my ambitions."

"That poor girl died giving birth to your child, Ebenezer."

"I didn't know she was with child at the time. You know that. I am not to blame."

"You didn't care. You used a poor girl for your own pleasure and then abandoned her. She fell and landed in the workhouse and you washed your hands of her."

"I didn't know she was—"

"When she told you, you cared nothing for her. She died in childbirth, and with her everything that was decent and kind in you also died. Yes, I saw what man you were back then and there was some good in you. But you became bitter. You walked on through life resenting it and amassing money, as if that would absolve you. You became a monster, Ebenezer."

"And this is why you wish to sunder my proposal?" he said. "This is why you seek to prevent me marrying Miss Belle."

Mrs Jowett shook her head and gave a sad little laugh. "Oh, Ebenezer, you still do not see it."

"I remember it," Swingeford snarled. "Twenty years ago this night. And you wonder why I spit on Christmas and your season of goodwill. My greatest mistake lies there, that woman and that child, and yes, the railway in which I invest shall come and wipe away all of this, but I will not care if their bones are swept away by progress."

"What a magnificent monster is this," Dickens said, almost in awe.

"You are wrong," Mrs Jowett said. And here she smiled the painful smile of a fatally wounded man who knows he has won.

"I'm glad you defend me, sister."

"I don't," said Mrs Jowett. "He's absolutely right: you *are* a monster. But it is you who are wrong, Ebenezer. Your child does not lie in this grave."

"What do you mean? I buried them both here."

"You buried poor Susannah Bell. Not your child."

"What is this humbug?"

Mrs Jowett nodded and her smile soured. "Your child is not there."

She raised a bony finger and pointed at the grave. Everyone followed that finger as it moved from the grave and traced a slow arc through the cold air, past Swingeford, past Fred, Mrs Hudson, Dickens and Forster, and settled on…

Belle.

"There is your child."

They all looked from Belle's astonished face to Swingeford's. The blood seemed to retreat from his cheeks, till his lips became pale. He stared dumbfounded, looking from his sister to…

His daughter.

"What lie is this?" he spluttered.

The blood came rushing back to his cheeks, so violently he moaned in pain and clutched his heart. He fell to his knees as if to get a closer look at that gravestone, as if those few sad chiselled letters might reveal the truth.

"Dig it up if you must, Ebenezer. You will only find your wife's bones there. Your child lives and stands before you."

"No," said Swingeford. "This cannot be. You lie!"

Belle clutched her throat. "This is my mother?" she said. "This is my father?"

Fred put his arm around her shoulder and felt her sink against him. And for a moment it felt as if he was falling with her. He shuddered and snapped back to the moment. That old familiar feeling — the same as all those times he'd flitted through time before and come back to his present. A sickening vertigo. Not now, he thought. Let me stay here, with her.

"You see, dear brother," Mrs Jowett said with a glint of malice, flashing like a knife. "Not everything that was good in you died; one thing survived and lived on: your daughter."

"This cannot be," Swingeford moaned, with a sickening low of horror, rather like he might have sounded had he lost his entire fortune.

"You haven't seen it at all, have you? So much did you put her behind you. Your attraction to this girl is a memory of her that is dead. Doomed to repeat your ghastly mistake over and over again. A man truly in Purgatory."

"You knew this?" Swingeford spat, a thread of drool falling from his mouth. "All these years you knew this was my daughter? Why did you not tell me, damn you!"

"You wanted no daughter! You wanted nought of this shameful episode. You detached yourself from this poor woman and her fate lest she drag you down into the Froggery with her. So desperate were you to climb out of the pit, you stood on her face and she fell into the abyss."

"You evil woman. What have you done?"

"I raised your child and saved her from the worst of this. I will not see you further ruin her."

"God damn you!"

Swingeford rose and stumbled towards Belle, one hand reaching out. She cowered away from him and Fred stepped before her. Swingeford stumbled past them, grasping cold air, and scrambled on and on and didn't stop. He fled into the night, howling, his feet crumping in the snow, threading a path through the gravestones. He left no trail of blood in the snow but staggered like a man who had been mortally wounded and might fall any moment.

His pathetic form disappeared into the gloomy silhouette of the chapel, as if it were the gateway to Hell, the black mouth of the Inferno.

A coachman cracked his whip. A carriage rattled away into the night.

Forster mumbled, "This is like something from one of

your stories, Charles. I always thought in real life there weren't these threads that bind us all."

"Oh, we are bound to everyone," said Dickens.

Belle gazed on the sad little gravestone. It seemed none of them could take their eyes off it.

"All my life, I thought my mother threw me away, and now I know she died bringing me into this world. It was your brother who cast her aside and me with her. And it was you who covered up the crime."

"What I did, I did for the best," Mrs Jowett said. "I did it to protect you."

"To protect your family name."

Mrs Jowett went to Belle, holding out her hand.

Belle shrank away and into Fred's embrace.

Mrs Jowett looked at the cold ground and nodded and gave out a sad sigh. "I was wrong," she said. "I was wrong about everything." Without another word, she turned and trudged back to the chapel.

They watched her lamplight fade through the darkness. A swirl of snow and then she was gone, like a ghost.

"Did you see his face?" said Dickens. "Swingeford's. Such a sledge-hammer blow."

"And to poor Belle too," said Mrs Hudson.

Belle buried her face in Fred's chest and he held her tight. *The Holly and the Ivy* was playing on the wind. He looked around to see where the tune came from. A brass band echoing on the cold night air. He felt the ground tilt again. He was falling.

"I feel…"

"Fred?" Mrs Hudson said. "What is it?"

He felt Belle tighten her grip on him, though he was falling, the starry sky spinning all around him. That familiar swooning vertigo.

"Not now!" he heard himself cry, his voice disembodied, as if it came calling from across the graveyard.

His legs buckled under him and he fell into the yawning

black hole of a grave.

— 33 —

Mrs Hudson's heart dropped to her feet. Belle and Fred had shimmered in blue for just a moment and then faded. They were gone. God knows where. At best, he'd taken her with him to his own time. At worst, he'd cast her into some other time and she was lost. For a moment Mrs Hudson calculated the odds of reaching her, casting out a signal to find her, but it was like throwing a message in a bottle on the ocean waves. Futile. She had no strength for it.

"What happened?" Dickens said. "They've vanished."

"There's an awful fog coming in," said Forster.

A thick mist all around. It had come from nowhere, swirling around their feet and burying the sad little gravestone that had guarded poor Belle's secret and utterly destroyed Ebenezer Swingeford. And Mrs Hudson's own name carved there. *Susannah.*

Her soul lurched and she reached out to steady herself.

Charles grabbed her hand.

"No," she said. "You shouldn't touch me. Not now. Not when this is happening."

"You're faint," he said.

She was falling.

The air changed around them, like Mr Wilber's magic lantern show, the backdrop melting into a new vista.

Snow beneath their feet, but they weren't in the graveyard

anymore. The giant Greek columns of the Town Hall towered above them. They were standing in the little square before Christ Church, under the gas lamp.

"What magic is this?" Dickens asked. "We have been transported across the city in a moment?"

"Not through space," Mrs Hudson said. "Through time."

"But the theatre is just down there. I can see the portico from here."

"Look," Mrs Hudson said. "Over there."

She pointed to the corner of the Town Hall that jutted into the cramped square. A poster on the wall there.

Dickens stepped off the little island at the centre of the square, testing with his toe first, as if he might fall through the snow, as if the ground was ephemeral and this was all a dream. He crept over to the corner of the Town Hall and Mrs Hudson went with him. There, in large letterpress block type, a poster read:

CHARLES DICKENS
Public reading of his famous Christmas tale
On the nights of 27th, 29th & 30th December, 1853

They had travelled eleven years into the future.

Dickens bent down to read the smaller print at the bottom. "On the 30th December all seats except the side galleries to be sold at a fee of sixpence to enable the working man and woman to gain admittance."

What was it she had to do here? Mrs Hudson thought, looking all about her for clues.

She recalled the old library. Not the beautiful old Victorian library behind the Town Hall that hadn't been built yet, but the Central Library, the Brutalist concrete inverted ziggurat that had replaced it in the 1960s. She had gone there. A memory of acres of orange carpet and fluorescent strip lights. She'd asked a young librarian about Charles Dickens. *When did he come to Birmingham?* The question had seemed very important to her.

A young librarian with red hair. She knew her. Oh, what was her name again?

"What is it?" Charles asked.

"Oh, there was something I remembered. Something to do with you and when you came here. I was looking it up. The answer was very important to me."

"Why?"

"I don't know. I can't remember."

Katherine! That was her name. Yes, the librarian who'd become a friend. Of course. Katherine had the ability too. She'd travelled in time. That was why Mrs Hudson had befriended her. They had worked together to solve mysteries, correct time breaches and save lives.

A dark shadow passed over her heart.

Something had gone wrong with Katherine. Something in the future or in the past. If only she could remember what it was.

Shouts up the street, from the darkness where the old library used to be. Would be. A commotion of calls.

A woman came running out of the darkness. Men chasing her. Shouts and cries.

The woman sprinted past.

It was…

"Katherine!" Mrs Hudson shouted. "Katherine, my dear!"

The girl ran on, but glared at her name being called.

"Wait! Stop!"

Katherine ran on past her and disappeared down the dark hill of Pinfold Street. The chasing pack of men in uniform gave up and walked back.

That frightened glare. The poor girl. Katherine hadn't recognized her as she had never seen Mrs Hudson before.

Yes, she'd told her that first time, in the old library. *I saw you by the Town Hall. There was a poster for a Dickens reading. It was a slum.*

That was the moment Mrs Hudson had always known was

yet to come. And here it was, at last. There were no more moments foretold to her.

Imagine not knowing anything about your future.

It suddenly felt a very lonely and uncomfortable place to be.

She turned to find Dickens was gone. Where was he? She'd dragged Charles Dickens eleven years out of time and now she'd lost him. Where would he go?

Her eyes fell on the poster. To see his talk. Of course!

But there were two of them. What if he met himself? She had to stop him!

She ran under the arched walkway at the front of the Town Hall and turned into the warmth of the reception hall.

There were no ushers guarding the tall doors to the auditorium. They were crowded around one open door all peering in themselves.

Charles was there, peeping over their heads.

She came to his side, sighing with relief.

Through the gap in the giant door, the hum of humanity. The sense of a great sleeping presence. Every seat taken, all along the stalls, and up on the balconies that ran the length of each side. Thousands of people staring with rapt attention at the stage. Under the giant cliff face of the great organ, one man in an evening suit and purple waistcoat stood at a lectern. Unmistakable even at this distance. His untidy hair, wild and flowing around his shoulders and with a rather large moustache. She fancied she could almost see the blue of his eyes.

He was half way between the Charles beside her and the old man on the ten-pound note, just beginning to develop that grizzled look.

His voice soared through the air. "Scrooge was better than his word! He did it all, and infinitely more; and to Tiny Tim... Who. Did. *Not*. Die..."

A sigh of relief, like a giant in slumber.

"... he was a second father. He became as good a friend, as

good a master, and as good a man, as the good old city knew, or any other good old city, town, or borough, in the good old world."

It was as if not a soul of the thousand or more people in there dared to breathe. Even the ushers crowded in the door did not stir.

"Some people laughed to see the alteration in him, but he let them laugh, and little heeded them; for he was wise enough to know that nothing ever happened on this globe, for good, at which some people did not have their fill of laughter in the outset; and knowing that such as these would be blind anyway, he thought it quite as well that they should wrinkle up their eyes in grins, as have the malady in less attractive forms. His own heart laughed: and that was quite enough for him."

One of the ushers sensed their presence behind him and glanced back at Dickens, the smile still fixed on his face. He looked back at the stage and then did a little double take. Didn't this man look an awful lot like the man on the stage?

"He had no further intercourse with Spirits," the great voice called out, rising to a crescendo, "but lived upon the Total Abstinence Principle, ever afterwards; and it was always said of him, that he knew how to keep Christmas well, if any man alive possessed the knowledge. May that be truly said of us, and all of us! And so, as Tiny Tim observed, God... Bless... Us... Every... One!"

He raised his glass to them all and the audience let out a great sigh, and then there was an explosion of cheering, clapping, shouting, acclamation. It was a roar that almost lifted the roof right off Birmingham Town Hall.

The man on stage took a step back as if the roar that was unleashed was a shot that had wounded him. Then he gathered himself and grinned, mopped his brow with a handkerchief and bowed.

The roar went on and on and on and on.

"Good God," the Charles Dickens by her side said. "Just

look at it."

The ground lurched and she had only a moment to feel herself slipping. She grabbed hold of Charles' hand. An usher turned to them and his face froze into an astonished O as she disappeared.

— 34 —

Fred's one thought was to hold onto her and not let go. Not to save himself, but because he knew, even as he fell, that he was falling into the future, a future that was beyond her own life. He knew, even as he fell in darkness, that he was going back to his own time. He knew, as he fell, that the spell that kept him in her time was broken, and that if he let go of her, he might lose her forever. Lose her in time.

The graveyard behind the Connexion chapel off Peck Lane disappeared and he landed on hard stone, a jolt through his knees, holding onto her and protecting her from the worst of the fall.

In a cloud of fog, he leapt to his feet and pulled her up, standing dizzy and disoriented.

The rising of the sun and the running of the deer...

People rushed by and Belle cringed into him. The fog cleared and Fred saw that they were on a train station platform.

Belle looked all about her in wonder and up at the vast glass vault.

New Street Station. They were on a platform at New Street Station.

Fred laughed. They were on the exact same spot. This was where Susannah Bell's grave had stood. And this was the station that Swingeford had threatened to build. The graveyard was gone, the chapel, the Dungeon, all the streets of the Froggery replaced by a grand, central station.

A woman pushed past in a broad hat and a long coat that fell mid-calf. Like the women of his childhood, before the skirts became shorter and the hats smaller. She looked them up and down and smiled, clutching her little boy in a sailor suit, hurrying on.

A brass band playing at the foot of the wooden staircase, all dressed in Dickensian costumes.

"Don't let go of my hand," he said.

"They dress just like me," she said. "Like us."

"They're in costume. It's a… it's a play." A pretence, he thought. A pretence about a happy Dickensian Christmas. The good old days.

Happy children watched and begged their parents for a coin to put in the tin.

Fred took it all in. Something so familiar about this.

A boy came through the crowd, ignoring the brass band, walking straight for Belle and Fred, a boy in a tweed knickerbocker suit and baker boy cap. He stood before them, gazing up at Belle. She looked down on him and pushed her hood from her face.

Fred stared, paralyzed, and though *The Holly and the Ivy* droned on, the world stood still, as if the entire fate of Earth hinged on the look that passed between this boy and this woman.

"Hello, young boy," she said. "What's your name?"

"Fred," the boy said. "What's your name?"

He held out his hand.

Belle's mouth fell open. Before she could respond, a woman came rushing up.

"Fred! There you are!" She came and yanked the boy away and hugged him. "You are not to walk off like that! I thought you were lost!"

A man in a tweed suit joined the boy and his mother, smiling with relief.

Fred stared, stunned. "Oh, I've missed them so much."

"Your parents," Belle said. "That was you."

The platform revolving slow, a carousel starting up.

"I remember you!" Fred cried. "I remember this."

"You were such a beautiful boy."

"This is my last memory of them."

She squeezed his hand. "They are gone? I mean, they will be gone? Oh, it's so difficult to think of."

"They died in a motor car crash. Not long after this."

He had met himself, as a child, and not recognized his older self. How could he have? Just that vivid memory of his mother and father finding him, angry, loving, desperately hugging him again. The beautiful dark-eyed Dickensian woman in the cloud of steam. This, all of this.

"I can't control it," he said. "I'm losing it."

She gripped both his fists in hers and held them to her breast. "Don't let go of me, Fred Smith. Don't lose me."

He fought against the spinning, whirling, swooning platform, the brass echoing, melting, all of it being sucked into a whirlpool. Her dark eyes on his. Hold onto her, he thought. Control this curse for once in your life, damn you. Hold onto this woman and don't let go.

Take her with y—

— 35 —

"Hallo!" Forster called. "Hilly ho! Anyone?"

His voice echoed back to him, forlorn and desolate. It proper spooked him if he was honest. Graveyards in the daytime were bad enough but at night, with a mist, and with all his friends running off and leaving him alone, it just wasn't bearable.

Charles' lantern was there on the ground, next to the gravestone. He picked it up, still alight, and felt a little safer with two lanterns. But even the light of both of them couldn't illuminate Charles, Mrs Hudson, Fred or Belle. They had all somehow slipped him in the mist.

A strange mist it was too. A fog like nothing he'd ever seen. It had come in all of a sudden and hung in the air. It was warm instead of cold and clammy, and it almost had the smell of coal about it, sort of sulphurous. It was more like the clouds of steam you got at a train station.

Perhaps this was what it was like here in Birmingham, with so many houses devoted to workshop and factory activity. There had been a dark cloud hanging over the city all day from the chimneys, and perhaps it turned to this smoky fog at night.

He wandered through it and found the edge of land where they'd walked into the graveyard earlier at the start of their mission. Such a funny old to do: the Cratchit boy, scaring off those criminals and then the graveside revelations. He managed to hold both lanterns in one hand and patted the wad of money at his chest. At least that was safe. But in this part of town. He needed to get back to civilization as soon as possible.

He retraced his steps through the dark streets and thought he must be the only man out at night, except for the woman he passed who was sleeping in a doorway, settling down for the night with a blanket around her.

He shivered and walked on and tried to forget her. Were there no workhouses? And still, he had such an enormous amount of money on his person. But it was not his; it was Charles', and it was to be invested in a very important business venture. It wasn't his money to go handing out to all and sundry, and surely doing so would only draw attention to himself from all sorts of criminals and ne'er-do-wells. And wasn't that what he'd only just rescued the money from?

He came to New Street and the welcoming glow of gaslight. The Shakespeare Tavern on the corner sounded boisterous. A carol vibrating on the windows. He could nip in there for a pint of ale. But not with so much money on his person. That was a recipe for disaster. An ale to loosen his tongue and he'd be telling all and sundry about his adventure tonight and before he knew it, he'd be pickpocketed or held at knifepoint. There was just no trusting anyone in the world at all.

He shuddered and passed on, letting the lanterns fall to his knee now that he didn't need them to light his way. His arm was aching terribly.

If only Charles and the others had returned via some other route, he could tell them all the story of his dangerous odyssey to get back here, all alone and at the mercy of the worst criminals in the Froggery.

He quickened his step towards the theatre, eager to be reunited with his merry band of adventurers. He could regale them with his adventure and they would surely think him quite the hero. He was sure they hadn't experienced anything to rival his adventure.

— 36 —

Mrs Hudson gazed up at snow falling through gaslight. They were on a dark street of grand terracotta buildings. Another Christmas. Later, she felt.

Dickens was bent over. "I feel quite dizzy," he said.

"Come along," Mrs Hudson said, taking the stone steps through the arched doorway. He followed her inside the grand building. An empty reception hall. Yes, she knew this building. She'd visited it many times for talks and readings.

The sense of a hubbub deeper inside. She climbed the stairs, her skirts swishing about her ankles. There, the grand meeting room. She pushed the brass door handle. It creaked as she entered and slipped inside. Charles remained in the doorway, peeping inside, and took off his top hat. A hundred or more people were seated inside. A few turned to look.

The speaker standing at the lectern noted her and paused.

He looked older and this, finally, was the man she knew as Charles Dickens: this was the man from the ten-pound note and every portrait of him. Frizzy hair and a long beard. Grizzled and worn.

He came to the conclusion of his speech, his eyes on her. "And thus I say, a mere spoken word — a mere syllable thrown into the air — may go on reverberating through illimitable space forever and ever…"

He bowed. Polite applause crackled. All the men in the

room stood and clamoured to congratulate him. Charles Dickens pushed through the crowd, his eyes on her and her alone.

She cast a wary glance back at the younger Dickens in the doorway looking on, astonished, and felt it was vitally important that these two men did not meet.

Charles Dickens pushed through the crowd of glad-handing men. "It's you, isn't it? The Ghost of Christmas Past?"

"Now, Charles, you know full well I'm not a ghost."

"Why have you returned?"

"I can't control this. It takes me where it will."

"It's like a story," he said.

"I wouldn't know about that."

"Is it the same night? By the way you look, I see it is."

"I wish I knew what it was all for," she said.

"Don't you know why? You haven't seen it yet?"

"Seen what?"

"Why, Miss Belle and young Master Fred," he said with a delighted chuckle.

"What about them?" she asked.

But he craned his neck to see his younger self at the door. "I'm here, aren't I?" he said. "I remember it."

"I can't let you talk to him. That really wouldn't do."

"No. You didn't let me. You didn't. I remember." Dickens smiled wryly. He was ahead of her on this one. "But it meant all the world, to see me like this. I was young then and still so desperate. On the verge of bankruptcy. It was the *Carol* that saved me."

"And it was Belle's story," said Mrs Hudson.

"And yours," said Dickens.

He seemed unperturbed, not a bit concerned that he might have stolen the tale that truly cemented his name as Britain's favourite author. There was no shame in that gaze.

He was looking over her shoulder now. "Perhaps I could just say one thing to myself…"

"No you don't, Charles," Mrs Hudson said.

She backed away through the scrum of men who all wanted a piece of the great author.

"Just one word," Dickens insisted.

But he was trapped by his adoring public. Mrs Hudson retreated to the great oak doors, where Charles — a younger Dickens — peered, astonished.

"I look so old," he said. "And with such a foolish beard."

"It's your look."

"Perhaps I could just talk to him. Briefly."

"No," Mrs Hudson said. "We're going."

"I could just nip back."

"No," Mrs Hudson replied firmly. She held out her hand.

"Where are we going?" he asked.

"I don't know," she said. "But I think your older self knows."

She took his hand, closed the door and found herself staring into the face of a snowman.

Snow on the ground. Deep night.

Mrs Hudson thought for a moment that they must be back in the graveyard. There was the same half moon in the sky but there were no crooked gravestones about.

They were in a little square of garden edged by a picket fence. A terraced house. Was this? Yes, it was home.

A snowman in the middle of the lawn, wearing a metal helmet. Standing to attention with a wooden rifle. A row of brass buttons embedded up his torso. A carrot nose.

Yes, she remembered making this on Christmas Eve. The first Christmas after the war. A whole day making her Victory Snowman. It was Christmas Eve, 1945.

A light from the window at the back of the house. A side alley leading to the parlour window. A glow of light from inside.

"Where are we?" Dickens asked.

"My home. My childhood." She was about to say *after the war,* but checked herself. No point getting into that. "A hundred years from your time. One hundred and three years, to be exact."

She crept forward, leaving footprints in the snow, wondering if they would be there in the morning and leave a puzzling mystery for a young girl to ponder on Christmas morn, but she remembered no such mystery.

Along the side of the house, down the narrow yard, she crept to the window, and Charles came behind her.

The glow of a coal fire from inside, pools of lamplight around the room.

A girl lying on the rug before the fire. Her parents in adjoining armchairs, holding hands. The parlour at home. She was a girl. The complete leather-bound set of Charles Dickens volumes in the glass cabinet. Her mother reading *A Christmas Carol.* Their Christmas Eve tradition. The tree all spangling, golden. She thought she could almost smell the sweet scent of pine needles. Magical and warm. Christmas 1945. The war was over and there was hope in the world.

The girl lying on the rug, listening to the tale of Scrooge and the ghosts of Christmas Past, Present, and Yet to Come, was herself.

Mrs Hudson fought the urge to knock the window, to greet them. So many times in recent years she'd felt that pang of longing to see her parents again, to spend just one more day with them.

Charles came beside her.

"That's me," she whispered. "My parents. We're reading your… Christmas book."

"My Christmas book. How curious."

Her father sat in an armchair, his face in shadow. Her mother had her back to the window, silhouetted by the candle that lit up the pages of the book. The girl gazed up at her in rapt attention.

And then her mother turned a page and handed the book to her husband, passing the candlestick over so that it lit up her father's face.

Fred's face.

"Oh," said Dickens. "It's Fred."

The girl got up, kneeling by her mother, who leaned over and kissed her. The mumble of their voices, and the firelight catching the side of her face.

It was Belle.

But a different Belle. She had been transformed into a 1940s housewife.

"But this means that Fred and Belle are—"

"My parents."

But this wasn't right at all. Her parents had met at a dance in 1934. Mrs Hudson had travelled there herself to ensure it happened, when it was under threat, when she thought someone was targeting her very existence. Her parents, looking so young and awkward at that dance, with a couple of chaperones between them

That had been their first time, hadn't it?

But it hadn't, she knew now.

They'd told her that lie. Because they couldn't tell their daughter that they'd met in 1842 when Charles Dickens was in town and dad had saved mum from a Victorian living hell.

She'd gone to that night in 1934 and seen an awkward couple and nothing more. Perhaps the chaperones weren't anything to do with them. Perhaps her mother and father had simply gone to a dance and had their first argument, and that was the awkwardness she'd seen.

"Fred and Belle are your parents," Dickens said. "You didn't know?"

"I couldn't remember their faces."

Fred took the book and the candle and continued the reading. The girl lay down on the rug again and glanced at the hearth and the stocking hanging there.

So Fred had taken Belle to 1934, Mrs Hudson thought. And while the 1930s weren't the best decade to choose, there was a war around the corner and terrible devastation, but here they were in 1945, having come through it, and now there was hope and renewal. There'd be a National Health Service. They would rise with that social care and create a family and their own daughter would go to university to study History. And while that precarious freedom and comfort was always under threat from despots and greedy men who wanted everything for themselves, and it always had to be

215

fought for and defended — it was still there, as a right, and it was infinitely better than that Victorian prison.

She took in her parents' faces, as Fred read the story and Belle gazed on him with such a look of love. She'd been so desperate to see her parents again and she'd been with them all day long.

The girl sat up and leaned against her father's leg, hugging her knees. Her gaze went to the window.

Mrs Hudson stepped back, though she felt certain her younger self could see nothing out there.

She nudged Charles and they retreated to the garden and the snowman standing mute and sad. Snow was falling.

She took Charles' hand.

At the window, her younger self peered out, shielding her eyes, trying to see what was out there.

Yes, she remembered this. Looking out at the snow falling on a Christmas Eve, wanting to see Father Christmas riding across the night sky on a sleigh, and instead seeing a man in a top hat and an old woman in a cloak and hood.

Two ghosts and a snowman.

The house faded, her younger self at the window slipping away, and Mrs Hudson found herself back on New Street in 1842.

— 38 —

Fred opened his eyes. He still had hold of Belle. Her hands locked in his.

"We've come back," she said. "You held onto me."

They were before the theatre, under the portico. The placard for the Harlequinade still outside. The theatre was shut up. His feet gave way and he slumped against her. She held him up and pressed him against the door.

"I don't think I can hold on here," he said. "I'm fighting to stay with you, but it's too strong."

"Take me with you," she said.

"I don't think I can."

"You took me to your childhood. Take me with you again. Take me to your time. Don't leave me here." She clung onto him, grasping his hands in hers, and kissed him.

"I can't hold on anymore. I'm slipping. I'm sorry."

"Just don't leave me here. There is nothing for me here."

"Where I come from, it's a cruel place." Sneering fascists everywhere, he thought, fighting in the streets. The world was falling apart. The centre could not hold. "I can't take you there. It's too harsh a place."

"Harsher than this?"

It was better, he had to admit. As bad as 1934 was — and it was truly awful for a great many people — it was not as brutal and cruel as this.

"I won't let go," she said. "I'll hold onto you."

It was no use, he thought. It would take him any moment now. He would fall through decades and disappear from her arms. This was the desperate state of love in the world: a couple huddled in a doorway trying to fight off the world's cruelty.

"Forster! What ho!"

Dickens' voice.

Belle held Fred up against the door and leaned back to peer up the street. "It's Mr Dickens," she said. "And Mrs Hudson."

"Don't let go of me," Fred said.

They came to them, Dickens and Mrs Hudson, and Forster rushed over from the other direction.

"Hallo. What happened?" Dickens said.

"You all ran off," said Forster. "I the most amazing adventure."

"What's wrong, Fred?" Mrs Hudson asked.

Their voices swam in a slurry. Mrs Hudson came to him.

"I can't hold on," Fred said.

"I've got you," Mrs Hudson said, putting her hand on his brow.

Soothing, cool. He felt a wave of calm bloom through him like a shot of morphine.

"He looks feverish," said Dickens.

Belle took the keys from her cloak pocket and opened the door. "Let's get him inside."

They lumbered through the ballroom space, dark and cold. There was a hubbub from the Shakespeare tavern to the side, but the door to it was locked. The coffee house on the other side was closed too, but Belle rushed over to it and used her keys again.

Fred reached out for her. She'd let go. Mrs Hudson had him, but if he flitted now, he'd lose Belle forever.

Belle opened the door to the coffee room and invited them in. As Mrs Hudson and Dickens carried him through, he

218

grabbed hold of Belle again and whispered, "Don't let go."

"I won't," she said.

She held his hand as they guided him to a row of wooden booths against the outer wall. She slumped onto the bench beside him and Mrs Hudson and Dickens sat opposite.

"He looks most disoriented," said Dickens.

"Hmm," Forster said, standing over them. "That does remind me of the most amazing adventure I had in returning here."

Belle clutched at Mrs Hudson's sleeve across the table. "We need your help, Mrs Hudson."

"She won't." Fred shook his head. "She's been against us all day."

Mrs Hudson stroked his brow again. Soothing. Calm. "I'm not against you," she said. "I'll do everything I can to help you. Let me get my strength back."

"Coffee," said Belle. "We need coffee."

She looked to Dickens. Dickens looked to Forster.

"I suppose I'll get us all coffee," Forster said.

"There's a stove over there behind the counter," Belle called. "There might be coffee left in the big blue enamel pot. I often heat up the leftovers."

Forster clattered around back there. "Yes, there's coffee left. I'll heat it up. Then I'll tell you all such a tale…"

Fred relaxed into the bench, Belle holding one hand, so tight, Mrs Hudson his other, gentle, hardly touching at all. His agitation sank to a faint hum of interference behind a radio broadcast. But he still wasn't sure Mrs Hudson wouldn't pull some sort of trick to keep him and Belle apart.

"Why?" he asked. "Why would you help us now?"

"Tell them," said Dickens. "Tell them about your parents."

"My parents married for love," said Mrs Hudson. "I was telling Charles about it just now. And I can see that you're in love. Very much. Just like my parents used to be."

"You said you couldn't remember your parents," said

Fred.

"I said I couldn't see their faces anymore." There were tears in her eyes. She looked from his face to Belle's and then stroked his cheek ever so tenderly. "But their love I do remember. My mother was very happy. The happiest woman in the world."

Belle looked up and smiled at this, hope gleaming in her eyes.

"How could she not be?" said Mrs Hudson. "My father gave her all the love in the world."

And her voice cracked. Perhaps she'd only just remembered them and it was all new and raw. Or she was just worn out, like she'd said. It had been such a long day. He thought back to the man who'd arrived this morning, his head bleeding from a fascist's boot. A different man. A different life.

"You were a lucky girl to have such parents," said Belle.

"Oh, I was. They showed a deep affection for each other till the day they died. It's a great example to have for a young woman growing up. And they were strongly of the belief that I should choose my own future."

"Imagine such a thing," Dickens said. "Quite revolutionary."

"Talking of revolutionary…" Forster called from behind the counter.

"Isn't a woman worth as much as a man?" Belle asked. "Why should she be denied what every boy expects as a right?"

"Not all men expect such things," said Dickens. "The great many men of this or any city have no opportunity to look above the dirt at their feet. They live lives of great desperation."

"They do, Charles," said Mrs Hudson, "and the richest women in this city, born to wealth and privilege, have less rights and less expectation than the poorest of men. There are no Chartist riots calling for women to have the vote."

"Such a thing would be absurd."

"And that is the problem," Belle said.

Fred squeezed her hand. He was so proud of her.

"I encountered a very interesting woman on the way here…" said Forster.

"I'm sorry, Mr Dickens," Belle continued. "But I've always felt myself to be a woman out of time. I've always felt that I was cursed to see through the hollow pretence of this time. I do not wish to settle for what little it allows me. Like a slave, I wish to smash these shackles and run free."

"You shall," said Mrs Hudson. "I'll help you."

And she had such a tender smile. It was a total transformation, Fred thought. They had all been changed so much by this day, even Mrs Hudson.

Forster came from the counter with a tray and slid it across the table between them. Five bone china coffee mugs, steaming. "So as I was saying," he said. "You won't believe the amazing tale of my journey."

"Charles," said Mrs Hudson. "Don't you need to talk to Belle about her story?"

"What do you mean?" asked Dickens.

"You are formulating the idea of a Christmas story, largely based on the play you have seen tonight."

"Hmmm, well, not exactly based on the play," said Charles, chuckling nervously.

Fred took his coffee and breathed in its earthy fragrance.

"Charles," said Mrs Hudson, "it's time for a bargain to be made."

"A bargain?" said Forster, squeezing in his massive bulk beside Dickens and still half hanging out of the booth. "What kind of bargain?"

Dickens wagged a finger. "As I pointed out today, there are certain elements of one of my own tales from the *Pickwick Papers* — the tale of Gabriel Grub, visited by goblins who show him his past and future — that precede Miss Belle's story. So in a sense, it is already my work. Hmm?"

Mrs Hudson shook her head with the confident smile of someone who knows they have a winning hand. "I think the tale you have in mind, dear Charles, bears rather more resemblance to Miss Belle's play than to your Gabriel Grub story."

"What is this?" Belle asked.

"Of course," said Fred. He saw it now. He knew exactly where Mrs Hudson was going with this.

"Well, I wish someone would explain it to me," said Forster.

"In a way, I shouldn't really need to pay her anything at all," said Dickens. "The story is mine."

Forster banged the table. "You're not suggesting that Charles has plagiarized Miss Belle's work, are you? He wrote his story six years ago."

"Not what he *wrote*," said Mrs Hudson. "What he *will* write."

"You mean to sue Charles for something he hasn't even written yet?"

"It's all right, Forster," Dickens said. He took a sip of coffee, smacked his lips and settled down to business. "Mrs Hudson knows the outline of the story I am to write. I have shared the details with her. It is all but written."

"You haven't mentioned this at all, Charles!"

"It was inspired by tonight's events. In part. But I will write it and it will be a magnificent success."

"Perhaps it's not so inevitable as you think," Mrs Hudson said. "Your life's course will foreshadow certain ends. But if the course be departed from, the end will change."

"But I've seen the ghost of Christmas Yet to Come. I've seen my future."

Mrs Hudson considered this. A sly smile. "You've seen *a* future."

"What do you mean? I saw that throng listening to my every word. I saw myself reading. I saw my future fame. That cannot be sponged away any more than the writing on poor

Susannah Bell's gravestone."

"You saw the shadows of the things that *may* be, Charles, not necessarily the things that *will* be. The future is not set in stone. It can always be changed."

Charles gasped. "You would seek to rob me of my future fame?"

"I didn't say that, Charles. I said that it was only possible to change the future. The good or bad we do today creates the good or bad we reap tomorrow. You know that."

"Well, I think I've slipped into a dream," Forster said. "Because I have no idea what anyone is talking about."

"I cannot share the writing of a tale," said Dickens. "It can't be a story by Charles Dickens after a play created by some woman in Birmingham. That would never do. The public, the readership, need to see something new that has sprung from the imagination of Dickens! That's how the business works."

"Then pay the author for the story," said Mrs Hudson.

Charles laughed. "Oh, Miss Belle. You have an excellent literary agent. Look you, Forster. See how it's done." He held out his hand to Forster.

"Charles," Forster said, "you can't be thinking of handing over this money to her?"

"I'm afraid a deal has been made. Did you not hear it struck?"

"But Charles," said Forster, "that money is to secure a competitively priced print run for your next book."

"The provincial publishing world is too fraught with difficulty. We're best to stick to London, which may be more expensive, but you pay for the convenience of avoiding all of this." Dickens flapped his arms to take in the coffee house, the theatre and all around it, as if New Street was a great inconvenience to him.

Forster reluctantly dug into his pocket, frowned, reached into another pocket, panicked, delved into a third pocket and pulled out a thick envelope with a sigh of relief. He gazed on it, like a man finding his favourite childhood book again, winced, and held it out to Fred.

Fred looked to Belle.

Belle reached out and took it.

Forster gasped.

Dickens said, "My word."

"Well, I've seen quite enough of this mad place," said Forster. "I'm to bed to grab what little sleep I can before our train home, Charles. I'll call on you at half to seven." He knocked back his coffee, squirmed out of the booth, retrieved his top hat and bowed to everyone. "I wish you all a good night."

"Merry Christmas," said Mrs Hudson.

"Humbug!" Forster said and stomped out, muttering about the inconvenience of snow.

Fred was already imagining how to cash the money. One hundred Victorian pound notes would surely be worth more than £100 in 1934, as collector's items if not as legal tender.

"I want to go right this minute," said Belle. "There is nothing for me here."

She shuffled out of the booth, holding onto Fred's hand, pulling him with her.

Dizziness and the sick swoon of nausea. Like he was already melting. Soon he would resolve into a dew and be gone.

Mrs Hudson brought them together and Dickens watched.

"Now, my darlings," Mrs Hudson said. "I'll try my best to help you go back, Fred. You just hold onto this woman and don't let go."

He would hold on for dear life, he thought. The one true thing in this world that mattered to him. He gripped Belle's hands more tightly. Her fingers laced with his.

Mrs Hudson put her arms around them and took in a long, deep breath. She closed her eyes and hummed a low note.

As he felt the ground giving way beneath him, Fred tightened his grip and knew one thing only. He would not let go.

And with a sudden rush of wind, everything went blue and he and Belle soared straight for the place he called home.

And they would call home

— 39 —

Mrs Hudson stumbled. Charles reached out to hold her, motioning her back to the booth. She shook her head.

"I can't stay. I'll be going myself. Just a minute."

They stood in the centre of the dimly lit coffee house, the gaslit glow of New Street shining through the stained-glass windows. Snow falling again.

"I'm so tired," she said. It had wiped her out.

"They've vanished," said Dickens. "By Gad, that's a stupendous magic trick. Better than my feeble efforts at conjuring."

"Not a trick you could ever learn," she said. "Sometimes I think it's a curse."

"But such wonders you see," he said. "You saw your parents again."

"There is that. Although, they were here all day by my side. I just didn't see them."

Fred and Belle. Her parents' faces had been a blank for so long. Their names stolen by this terrible disease that was eating at her brain. But this thing that was inside her, this curse, this magic, whatever it was — it had brought her here to make sure that her parents met and found home. And she'd tried to prevent it, like a fool.

"I don't know if I've got anything left to get home," she said. "I'll have to try."

Charles stepped back, as if she might explode at any moment. "You're one of the spirits. The spirits can do anything they want."

"I'm old and forgetful and I don't know what power I have anymore. I only know that I can't stay here." She nodded to the windows and the snow teeming in the air outside. "This place is death to the old, the sick, the vulnerable."

"It shouldn't be like that."

"It shouldn't. And in my time, it isn't. But there are always men who want to take us back to the darkness. Men like Swingeford."

"We must stop them," said Charles, "speak out against them. Surely there can be a government, a system of governance that does not crush the poor so that grasping misers can sit on a mountain of gold."

"We'll always have to fight for that, I'm afraid," she said. "But we'll always need voices like yours to remind us. Use your voice well, Charles Dickens. Use it for good. Bring out the best in us."

"I will," he said. "I promise."

She took a deep breath and closed her eyes and thought about home. Christmas Eve, 2019. She reached out to that time, in her heart. It was a little like the feeling of love. It was a little like sending out the spirit in your heart to walk abroad. It was a little like the feeling of Christmas.

She reached out with all her strength, and succumbed to it.

A flurry of snow, teeming all about her, the clang of bells and the faint echo of a choir.

She opened her eyes. The coffee shop had gone. Charles had gone. She was standing in the street.

A tram was bearing down on her.

The bell clanged.

Someone rushed to her and pushed her to the pavement. The tram shuddered past, its bell clanging once more.

"Mrs Hudson," the girl said. "Are you all right?"

A sweet young face, a brunette. A face she knew.

"It's me, Rachel," she said.

The girl she'd saved. The girl who'd lost everything to Time, lost her life, her parents. The girl who'd fought to correct time and get her life back. Yes, she remembered her now.

"Rachel," Mrs Hudson said. "How lovely to see you."

"I heard you call," Rachel said. "I heard you call for help, so I came."

"I don't remember," the old lady said.

Rachel linked her arm in hers and walked with her to the glass doors of New Street Station. "Come on. We need to move quickly."

They pushed through to the warmth of the crowded concourse. She was back home. She was safe. "Where are we going, my dear?"

"Something has happened," Rachel said. "Something awful. To do with the station."

Mrs Hudson stopped and looked all around at the Grand Central concourse with its glittering Christmas lights. "This station?"

"No. Kings Heath station. Come on. I'll explain it on the way. As much as I can. It's the station at the end of time."

She let the young girl guide her through the crowd, past the brass band playing *Hark! The Herald Angels Sing,* all dressed in their Dickensian costumes. There was fear in the young girl's voice, but it was a kind face, and for the moment, Mrs Hudson was happy that she was home and someone needed her again.

— Epilogue —

When Charles Dickens awoke, it was so dark, that looking out of bed, he could scarcely distinguish the transparent window from the opaque walls of his hotel room. The chimes of a distant church struck two quarters. He fumbled for his pocket watch and squinted in the dark. A half to seven.

Ghosts, he thought. All three gone like ghosts.

A knocking at the door from the adjoining chamber.

"Charles. It's time."

"Yes, Forster. Yes."

He leapt off the bed. He'd fallen on it fully dressed last night. A letter in his hand, from his wife, handed to him when he'd returned to the hotel at midnight. He'd only half read it. He stuffed it in his jacket pocket and scrambled for his things, shoving them all into his travelling case.

He was out and down to the hotel reception in moments, where Forster was fussing over a coach he'd ordered.

"I'm not walking to the station," Forster said. "No fear."

Charles shrugged. It was all the same to him. Still surly with sleep, he rushed up the red carpet of the pergola, cringing against the cold, dark morning, and leapt into the carriage.

They said nothing as the rusty old chariot with post-horses rattled down New Street and through the warren of gloomy streets to the distant station at Curzon Street. If only they'd build one in the centre of town.

Once they'd arrived, Forster rushed off to get a porter to take the cases to their carriage. "And The Times," he said. "I must get The Times for the journey."

Charles lingered on the steps of the building, the Roman temple, and looked all about. That old beggar woman he'd passed when he'd arrived yesterday. He'd hoped to see her again. Give her something. He chided himself. The chance to be charitable was ever a momentary thing. Pass it by and the chance was gone.

Other carriages came and emptied out travellers and their luggage, all eager to be off to join their loved ones. It was Christmas morn, but cold and dark still. He trudged up the stone steps and went to go through the giant open doors when he glanced to his side.

Behind one of the great pillars, a bundle of rags, from which a hand protruded, a palm held out in supplication.

He instinctively patted his pockets to show he had nothing and was chastened by the telltale chink of coins.

It was the same beggar lady he'd passed yesterday. He went to her and crouched before her. She looked up from under her ragged hood. A dirty, grimy, creased face but with kind eyes.

"Good morning, lady," he said. "I'm glad I found you. Only I noticed you yesterday and wondered if you are all right."

Stupid. Of course she wasn't all right. She was sleeping in front of a railway station.

"Yes, sir," she croaked. "I'm fine, thank you."

"Why are you here like this?" he asked. "Why do you have no home?"

"My husband beat me," she said.

"Are there no..." He stopped himself. The word *workhouse* caught in his throat. "Is there no provision for you?"

"The Poor Law doesn't provide," she said. "There is

230

nothing for it."

A surge of anger balled in his throat. Sir Robert Peel and his blasted Tory government. A parliament of braying Swingefords. They had brought this about as surely as if Peel himself had kicked this woman onto the street.

"What's your name?" he asked.

"Mary," she said.

An icicle through his heart. *Mary*. Like his own little girl. Why was this Mary sleeping on the streets with nothing? Would that ever happen to his own Mary?

"Well, Mary, I'd like to give you something to ease the burden at this time of year." He dug in his pocket and pulled out his purse. A few coins. Not enough to change a life, but enough to change this day. He emptied it out in her hand. "Here. It's all I have."

"Thank you," she said. "God bless you, sir."

He leant in and kissed her cheek and walked off through the great doors and the palatial ticket office, and through to the platform. He found tears stinging his face. He wiped them away, angry. No, ashamed. There would be more of this, so much more of this with this blasted government of unfeeling monsters. The country was done for.

He marched up the platform, wiping his eyes, swallowing the knot in his throat, and found Forster packing the cases into a carriage.

"You all right, Charles?"

"Blasted smoke in my eyes," he said, skipping into the carriage and slumping into a springy seat.

"We'll have this one to ourselves," said Forster. "Not many travelling this Christmas morn."

Forster was babbling, trying to fill the uneasy silence between them. There would be almost six hours of this.

Charles slumped against the window and gazed through clouds of steam while the train sat still and doors slammed.

Forster opened The Times and hid behind it; an effective screen from his churlish companion.

Ghosts, Charles thought. All three gone like ghosts.

What wonders there were in the world. He must write of them. But how to make his readers believe something as fantastical as the things he'd seen last night? It was impossible. He would be laughed at. It would be the end.

Perhaps he could turn *Martin Chuzzlewit* in the direction of magic, the supernatural. No, that wouldn't do. The story had its own impetus now, driving itself where it wanted to go. He liked to think he was steering the vehicle, and most people thought he was, but he was not the engine driver. The locomotive of the novel went where it would without his intervention. He was merely a passenger in a first-class seat. He had merely bought a ticket.

Another story. Something he might tackle when this gargantuan novel, this long journey was over.

The Christmas story.

He'd heard himself reading the final words, which he only half remembered over the surreal, haunting, terrifying moment of seeing his future self.

A Christmas story.

A mean old miser is visited by three ghosts on Christmas Eve who show him the past, the present and the future.

He would put them all in it. Belle and Fred. Bob Cratchit and Tiny Tim. Though he'd most likely have to sweeten the boy up a little. Mr Fezziwig would certainly be in it. Such a character. But not the Pike ruffian; far too mean and violent for a Christmas tale. Though that story of old Jacob Marley coming back from the dead. That was gold. Well worth the money he'd paid to secure it, whatever Forster thought.

It was all before him and he was eager to make a start.

He counted off the months.

Chuzzlewit wouldn't be finished until July 1844, then compiled into a single volume. He couldn't wait that long. No, it would have to be written for next Christmas. Perhaps he could take a break from *Chuzzlewit* around October. And yes, release a Christmas book in time for Christmas. It would have to be on the short side, a novella, perhaps.

He tucked the thought away. Let it germinate until October while he worked on *Chuzzlewit*. All the more likelihood that this Christmas story would come fully formed when he was ready to bring it to the forefront of his mind, his unconscious mind having worked on it all this time.

But he would not write a word until he had a title. He never could. What would it be called?

A Christmas Present.

The Ghost of Christmas Yet to Come.

The Ghosts of Christmas Past.

No, none of those were right. The title was just out of reach, frustratingly at the edge of his consciousness.

A tune carried on the wind over the hiss of steam and the dull roar of seething engines. Someone singing a Christmas carol.

No, the title wouldn't come. He put the thought away. It would come to him at some later time.

Finally, there was a whistle. The train shuddered into life, creaked and groaned, a colossus waking, and it pulled away from Curzon Street and from Birmingham.

He settled into the journey and relaxed into the pleasant hum of the rails. The charm of transit. He dug in his jacket pocket and pulled out the letter from Catherine.

His wife's neat handwriting, the sight of which instantly brought him back home. He had only been gone a day and she longed for him to return. And yes, it had felt like a lifetime to him too. The turkey had arrived, she wrote. The turkey that his printers in London, Bradley & Evans, sent every year. They were rather capital fellows to do that. Of course, it was a gift to maintain his patronage, but they were good fellows all the same and it brought cheer to his heart and to his family, and that was the main thing.

We shall have a dinner, she'd written. A very big dinner. And guests. A party with our dearest friends. Let the house be full of warmth and love.

He folded the letter and tucked it away and felt that knot in his throat again.

Fred and Belle. Such a fire of love blazing between them. It was a thing to see. He and Catherine had not been so ardent, but he loved her and was eager now to be with her and the four children. Christmas was a time for home and family and above all else, love.

He'd come here on Christmas Eve when he really should have been with his wife and children. Much as he felt the need to launch himself abroad, to seek other things, this last day had reminded him that he only truly found himself with home and fireside.

Home! Home, home, home.

"Forster," he said.

Forster popped his head from behind the barricade of The Times. "What's that, Charles?"

"My darling Catherine has written me—"

"Oh, that's nice. Gone for only a day and she writes."

"Yes. Yes, it is."

"You're a very lucky man."

"I am. I know it. She says we're having a Christmas party this afternoon. Would you come?"

"Me? Come?"

"Yes. A party with our dearest friends, she says."

Forster smiled and puffed his chest out. "Why, I'd be honoured to spend Christmas Day with you and your charming wife, Charles. And your lovely children and your friends."

"Excellent," Charles said. "It'll be a merry Christmas."

"God bless us," said Forster. "Every one."

The train rumbled out of the gloomy city and the glow of dawn cast a rosy hue over fields of white snow.

The man who had come here yesterday had failed in his mission. But that man was a different man now, a changed man who had succeeded in so many other things. He'd brought together two young lovers and seen them home safely to a new life. He'd helped to rescue a boy from a life of crime, performed on the stage and given delight to hundreds of poor children. There really was nothing so rewarding as a child's smile. He'd seen his future self, assured his future success, but more importantly seen that man he was to be giving the joy of the season to thousands, urging them to keep Christmas in their hearts all the year round.

He had not a penny on him and felt the richest man in the world.

Also in the Touchstone saga

The Ghosts of Paradise Place [Touchstone Origins]
Taking up a new job at Birmingham Central Library,
Katherine Bright is haunted by sinister occurrences in the
brutalist concrete complex.
The dark anti-heroine of the bestselling time travel saga gets
her own personal origin story in this novella that reveals how
she first found her touchstone.

Make sure you're the first in line to read it by joining Andy
Conway's Touchstone mailing list at andyconway.net

Thank you…

… for buying and reading *The Ghosts of Christmas Past*

If you enjoyed it, please do spend a minute to give it a review on Amazon or Goodreads. You won't be seeing adverts for Touchstone books on TV or station platforms, but a simple review is like a billboard ad for an independent author like me.

Acknowledgements

The greatest thanks go to David Wake, who acted as editor while I wrote this book to a Christmas deadline that resembled Dickens' own insane schedule when delivering his *Christmas Carol* on the same day — December 19th — 176 years ago. David edited this book on the fly, chapter by chapter, when neither of us knew where it was going, and it is a much better book for his efforts.

The usual thanks go to my amazing launch team — Paul Gray, Lee Sharp, Audrey Finta, Roger Chadburn, David Cline, Marie McCraney and Helena George — who couldn't read an advance copy but who have helped greatly with previous Touchstone books and will always be dear to me.

*

There are several important books and blogs whose historical research on Birmingham's past I have drawn on here.

The delightful book, *Maps & Sketches from Georgian & Early Victorian Birmingham* (in the brilliantly named Armchair Time Traveller Guide series), by Paul Leslie Line and Adrian Baggett, with a foreword by William Dargue, provided an invaluable visual reference for the Birmingham of 1842. (2013, Mapseeker Archive Publishing Ltd)

William Dargue's blog, *A History of Birmingham Places & Placenames from A to Y*, was useful in cataloguing many of the lost streets of the 'Froggery', replaced by New Street Station.

Another wonderful blog is that of *Mapping Birmingham, Birmingham in the Long Eighteenth Century (mostly)*. Jen Dixon's research into the history of manufacturing and in particular the culture of 'toy' making proved invaluable in the writing of this novel.

My main reference on the life of Charles Dickens was Peter Ackroyd's gargantuan biography, *Dickens* (Minerva, 1991).

Historical Notes

Dear Boz. Dickens' first published writings were written under the pen-name 'Boz' — a series of journalistic sketches published in various newspapers and periodicals between 1833 and 1836.

Dickens in Birmingham. Although Manchester tries to claim the inspiration for *A Christmas Carol* (erroneously, as the ragged school Dickens visited in 1843 was in London, not Manchester, and he merely visited a relative in Ardwick while attending a talk in Manchester), my fantasy of a Birmingham connection does hold some water. Dickens' first ever public readings of *A Christmas Carol* were at Birmingham Town Hall on the nights of 27th, 29th & 30th December, 1853. On the last night all seats except the side galleries were sold at a fee of sixpence 'to enable the working man and woman to gain admittance.' Before that, Dickens' first public engagement in Birmingham was on Feb. 28th 1844, when he presided over a *conversazione* at the Town Hall in aid of the Polytechnic Society. He then became president of the Birmingham & Midland Institute in 1869. This association with Birmingham had begun much earlier when he gave a talk to the Society of Artists in 1852.

But could it be that Charles Dickens had visited Birmingham before writing *A Christmas Carol?* A passage from *The Pickwick Papers* suggests very much that he could.

In Chapter 50, Pickwick goes to visit Mr Winkle who lives on a Canal Wharf in Birmingham, and Dickens gives a vivid description of 'the great working town of Birmingham' with its streets *thronged with working people. The hum of labour resounded from every house; lights gleamed from the long casement windows in the attic storeys, and the whirl of wheels and noise of machinery shook the trembling walls. The fires, whose lurid, sullen light had been visible for miles, blazed fiercely up, in the great works and factories of the town. The din of hammers, the rushing of steam, and the dead heavy clanking of engines, was the harsh music which arose from every quarter.*

What happened in Cornwall… Dickens, John Forster and Daniel Maclise had recently had a 'bachelor' excursion to Cornwall. There is no indication that anything untoward happened on this bachelor getaway, but later, Dickens did behave inappropriately on a holiday in Broadstairs when he ran off with Eleanor Christian, the young fiancée of his solicitor's best friend, grabbing her and running with her into the sea. He declared they were both to drown there in the 'sad sea waves'. She got free but afterwards kept her distance. I have here imagined something similar might have happened in Cornwall. The men returned to London on 4 November, 1842.

Martin Chuzzlewit. The MS of *Chuzzlewit* went to the publishers on December 18th, 1842, and was first published on New Year's Eve, so at this point in the story, Dickens is between submission and publication and optimistic about his new serialisation.

Dickens as miser. The Dickens of the opening pages of this novel is perhaps a surprisingly curmudgeonly figure — closer to Scrooge than, say, David Copperfield — but at this precise juncture of his life, he was a young man whose mission had failed. He had taught the world to reach out to the poor in *Oliver Twist*, but that success had passed and his recent ventures had failed (*Barnaby Rudge* was a flop and the periodical via which Dickens published the work, Master Humphrey's Clock, had folded). He was also trapped in a marriage that he was already regarding as a mistake. Much has been written about his grief over the death of Mary Hogarth, his sister-in-law, but it is clear, to me at least, that he was really in love with his wife's sister and her tragically young death had affected him profoundly. He mourned her like he would mourn a lover.

A Christmas Carol was published on 12 December 1843 and Dickens first thought of it seemingly in October that year, which makes this fantasy, of course, precisely that.

The Theatre Royal, New Street, was founded in 1774. Originally the New Street Theatre, it gained its Royal appellation following the 1779 rebuild featured 'a ballroom which stood at the front of the building, and where refreshments would be served. There were also The Shakespeare Rooms, for alcoholic drinks, and a coffee house, which were both run by Mr. Wilday.'

It was damaged by fire twice, in 1793 and in 1820, and was eventually demolished in 1956. It was located at the top end of New Street, roughly where the Woolworths building sat (which features in the Touchstone novel *Fade to Grey*).

Ebenezer Swingeford is a fictional character and an entirely imaginary prototype for Ebenezer Scrooge. I have borrowed parts of his name from Samuel Wilson Warneford, the English cleric and 'philanthropist' who was instrumental in founding the Birmingham Royal Medical School, later known as Queen's College, Birmingham, in 1838. The Queen's College building still stands opposite the Town Hall and is now a luxury apartment complex. While he was instrumental in bringing higher education to the city of Birmingham, the historian William Whyte says that Warneford was 'a grasping, avaricious, bigoted reactionary.'

Tories. Though vehemently opposed to the new Tory government, I have portrayed here Dickens as a man who, in despair at the political situation and his own financial dire

245

straits, is succumbing to a lack of feeling. It is not hard to imagine him joining the cynics and the Tories in saying damn the poor at this stage of his life, due entirely to his primal fear of sinking back into poverty.

New Royal Hotel. Charles Dickens often stayed at the Old Royal Hotel on Temple Row, facing St Philip's cathedral, but in this imaginary clandestine visit to Birmingham I have chosen to lodge him in the New Royal Hotel on New Street, due to its convenient proximity to the Theatre Royal.

Half farthing. The British half farthing was one eighth of a penny, and in 1842 had only just been declared legal tender in the United Kingdom. It had previously been used only in Ceylon. There was much cynicism of the need for such a coin in Britain, but its purchasing power was not as small as middle-class writers of the day imagined. The real price value of a half farthing in 2019 prices is approximately five pence or a nickel. (Real Price is measured as the relative cost of a bundle of goods and services such as food, shelter, clothing, that an average household would buy.)

The Dungeon. Also called 'the Prison', this building was situated on the corner of Peck Lane and Pinfold Street, therefore opposite the Connexion Chapel. Thomas Underwood's Buildings of Birmingham, Volume One 1866 describes it as 'the site of the Gaol — the materials of which were sold 28th November, 1806, for £250 — was very near the site where the Madras School subsequently stood. The prison-like look of the place made it famous in local memory...' It is quite possible, judging from the 1839 map of Birmingham, that the Dungeon was demolished by the time of this story, but I have gone with it to provide a major presence for the sake of my fiction.

It has been my invariable practice to attend to the morals of the people in our employ, discountenancing vice by every means in my power. This is a direct quote from the Disposition of John Turner, sworn to before Leonard Horner and John Spencer, Esquires, 1st May 1833 in the matter of

Hammond, Turner & Sons, button manufactory. John Turner was answering the question: *What is your impression of the moral character of the children, male and female, in your employ?*

Countess of Huntingdon Connexion chapel. Selina, Countess of Huntingdon, who died in 1791, was an English religious leader who left an affiliated group of churches (Countess of Huntingdon's Connexion) in England and in Sierra Leone in Africa. She financed the building of 64 chapels in England and Wales. The Connexion chapel in Birmingham was demolished to make way for New Street Station in 1846, four years after the events of this story. From the description of its location on William Dargue's website, I have worked out that it faced the Dungeon.

New Street Station. William Dargue writes in his blog: 'The London and North Western Railway obtained an Act of Parliament in 1846, to extend their line into the centre of Birmingham, which involved the acquisition of some 1.2 hectares (3 acres) of land, and the demolition of 70 or so houses in Peck Lane, The Froggery, Queen Street, and Colmore Street. The Countess of Huntingdon's Connexion chapel (Methodist), on the corner of Peck Lane and Dudley Street, which had only been built six years before, was also demolished.'

Dense cloud of smoke that hung over the town. James Drake in 1839 wrote of Birmingham's 'dense cloud of smoke issuing from its confused mass of buildings, and brooding over it in sullen gloom.' (James Drake, 1839 Road Book of the London & Birmingham and Grand Junction Railways.)

Samuel Titmarsh and the Great Hoggarty Diamond by William Makepeace Thackeray, Dickens' biggest rival as a novelist, was published in Fraser's Magazine in instalments from September to December 1841, but was not reprinted in book form until January 1849, after the publication of *Vanity Fair*.

Forster's broken engagement. John Forster was engaged to

Letitia Elizabeth Landon, the poet and novelist, better known by her initials L.E.L. She broke off the engagement when Forster launched an investigation, at her behest, into rumours of her having affairs and secretly bearing children. To save him from scandal, she let him go, but privately expressed that it was his lack of trust: 'If his future protection is to harass and humiliate me as much as his present — God keep me from it.'

His heart grew dark. An ironic quote from *L.E.L.'s Last Question,* a poem by Elizabeth Barrett Browning, written on L.E.L.'s death in 1844.

Warren's Blacking Warehouse. When Dickens' father, John Dickens, was declared bankrupt and forced into Marshalsea debtors' prison, the 12-year-old Charles was forced to leave school and work ten-hour days at Warren's Blacking Warehouse, on Hungerford Stairs, near the present Charing Cross railway station, where he earned six shillings a week pasting labels on pots of boot blacking. The experience is often cited as the foundation of his interest in the reform of socio-economic and labour conditions.

Master Green. Paul Green, along with Fred Fagin was one of the boys at Warren's Blacking Factory where the young Charles Dickens was condemned to work for a short time. While some biographical depictions of Dickens portray these lads as mean-spirited bullies who delighted in dragging a toff down into the dirt with them, they were, by his own account, very kind and supportive. Dickens' guilt over escaping their fate haunted him for the rest of his days.

Cornish's Cheap Book Establishment was on New Street for a good many years and features in several Touchstone books, most notably *The Sins of the Fathers.* At this time it was at 37 New Street, but occupied various other numbers along that same corner. It can be seen in the famous photograph of Buffalo Bill's Wild West show promenading down New Street, which was the inspiration for the Touchstone short story, *Buffalo Bill and the Peaky Blinders.*

J.W. Showell, Printer and Stationer, 45 and 46 New

Street is listed as one of several businesses, along with Cornish's, that occupied New Street in an engraving from 1860.

Dickens' anti-Tory feeling. Dickens was a staunch supporter of the Whig party and thus vehemently anti-Tory. He went so far as to put his feeling in verse in the pseudonymously published poem, *The Fine Old English Gentleman,* published in the liberal journal The Examiner in 1841, only two years before the events of this book, in which he rails against 'the fine old English Tory times' with savage satire.

Robert Peel government. Dickens reacted angrily to the election of Sir Robert Peel as British prime minister in 1841, replacing Lord Melbourne and his Whig ministry. The power shift was a serious threat to the liberal cause and its reforms, personified by Dickens as 'strong-wing'd' Tolerance, who triumphs briefly over 'the pure old spirit' of Tory repression in verse seven of *The Fine Old English Gentleman.*

Gammon. While this pejorative term for dreadful old reactionary men is thought to be a recently-coined slang term, it in fact has great historical pedigree. Dickens uses it in *Nicholas Nickleby,* published in 1838. *The time had been, when this burst of enthusiasm would have been cheered to the very echo; but now, the deputation received it with chilling coldness. The general impression seemed to be, that as an explanation of Mr. Gregsbury's political conduct, it did not enter quite enough into detail; and one gentleman in the rear did not scruple to remark aloud, that, for his purpose, it savoured rather too much of a 'gammon' tendency.*

You know nothing of my life. John Forster, of course, became Dickens' biographer, and it wasn't until much later in life that Dickens revealed the trauma of his time at Warren's Blacking Warehouse. Apart from his parents and siblings, who never spoke of it again, it is likely that no one knew of it, not even Dickens' wife and children, until Forster's biography was published in 1872, two years after Dickens' death.

Time's Laughingstocks is the title Thomas Hardy's collection of poems published in 1909. It's a phrase I've been itching to use somewhere in the Touchstone world right from the beginning and it's only taken me 13 books to fit it in.

Ira Aldridge was an African-American actor and something of a star in Victorian England, marketed as the 'African Roscius — a Most Extraordinary Novelty, a Man of Colour'. Birmingham's love affair with Aldridge began in January 1828, when theatres were usually closed following Christmas. He starred in the musical melodrama *The Slave,* followed by *Othello,* and the Birmingham Gazette said, 'We were greatly astonished... (and) totally unprepared to meet with a performer' who could challenge criticism at the highest level — who 'possesses a voice... as fine, flexible and manly, as any on the London stage.'

Margaret Gill, born in Yorkshire, England, was the first wife of Ira Aldridge. They married in 1825. Their inter-racial marriage caused great anger from the pro-slavery lobby. She died in 1864.

Harlequinade. It was traditional for children to visit the theatre at Christmas to see the Harlequinade. This proto-pantomime developed out of the Commedia dell'Arte. The plot was always the same and involved. a pair of star-crossed lovers (Columbine and Harlequin), a belligerent old father (Pantaloon) trying to marry his daughter off to a rich fool, though she is in love with a good-hearted man of lower stock. He is slowed down by his bumbling servant, Clown, and a slow-witted policeman. The Harlequinade always climaxed with a magical scene of transformation presided over by a fairy godmother. Harlequin was a figure of chaos, pricking pomposity and revelling in disruption to the established order.

Gabriel Grub. Seven years before *A Christmas Carol,* Dickens published a short story as Chapter 29 of *The Pickwick Papers.* 'The Story of the Goblins who stole a Sexton' is very much a prototype of the Scrooge story, in which an 'ill-conditioned, cross-grained, surly fellow — a morose and lonely man, who consorted with nobody but himself' is abducted by goblins who show him scenes from his past, present and future in order to transform him into a better man. The action takes place on Christmas Eve.

Mr Allin's curiosity shop was formerly the castellated building at the end of Ann Street, right next to the Town Hall and something of a landmark for many years. Mapping Birmingham says that Allin moved the shop to High Street at the time of this book, but the Kelly's Directory for 1839 does not show any Allin-owned shop on High Street.

What a flare that was! Dickens reportedly used this peculiar phrase for a variety of meanings: for publishing, a party, an argument and for a fight.

The blood came rushing back to his cheeks, so violently he moaned in pain and clutched his heart. Dickens writes this in *Martin Chuzzlewit* at about this time so I have here suggested this might be the inspiration for the line.

A sledge-hammer blow. Ackroyd notes that this was a common phrase in Dickens' writing at this time, and yet it is not to be found in either *A Christmas Carol* nor *Martin Chuzzlewit*. (Ackroyd, page 447).

A rusty old chariot with post-horses. This mode of travel is precisely that mentioned in chapter three of *Martin Chuzzlewit,* which Dickens had already submitted for publication by this day.

The London and Birmingham Railway. The first train back to London was at 7am and arrived in London at 12.45. The cost for an 'A' standard ticket was 32 shillings and sixpence.

Dickens' children. Dickens had ten children in all, but at the time of this story, he had fathered only the first four: Charley, Mary, Kate and Walter.

FREE DOWNLOAD

**A chilling investigation into the truth
behind the Touchstone series...**

"A cracking, spooky short story which is a real head-wrecker..."

Jack Turner, author *Valentine's Day*

Sign up for Andy Conway's Touchstone mailing list at
andyconway.net to get a free copy of
The Reluctant Time Traveller.

Printed in Great Britain
by Amazon